# SUZANNE FORSTER
## JULIE KENNER

*Beyond Suspicion*

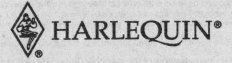

**HARLEQUIN®**

TORONTO • NEW YORK • LONDON
AMSTERDAM • PARIS • SYDNEY • HAMBURG
STOCKHOLM • ATHENS • TOKYO • MILAN • MADRID
PRAGUE • WARSAW • BUDAPEST • AUCKLAND

ISBN 0-373-83631-7

BEYOND SUSPICION

Copyright © 2004 by Harlequin Books S.A.

The publisher acknowledges the copyright holders of the individual works as follows:

THE MAN AT IVY BRIDGE
Copyright © 1987 by Suzanne Forster

DANGEROUS DESIRES
Copyright © 2004 by Julia Beck Kenner

Dear Reader,

Baby's got a brand-new dress! That was the thought that popped into in my head when my Harlequin editor called to say they were going to be reissuing my 1987 Silhouette Desire novel. *The Man at Ivy Bridge* was my third book and had always been a great favorite of mine. And now, paired with an original novella by rising Harlequin star Julie Kenner, it was going to have a whole new look!

I was also excited by the chance to update the original story. And now it can be told—I did a little more than update *The Man at Ivy Bridge.* I got out my red pen and went to town. The language was pretty lush back in those days, and apparently I was a great believer that more is more. Why use one adjective when you can use three? So I pruned here and snipped there, and felt good about the writing skills I'd picked up over the years.

For those of you who've already read *The Man at Ivy Bridge,* I hope you'll give it a second chance—and let me know if you like the changes. For those who haven't, I invite you to try a dark and dangerous man from the past of the romance genre as well as the past of my heroine—my hero, Nathaniel Cutter.

I know you're going to love Julie Kenner's story, *Dangerous Desires.* It's a brand-new novel, but liberally laced with many of the intriguing elements of the beloved gothics of old. And of course, Julie provides a wonderfully mysterious hero to pique your curiosity. Two books in one? Two compelling men to make your heart beat a little faster? Perhaps you should brew yourself a big cup of tea, curl up by the fire and enjoy them both!

My warmest regards,

*Suzanne Forster*

# CONTENTS

# THE MAN AT IVY BRIDGE

## Suzanne Forster

# 1

"THERE HE IS," she whispered to the dust-streaked windowpane. Chloe Kates shivered with anticipation as the tall, dark-haired man materialized through the early-morning mist and hesitated at the shoreline to peer out over the foaming surf. His denim-clad legs formed a defiant triangle against the horizon as he pushed the sleeves of his fisherman's sweater up to his elbows and crossed his arms. Chloe's heart tapped out a Sousa march against her ribs.

She'd been watching him for two days now.

Since her arrival at the small, Maine seacoast resort motel the day before yesterday, she'd kept vigil at the window where, partially hidden by fraying drapes, she'd observed his every move.

Standing not more than fifty feet from her, he warned intruders away with the stony set of his shoulders. She'd only seen his face once, when he'd turned around abruptly, and she'd had to duck behind the curtain.

But sometimes once is enough.

Chloe inhaled a steadying breath. His shadowed features still haunted her. The glint in his eyes reminded her of a wolf intent on its prey.

Did he know she was watching?

He uncrossed his arms and, for a second, Chloe thought he was going to turn around again. When he didn't, she released her breath in a tight sigh. "Damn," she muttered. She almost wanted him to see her and finally put an end to the anxious waiting. She hadn't the courage to approach him and introduce herself. Breaching that angry, wind-whipped aura was beyond her mettle.

She tensed as he began to walk toward the sandy point that jutted out into the ocean. She knew from experience he would cover the quarter-mile distance quickly, then round the projection and disappear.

Gathering her courage, she slipped on a hooded, zip-up sweatshirt over her tattered Harvard T-shirt and faded jeans. At the bureau mirror, she stopped a moment to comb her fingers through the wild scatter of her coppery curls and grimace at her hopelessly cherubic face before she slipped out the door.

Still half expecting him to turn around, she stayed a safe distance behind him and hoped the wind and surf would muffle whatever noise she made. An Indian scout, she wasn't.

Her canvas sneakers tried to match the path his prints made in the hard-packed sand, and the effort it took made her realize how much larger his feet were than hers, how much longer his stride. Matching her footsteps to his became a momentary obsession, until a swooping sea gull dropped its shadow in her path, startling her before it whisked away. Its cry asked a plaintive question: *Why?* The chill mist held her in a forbidden caress. Why was she following this virtual stranger?

*Because he resembled the man at ivy bridge?*

Her heartbeat jumped tempo. She *must* be going crazy. This damp, dank place was shorting out her circuitry. All right, she admitted, the man's features *were* similar, especially those blood-chilling eyes, but was that a reason to pull up stakes and follow him to the ends of the earth?

As she refocused her sights on the striding form ahead, her thoughts flashed back to the writers' conference in Cape Cod where she'd seen him three weeks before. The fleeting brush of his dark eyes had stirred memories...haunting, half-formed images that told her he was connected to her past.

For several days afterward she'd tried to convince herself that the disturbing flashes of recall were unrelated to the man she'd momentarily caught sight of. But it was no use. His appearance had triggered a rush of déjà vu that no amount of logic could dispel.

She found out his name and even though it wasn't the name she sought, something urged her on. She learned he was a mystery writer and, with some difficulty, ferreted out that he'd taken a monthly rental in a motel an hour or so down the coast from Rockland, Maine. He was reclusive. He'd once been a poet.

But a spate of questions remained unanswered. Was he the man who, fourteen years ago, had turned her young life and the little town she lived in upside down? The man she'd seen on the bridge? She'd been twelve then, not quite a child, not yet a woman, that vulnerable time when a young girl's romantic imagination was stirring, ready to be awakened.

A shiver raised the fine hairs on her neck. Sara, her eighteen-year-old stepsister, had disappeared the same week Chloe had first noticed him near their land. Had Sara run away as they said? Or had *he* had something to do with it?

Her quarry increased his pace, and she broke into a trot to keep up. A tangy, salty wind snapped at her chestnut hair. There were so many reasons to stop, to turn around, pack her bags and catch the first flight back to New York. Her struggling public-relations firm needed her! She couldn't expect her partner to carry on alone indefinitely.

Not only that, she reminded herself, it had been fourteen years since she'd seen the man in question. Considering the tens of thousands of tall men with dark hair and dark eyes, what were the chances she had the right one?

But she couldn't stop—for lots of reasons she didn't understand, and for one she did—her stepfather's recent illness. He'd summoned her to his hospital bedside to ask for her help in finding his daughter. She hadn't seen James Guthrie in more than a decade, and his pallid features had shocked her. She'd feared him as a child, even hated him at times, but ill as he was now, she couldn't deny his request.

A gull's sharp cry pulled her attention back to the man ahead of her. Uncanny, she thought, observing his deliberate stride. Even the way he walked triggered flashbacks. Was it memory or wishful thinking? The man she remembered had awakened her romantic imagination and more…he'd fascinated and frightened her.

The thought that she might have found him again set off a flurry of nervous anticipation. She increased her pace, aware of another sensation deep in her belly, a lurking tickle of fear. It should have warned her. Instead, it seemed to heighten the sense of urgency she felt.

As he rounded the point, she broke into a run, some part of her afraid he would vanish. Her hurried dash along the shoreline brought him back into her sights.

He was ascending a ramp to a weather-beaten pier that looked as if the next wave would sweep it out to sea. By the time she reached the ramp, he stood at the end of the pier, his hands braced on the slatted railing, arms spread wide. As he stared off into the horizon, Chloe saw his shoulders rise and fall with a sigh. A troubled man, she concluded, an odd resonance brushing her heart.

At the pier's anguished creaking, she wanted to warn him to be careful, but almost as soon as she'd talked herself out of the idea, she saw him do something extraordinary. Staring down into the water some twenty feet below he pulled off his sweater and bent over the wooden railing, so far over that Chloe heard herself gasp.

What was he doing? Was there something in the water? she wondered, squinting to see where he was looking. She scanned the area carefully but detected nothing in the inlet's murky depths other than surface ruffles built by the gusty winds. Certainly nothing to get excited about.

His next move made her wonder at his sanity.

Straightening, he hoisted a leg over the railing and planted his foot on the narrow outside ledge, then shifted his weight and began to follow suit with the second foot.

What *was* he doing? A crashing realization slammed her heart against her ribs. He was going to jump!

She bolted up the ramp and sprinted over the wooden planks.

"No!" she cried. "Don't do it!" But the wind caught her words and tore them away.

The man didn't hear her. He seemed oblivious, even to the shaking pier, and he struggled to free his pant leg, which had snagged on the wood. Chloe's feet flew over the swaying structure. "Don't do it!" she pleaded as she got closer to him. With an urgent lunge, she caught his foot before he could pull it over.

He looked around, startled, aware of her for the first time.

"D-don't do this," she cried, gripping his foot and tugging with all her strength. What would a crisis counselor say? "Where there's life there's hope!" she ad-libbed frantically. *"Please—"* She hugged his foot. "There's so much to live for!"

His wordless astonishment faded to annoyance. Dark eyes narrowing curiously, he gave his foot a determined tug.

Chloe held on for dear life, her fingernails scraping across the white canvas Adidas sneakers. "Oh please, no," she whispered, digging in her heels and gritting her teeth.

"For God's sake, let go of me," he said, his incredulous frown deepening as he tugged again then shook his foot to disengage her. Chloe felt his shoe wobble and her grip along with it. In a flash of blinding insight, she foresaw the awful consequences of his loosening footwear, but her leverage and backward momentum were too much. Let go? *She couldn't!*

The shoe gave. Hanging on to it helplessly, she lurched into reverse, skittering away from him, arms flailing, tennis shoe flying, feet scrambling to change gears. The opposite railing stopped her tailspin short as she hit the rotten wood with a soft *thummk* and a startled cry.

The railing heaved a groan of protest. Sickening crackles resounded as the slats began to give away.

With a shrill scream, Chloe grabbed for something, anything!

The slat she caught broke off, and the entire railing sagged with her weight. Dear God, she'd had nightmares about dropping off the edge of the earth into a watery abyss, and now it was coming true! She saw herself hurtling, hurtling twenty feet to the dank water below.

Her breath left her as a wrenching force gripped her arms, and she felt herself being jerked upright. Powerful hands snatched her back and set her on her feet.

Her legs wanted to fold like a portable chair's, but he wouldn't let them. Steadied by his strong, sure-handed grip on her arms, she fought to catch up with her racing heart.

A moment later, a shock wave of delayed realization trembled through her. She was *safe*. Oh, thank goodness. The sun was in its heaven, the sea below—and with a little help from her dark-haired friend here, Chloe Kates was safe and dry on a creaky dock.

*Friend?* Still shivering, she opened her eyes and blinked. A stretch of tanned skin gradually came into focus.

Realizing her clearing field of vision was somewhere between his chin and his chest, she stared at the dark body hair that crept over tanned collarbones and into the hollow at the base of his neck. Unequal to exploring any higher, or lower, she simply gave in to her body's lead and sagged with relief. He'd caught her. Everything was going to be all right.

His arms wrapped her in a warm, powerful embrace, one hand spanning the space just below her shoulder blades, the other smoothing her tangled hair. Her cheek rested against the very same furry chest she'd witnessed earlier. "Hello," she rasped as soon as her voice would cooperate. "Name's...Chloe."

"Chloe." He murmured her name as though it might shed some light on what had just happened. "Do you always introduce yourself this dramatically?"

"Sorry," she whispered, still nestled against him. "I was supposed to save your life, not you mine."

His soft laugh vibrated through her. "Next time I'll be sure my shoelaces are tied." His hand was engaged in wonderfully soothing ministrations to her disorderly hair, her pulsing temple, her flushed cheek.

Easing back, she looked up into eyes that were blacker than a moonless night. Breath caught high in her throat, rushed out, then caught again. Was this the man she'd seen? The man at ivy bridge?

She searched a face that shouted of reckless discontent, it's harsh lines only briefly tempered by concern. His angular features were roughened by the shadow of a heavy beard and carelessly bordered by a dark mane of hair.

Her mind faltered—it's not him, this man is too tall, too lean, his features too stormy—but her senses, her body, dismissed all her objections. Her pulse beat said yes. Her heart rate said yes....

His narrowed gaze brought her back. "You okay now?" he questioned.

"You were going to jump," she said softly. "Why?"

"Jump?" The word was followed by surprised laughter. "You thought— Well, I guess that explains your impetuous attraction to my shoe."

He wasn't going to jump? "What were you—"

"I was rescuing my sunglasses. They dropped off · yesterday, and I gave them up for lost, but this morning there they were, dangling from a crossbeam, and—"

"*Please,*" she advised quietly, "buy yourself another pair."

"Sounds like a good idea," he conceded. "Unfortunately, they don't make glasses like that anymore." His brows flattened. "You sure you're okay?"

She shook her head, reluctantly disengaging herself from him, and held up a smarting, splinter-ridden palm.

"Uh-oh," he said and whistled softly, his mouth lifting in a wonderfully crooked grin. "You'll never play the accordion again."

A surprised gurgle escaped her. "Such a tragic waste of talent." She sighed, deadpan. "Lawrence Welk's loss."

His eyes returned to her, and his smile deepened.

Whoever he was, she decided, staring up at him, he *was* something. Falling-down gorgeous! Could this be the same mysterious man she'd been watching for forty-eight hours?

Proceed with caution, her mind whispered.

Nudging the advice aside, she smiled, too "How 'bout you?"

"Hmm?" His eyebrows knitted.

"You aren't hurt are you?" She glanced gingerly at his muscular arms, his hands. "No splinters...or anything?"

Eyes twinkling, he hunched his shoulders. "Nah, I'm tough."

Watching as he pulled on his sweater and put on his sneaker, she realized how relieved she was that he hadn't been about to do what she'd thought he'd been about to do.

"What's your name?" she asked nonchalantly. After her questionable first impression it might be wiser to make this look like a chance meeting.

"Nathanial Cutter," he mumbled, occupied. A moment later, he was back, inspecting her wounded hand. "I think it can be saved," he diagnosed, straight-faced, then winked engagingly. "Let's go find a pair of tweezers and I'll operate."

They departed the pier, side by side, Chloe struggling to keep pace with his long-legged stride until finally she was breathless. "Could we take this a little slower?" she suggested.

Noting her rapid footwork, he laughed again, soft and husky. "Can't have my patient expiring from exhaustion." He paused for a moment, staring at her with such intense concentration she felt her pulse beat waver. *Does he remember? Does he know who I am?*

But something told her the lights in his dark eyes were not motivated by recognition. They were curious, subtly analytical and very, *very* sensual.

She averted her gaze. "Where are we going, Doctor?" she asked, wishing her voice wasn't quite so breathy.

"Room 15, the Sunrise motel. I do all my emergency surgeries there."

She felt a quick tug in her stomach. "Wonderful," she said with feigned aplomb. "I'm staying there, too. I'll be able to do my post-op convalescence next door in room 14."

His head came around abruptly, distance in his eyes. No one had to tell her something was wrong. She could see the wariness growing in him, could almost feel it.

"How long have you been there?" he questioned, continuing to walk.

"Just a couple of days," she offered, wondering foolishly if that was the right answer. "You?"

"Not long."

Two words had never sounded so final.

The rest of their half-mile journey was completed in silence while Chloe's curiosity ran like an imp out of control. Her mind cartwheeled with questions about the insular man who walked beside her as if he didn't give a damn that his jeans had a tear at the calf and that one of his shirttails emerged rebelliously from under his sweater.

He was older than her twenty-six years, she knew immediately, and wondered by exactly how much. Eight years, she speculated, nine? *That would put him at about the right age.* His stride was purposeful, his body lithe and supplely muscled, but his eyes signaled trouble. Beyond their temporary diversion with her, they were the searching, hungry eyes of a malcontent.

His pensive profile held her in thrall.

"What is he thinking about?" she wondered so fiercely that she actually asked it aloud.

He turned his head sharply.

Instinctively, she drew up a hand.

Gradually his features surrendered some of their guardedness. His eyes glanced over her, brushing her with a fleeting spark. "I was thinking," he said, "about temptation and opportunity...and how to tell them apart."

SEATED AT THE kitchenette table of Nathanial's motel room, Chloe drew in a breath when he took her hand. "Be gentle, Doctor," she said, not entirely flip.

And he was, incredibly, as he removed the slivers from her red-welted palm.

Several times Chloe found it necessary to remind herself why she'd followed him to Maine, and even then the caution only held for a minute or two. There was something utterly distracting in the way he cradled her hand, almost as though it might be the most delicate thing he'd ever touched.

His capacity for gentleness mesmerized her.

Fascinated by the seeming contradictions in his nature, she sat wordlessly, shivering as she realized how totally she'd entrusted herself to the man who knelt beside her.

He'd rolled up his sleeves, revealing forearms dusted with sable hair. Watching his long agile fingers work magic with the tweezers, she smiled comtemplatively. These could be the hands of a classical pianist, a neurosurgeon, a gifted sculptor. They could be anything, she realized...even the hands of the phantom from her past.

When the last tiny lance was freed, he cleansed the area with soap and water and studied his handiwork soberly. His fingers brushed lightly, exploring the slight swellings. And then, without warning, he raised her palm to his lips as if to heal each wound.

Chloe's breath went high and thready.

"Kiss and make it better?" she said, trying to laugh, her heart in her throat. Soft and cool, his mouth touched each tiny mark, shimmering over her palm, the roughness of his unshaved jaw gently abrading her flesh. Lord, but it was startling, so startling she could feel her toes curl.

She felt a surge of delicious fear as he stopped, letting a beat pass before he raised his head to look at her. Time seemed to slow to half tempo and eddy around her as she acknowledged the most starkly beautiful eyes she'd ever seen.

His hand came up to touch her cheek, a whisper of skin against skin, and the contact, even in its gentleness, jarred her. She closed her eyes and wished herself away, far away, anywhere, somewhere, *safe*.

"Look at me," he said.

The air breathed with expectancy as she hesitated, half-raising her lashes. The area behind him faded to a soft watercolor blur as his dark eyes seemed to reach out from the past and touch her. They were irresistible, hypnotic. For a moment she could almost feel the beating heart of the breathless young girl she had once been.

"You're lovely," he said, the quiet reverence in his words drawing her back to reality. "Your face has the cleanest lines I've ever seen." Visually tracing the oval curves from cheek to chin, he added, "The contours are flawless, the skin tones rich and true."

"Flawless...?" she questioned. "No—I'm not even pretty, really."

"I didn't say pretty," he stated gently. "I said clean and true."

He stood up then, offered her his hand.

Acutely aware of him, she knew that even the touch of his fingers was more contact than she could handle at the moment. "No, I—" She pushed back, chair and all, as she rose. Brushing at her clothes, she stepped away, giving herself the distance she needed to regroup.

Outside the strange aura of energy he gave off, she remembered her mission. She'd come here for a reason. A deep breath steadied her. She edged a look at him. "Haven't we met somewhere before?"

"Haven't we—" He exhaled a soft gust of laughter. "I thought they'd retired that line years ago."

"No, it's not a line." Without thinking, she moved closer and presented her face to him. "I, uh, do I look at all familiar to you?" Her heart quickened expectantly.

"Chloe, if I'd ever met you before," he said, "I wouldn't have forgotten."

Their eyes held, and she felt that irresistible energy again. It was the oddest, most indescribable sensation of light rushing and sliding inside her, wind chimes and whispers beckoning softly in the distance.

"Oh—" She lost whatever she'd planned to say next in a hushed intake of air.

His lips parted and she found herself entranced. A low thrill swept her as she remembered how they'd felt on her palm. From somewhere an errant breeze, cool and light, caressed her face, her mouth. *What would it be like to kiss him?* she wondered.

She felt a sweet jolt of anticipation as he took her hand. They moved to each other, their eyes locked, and then she let hers drift shut as he bent toward her. Warm breath feathered her lower lashes. His mouth touched her parted lips, and she felt a descending sensation, and with it, a rush of giddiness.

The kiss deepened, a moment out of time.

Chloe was lost in his taste and his scent and the feel of his mouth on hers. The pleasure swirling inside her elicited a honey-sweet languor that made her want to soften against him. Breathy sounds of pure appreciation hovered in her throat.

A feather traced the arc of her neck...his breath, his fingers? "I know who you are," he whispered.

The words floated in her mind, unheeded for several

seconds before she realized what they meant. And then the thunder cracked, a bolt that brought her eyes wide open. She took a step back. "You do?"

Staring down at her, he nodded.

The next moments stretched endlessly. She was barely aware of him reaching out to touch her hair, taking a russet curl between his fingers. He said, his voice husky, "'I met a lady in the meads. Full beautiful, a faery's child; Her hair was long, her foot was light, And her eyes were wild.'"

"Faery's child?" Her heart was beating so erratically it took her a moment to put it all together. "Keats?" She looked up at him, her voice light with disbelief. "You mean— You were talking about a poem?"

He nodded slowly. "A poem. About you, I think."

She'd thought he meant— Trying to smile, she mumbled inanely, "Thank you, but Keats was a couple of years before my time."

"Hey," he said, tilting her chin up, concerned, "is something wrong?"

She pulled away, shaking her head and realizing what she should have known before. Nathanial Cutter was dangerous. He could throw a woman off the track with a word, a glance. In the course of a morning, he'd saved her life, brought her to his motel room, performed surgery on her hand, kissed her breathless and she still didn't know anything more about him now than when she had arrived in Maine. She could hardly keep track of why she was here!

Collecting herself, she gave him an appraising stare. There was only one way to find out what she had to know. *Ask.* But did she put it to him straight, or did she try an angle? Fortifying herself with a quick breath, she took a chance. "I hope this doesn't sound too presumptuous, but is...is Nathanial Cutter your real name?"

Was that a spark of recognition she saw, a fleeting instant of acknowledgement? She couldn't be sure. His gaze was narrowing, his eyes losing their warmth.

He studied her as though he could, by sheer effort of will, see inside her mind, read her intentions. And then he turned away to face the motel room's small kitchenette. His fingers riffled through his hair before he came back around slowly, his expression wary, faintly puzzled. "What are you—a reporter?"

"No," she said quickly. The change taking place in him was tangible, passion was being replaced by something increasingly hard and impenetrable.

"What then? What do you want?"

Did she dare tell him why she was here? *Not unless you want to be thrown out like yesterday's trash, girl,* she warned. Tension rippled clear to her fingertips as her body signaled its instinctive knowledge: Nathanial Cutter *was* dangerous.

"I'm a fan, that's all," she said, her voice hushed.

"A *fan?*"

The edge in his voice told her she'd made a mistake. Considering her options, she realized if she backed off now, she'd lose whatever ground she'd made, as well as any chance of gaining his trust. "Yes, a fan," she said deliberately. "Is that so hard to believe?"

He turned away again, stony and silent, much the way she'd seen him that morning when he'd stood in the mists facing the ocean. "Yes," he said finally, "it is."

When he faced her again, his expression was thoughtful. "I'm a private man. I don't apologize for that. And I don't have much use for *fans*. But let's say you are one," he acknowledged, a quiet challenge in his eyes. "Tell me then—I'm curious about something. What did you think of the abduction scene in *Siren's Song*?"

Aware that he had moved toward her, she steadied herself, desperate not to let him know she hadn't read *Siren's Song*, or any of his work. "I—I found it... frighteningly real."

"Really?" His voice dropped low. "I like liars even less than fans, Chloe, or whatever your name is. *There's no abduction scene in that book.*"

Instinctively she edged back, glancing at the door. "I—I must have been confused," she explained. "It was another book."

"Damn, but you're a clever piece of business," he murmured, nodding, his voice gruff and almost appreciative. "That bit of drama on the dock was first-rate." His features hardened. "Who are you?"

Chloe continued to edge back, her instincts sharpened with surges of adrenaline. *She had to know.* "Did you ever live in upstate New—"

With two strides he caught her, his hand urging her chin up, his eyes threatening dark consequences. *"No more questions."*

For a breathless moment he hovered near, a pulse beat from her lips, his gaze burning a message of peril along the nerve endings that honeycombed her spine. And then, just as abruptly, he released her. "I think you'd better get out of here."

Faltering, she backed away, hesitated for an instant, then turned and fled. As the door closed behind her, she took several shaky steps and then slumped against the shingled wall of the motel. Tension released from her in a trembling sigh.

Her head spun with confusion. What had just happened? And why? She felt as if she'd been dealing with not one man, but two. He'd been eloquent, gentler than any man she'd ever known...and then, not ten minutes later, his eyes had ignited and he'd turned menacing. Closing her eyes, she saw nothing but his dark fire, the way the sun blinds you long after you turn away. *What had she blundered into?*

# 2

SEVERAL MINUTES LATER, still shaken and confused by Cutter's reaction, Chloe hesitated at the door of her motel room. She couldn't go inside yet. She needed space to think and breathe.

Beyond the small, twenty-unit building to the south, a path wound up along the rocky bluffs overlooking the shoreline. Chloe reached it in minutes.

She slowly walked along the trail, staring out at the horizon with unfocused eyes as she tried to make sense of Cutter's volatile behavior. He was a writer, a private man by his own admission, but surely that couldn't account for his mood changes, or the way he'd tossed her out on her ear. Writers were a difficult breed, no one understood that better than she, but this man...

She hesitated, aware for the first time of the chill breeze, the gooseflesh on her arms. This man had something to hide.

Hugging herself, she caught sight of a weather-beaten bench nestled between clustered rocks and shrubbery. She reached it in a few quick strides, settling in, bringing her knees to her chest in a body tuck against the cold.

Gradually her shivering eased, and she saw all at once the breathtaking seascape stretched before her. The ocean looked as though an artist had chopped it out with a palette knife. Low in the sky, alabaster rays pierced gray haze; directly above her, mounds of cloud upon cloud glowed with a golden fringe, backlit by the risen sun.

Untucking her legs, Chloe let out a sigh. The answers she sought were in her past, locked in that single catastrophic week of her childhood...but more than that, the answers were all bound up in the secrets of the Guthries, the reclusive family she'd struggled so hard to feel part of after her mother's death.

Why had her mother married James Guthrie? What had she found to love in the forbidding textiles magnate? Chloe felt a flash of sadness, remembering the skiing accident that had taken her mother's life on the first day of her Gstaad honeymoon with Guthrie. Just eleven years old, Chloe'd been left in the sole care of a harsh, embittered man.

She'd spent two years at Northpointe, Guthrie's somber English Tudor-style mansion in upstate New York, a time that shimmered in her mind like a mirage...memories that vanished when approached. The few times she had been able to call the past up, the events had seemed almost surreal, a waking dream peopled with shadows and fleeting images.

A shudder sent the gooseflesh prickling down her arms.

But that had all changed three weeks ago...when her brief and fatal glimpse of Nathanial Cutter at the writers' conference in Cape Cod began triggering flashes of recall. Since that day, random details seemed to spring out at her from everywhere—splashes of color, certain sounds, even innocently printed words quivered like divining rods, tapping at her memory.

Sometimes it felt as though debris from a shipwreck was floating to the surface, bits and pieces taking shape in her mind. Seeing Cutter had started it, and her recent visit to her stepfather's bedside had acted like a catalyst, accelerating the process.

And now, since she'd arrived in Maine, whole chunks of that lost week of her childhood had come back with such clarity it left her breathless. She remembered the day Sara, Guthrie's graceful, soft-spoken daughter, arrived home from college in the middle of term, summoned by her father. Distraught, Sara had locked herself in her room after a hushed, urgent argument with Guthrie, and had never gone back to school.

Chloe had always admired her stepsister and longed to make contact, but Sara's quiet manner and ethereal beauty made her seem unapproachable. And she'd so rarely been home. After the fight with her father, Sara had withdrawn completely to her own inaccessible world.

The argument. *Was that when it all started?* Chloe's mind quickened as she remembered the events that followed Sara's return to Northpointe. Sliding down, she rested her head against the bench back and shut her eyes.

Instead of resisting, the memories beckoned, pulling at her so irresistibly it almost frightened her. A shiver rippled through her as she let herself go, let herself dissolve into the past and become that twelve-year-old girl again....

RUNNING, RUNNING like a frightened animal, she'd dropped and burrowed into the covering bower of an ivy-wrapped bridge. The high, quick racing of her heart beat in her throat as she rose from her crouch to peer over the wooden railing. Eyes as wide as search-lights, she tracked the approaching shadowy figure.

He'd appeared out of the forest across the creek, ma-terializing through the dawn haze, startling her so badly she'd instinctively darted for cover.

He was heading right for her hiding place, the foot-bridge that spanned the creek bordering their land. Was he coming to Northpointe? What could he want? They never had visitors here. Her stepfather despised strangers, despised most people he knew, too.

As he neared, Chloe crouched again and crept to a spot alongside the bridge, waiting for the sound of his footsteps on the pine planks as he crossed over. As the silence lengthened, fear rose inside her. Where was he? Did she dare look again?

She did look, her heart trembling, and found him gone, gone so completely that she was sure he'd never been there, sure she'd imagined him. She searched the area again, and her shoulders fell with a sigh. Was he only a dream? Just like all the other inventions of her imagination?

Returning to the house, she escaped to the dim, chilly confines of her room, curled up and let her mind drift away. Daydreams eased her loneliness, sweet rev-eries full of all the things she missed and longed for—her mother's gentle voice, even the laughter and whis-pers of old school friends sharing secrets about boys and clothes and their glowing future prospects.

That night, lost in another kind of reverie, Chloe was a captive princess, beautiful and fragile, languishing in her confinement, dying a slow death of the heart and spirit...a cageling princess pining for release.

.   The next morning brought a misty sunrise—and an extraordinary event. Chloe's mysterious stranger reappeared from the woods across the creek, and she knew immediately that he was no dream. He came into view several more times over the next few days, always surreptitiously, always watching the Tudor mansion as though he expected its massive doors to open and a host of angels—or devils—to emerge.

Chloe began to discover him at other places on the estate grounds, too: the deserted stables, the overgrown rose gardens, lurking by the rusted tool sheds. Sometimes he appeared and was gone so quickly, she wasn't sure if she'd seen a man or a shadow. Careful to remain unseen herself, she stalked him with dogged fascination, never daring to get close enough for a good look. And never telling anyone of her discovery.

Who would she have told anyway? she wondered late one night, struggling with her conscience. Sara never came out of her room, and James Guthrie, suspicious of even his own household staff, would undoubtedly have stalked and shot the intruder himself. Perhaps the housekeeper or her handyman husband? Before giving up, Chloe briefly considered even her year-round tutor, a thin, cheerless woman. No, she decided, every one of them could be counted upon to assume he was up to no good. They might even panic and call the police.

Chloe felt sure the stranger was up to something, too, something secret and wonderful. Without understanding how or why, she sensed a special purpose in him...and she had to know what it was.

The next morning, just as dawn broke, she slipped unseen from a side door of the house and raced toward the creek, her bare feet shiny and wet from the dewy grass.

She stopped when the bridge came into view, arrested by something, a quiver in the air, a presence she felt but couldn't see, and then she saw him through the ivy bowers, standing at the railing, illumined by a shaft of filtered sunlight. As always, he observed North-pointe.

She moved closer cautiously, drawn to him, her eyes rushing over his absorbed profile. Was this the same man? He looked different somehow. His hair was the color of the foothills at sunset—a rich, near-black hue. And his eyes, they were dark, too.

She edged closer, recklessly intrigued. If he turned and saw her she'd have nowhere to run.

He had the singular gaze of a man on a mission, a dreamer, a conqueror. Chloe paused, and in that one, shimmering instant, she believed, *wanted to believe*, he'd come there for her...to rescue her from her terrible loneliness.

The thought took possession of her heart and mind. Entranced, she felt a pulse thrumming in her temples, racing in her veins. Her throat warmed with a spreading flush as she walked toward the bridge, openly now, expecting him to notice her at any moment. What would she do when he did? What would she say?

She froze as he whirled around, frozen like a cat caught in the glare of headlights. Stunned, she watched him turn and walk off the bridge. Before she could speak or move, he'd disappeared into the trees.

He hadn't seen her...?

Or he hadn't cared. Her throat caught in a swallow. Eyelids lowering, dampening with a sharp sting, she felt so young and lost, a hopeless child.

How dared he not see her when she'd seen nothing else but *him* for days? Impulsively, she began to follow him, running over the bridge, faltering to a halt as she entered the dank, lightless chamber of soaring ever-greens.

She looked around her, alarmed by the encroaching shadows and the sudden snap of a branch overhead. Stumbling through the underbrush, she remembered how many times her stepfather had warned her never to leave the grounds. "They kidnap the children of wealthy families," he'd said, staring past her at unseen ghosts, neglecting to explain who "they" were.

A small clearing came into view and Chloe started for it, desperate to escape the darkness. A branch cracked behind her, then another and another in urgent, brittle succession. Someone was following her! She ran, her heart slamming against her chest. Panic grasped at her like unseen fingers.

A tree branch loomed up; she veered away, but the next one caught her by the shoulder, knocking the breath out of her, tumbling her head over heels until she landed, facedown, gasping out a cry of alarm.

When she tried to pull herself up, he was there, standing in the shadows, his eyes catching light, milk-white as a wolf's glare in the moonlight.

A crazy, mindless fear iced her veins. She tried to drag herself away as he moved toward her, bending over her like a hovering demon, his arms outstretched. A scream tore from her throat and died, muffled by his gloved hand.

"Be quiet," he warned softly. Quiet? Chloe's heart roared in her ears. She flailed and twisted as he lifted her into his arms and began to move deeper into the forest. "Nobody's going to hurt you," he promised, catching both her wrists and holding them immobile.

She squeezed her eyes shut, and dizziness spun like tiny whirling pinwheels in her head. When she opened them, the world seemed lighter, the trees thinner, and then, miraculously, they were out of the forest. *He was carrying her back to the bridge.*

He set her down on the wooden planks in the pale sunlight, kneeling to support her with an arm behind her shoulders. "You'll be all right," he assured her. "You've had a little scare, that's all."

She drooped against him, her breathing rapid and thready.

"What's your name?" he asked after a moment.

"Chloe," she said, looking up at him. His were black as midnight. She would never forget them.

"Chloe," he repeated thoughtfully. "Yes, it's perfect."

Muted light caressed his compelling features...and Chloe's fear gradually gave way to wonderment. Was it him? Was he really holding her, looking down at her with such concern? Her heart lightened and tiptoed up into her throat.

"What's your name?" she asked finally.

"Joshua," he said, smiling. "It's Joshua, but don't tell anyone."

The glow from his eyes seemed to fill her with light. For an instant, she experienced an uncontrollable swell of happiness, an inexpressible kind of joy that threatened to cut off her breathing. Pressing both hands to her chest, she tried to capture the wonder of it all, for something told her she might never feel this way again.

A moment later, much too soon, he took his arm away, and Chloe felt a cold shock of air across her shoulder blades. She stared up at him, longing suffusing her green eyes, her throat full of the need to say things beyond her understanding.

"Innocence," he murmured, a roughened tenderness in his voice. "Innocence of heart." His eyes darkened for an instant, sparkling with amused, compassionate lights, and Chloe thought she glimpsed a flash of wonder and longing before he looked away.

After a moment, he glanced down at her again and touched a forefinger to her cheek in a light caress. She shyly averted her gaze....

And he was gone, vanished in a eye blink, just as before.

She waited there all day, resting against the railing, oblivious to the calls from the house. Shutting her eyes, she squeezed them tight, and with all the energy she could gather, tried to bring him back. She didn't quite understand why, but to her waiting heart, it seemed the most important thing in her life that he come back for her. And he would, she knew it.

She held on stubbornly even as darkness settled around her. Huddled and freezing, she darted out of sight when the handyman tromped over the bridge, waving his flashlight and calling her name.

Much later, blue with cold and frightened by the night's lonely cries, she finally gave up her vigil. She approached the house, pausing in confusion as it came into full view. The mansion was ablaze with light. The Guthries were up? A lump lodged in Chloe's throat. Because of her?

She pushed tentatively on the heavy doors and gasped as they suddenly swung open. Muttering incoherently, the handyman caught Chloe's arm and pulled her inside.

"Where have you been?" the housekeeper wailed. "Sara's been taken! We thought you'd been, too."

James Guthrie clattered down the winding stairway and strode the length of the hallway, marching down on Chloe like a huge, cloaked devil. "What do you know about this?" he snarled.

"Nothing," Chloe breathed.

"Where the hell have you been?" he lashed out.

"I, uh," she said, faltering, looking down at her torn clothing and bruises. She knew she ought to tell him everything, but an unnamed fear stopped her. "I fell and hurt myself," she rasped. "I can't—I can't remember what happened. I think I must have fainted."

Guthrie turned his rage on the housekeeper next, berating her for calling the police.

"Your door was locked, sir," she pleaded, cowering. "You didn't answer my calls. I didn't know what else to do."

When the police arrived, Chloe learned that Sara's window had been found wide open. An overturned chair and shattered vase indicated signs of a struggle, but none of Sara's clothes or personal possessions had been touched and, oddest of all, no one in the house had been awakened by the noise.

"If it's a kidnapping, the guy can't have gotten far," a policeman observed. "Let's put the dogs on him. They'll hunt him down."

"They'll get him," another muttered under his breath. "Rip him apart."

Listening, Chloe began to tremble. A sick feeling filled her stomach. It couldn't be the man at the bridge, *not Joshua*. He wouldn't have done something like that.

Her head snapped up as one of the policemen, a detective, approached her.

"Did you see or hear anything suspicious out there?" the detective asked.

"No," she told him, her heart beginning to pound.

Two other policemen joined them, all three watching her. "Was anybody with you?" one of them asked.

Chloe felt blood heat her face. Everyone seemed to have turned toward her now, even her stepfather. She dropped her eyes, and finally, her heart thumping painfully, she shook her head.

But it wasn't enough. The detective wanted to hear her statement. "I didn't—" she vowed, her voice faint. "I didn't see anyone."

After a long, horrible moment he turned away. They all turned away, done with her.

Chloe caught her hands at her stomach, about to be sick.

That night she dreamed again and again that Joshua was waiting for her on the bridge. Each time she tried desperately to reach him, and each time he disappeared. She woke up exhausted, confused, wandering the house, finally arriving at Sara's empty room where she hovered in the doorway, filled with a vague, rising dread.

In the days and weeks that followed there was no news of Sara Guthrie. James Guthrie quickly and thoroughly squelched the police investigation and press coverage, and brought in private detectives to search for his daughter.

Despite the rumors that Sara had been abducted, no ransom note ever came. Other rumors surfaced, increasingly morbid predictions that Chloe couldn't accept. The housekeeper believed Sara had been drugged and sold to a prostitution ring; her husband thought she'd been assaulted and murdered.

But Chloe's tutor held a completely different view. "Sara's run away to be with her lover," Chloe overheard her whispering to the housekeeper one morning not long after the incident, "the young man she met at school...."

## SARA'S LOVER?

A wave crashed against the rocks like a low clap of thunder. Chloe's eyes opened, and she sat up abruptly. How could she have forgotten that whispered conversation between her tutor and the housekeeper? Had it been swallowed up in the intervening years?

Closing her eyes, she tried to quiet the rush of noise in her head, and after a moment, the whirling fragments began to come together, to coalesce into meaning. The emotional conflict had been more than a twelve-year-old could handle. Yes, Chloe realized, slowly nodding her head. The trauma of Sara's disappearance, the confusion of her own motives for protecting Joshua, the knowledge that Sara and Joshua might have been lovers. She hadn't been able to face it. She'd had to deny it, to bury it. *God, she could hardly face it now.*

She took a deep breath and pressed her palms flat against the wooden slats of the bench. She'd been grateful to escape when Guthrie had sent her away the week after her thirteenth birthday, first to a boarding school in Vermont, then on to finishing school and college. At her own request, she'd never returned to Northpointe.

*The young man she met at school,* her mind whispered, refusing to be sidetracked by any other thoughts. How had the tutor known Sara had a young man at school? If she was right, *it explained everything.* The chair, the broken vase—overturned in their haste to get away, of course. They hadn't even had time to take Sara's clothes.

Chloe sprang up and started down the path toward the motel. Could Nathanial Cutter be Joshua? She had to know. Her feet hit the packed dirt with an urgent slapping sound. Even if he had been Sara's lover, *even if he still was*, she had to know. She would find a way to deal with the truth whatever it was.

Negotiating the winding path, she recalled the moment at James Guthrie's hospital bedside two weeks ago when he'd asked her if she'd ever been contacted by Sara. She hadn't, and told him so honestly, but afterward, when Guthrie'd become too weak to talk, his assistant, Gordon Browne, had drawn her aside.

"It's his heart," Browne told her. "He's desperate to find his daughter, so if you know anything about her, anything at all—" He'd gone on, pressing for information, but something furtive in his manner warned Chloe against revealing the stranger she'd seen on the grounds.

She'd come away from the hospital with the nagging feeling that Browne and Guthrie knew more than they'd told her, and another stronger hunch that Sara Guthrie was still alive.

That night Chloe had made a decision. Nat Cutter was her only link. She would go to Maine and find him....

Breaking into a jog, Chloe let her mind work. Finding Cutter had been the easy part—now she had to get past his guard. Questions made him defensive. Her breath came faster, keeping pace with her feet. Answers, then. She wouldn't ask, she'd tell him—*yes*, she'd tell him everything. Once she'd spilled out the whole story he'd realize he had nothing left to hide.

As the motel came into sight, she eased up a little, aware of a possible flaw in her plan. She wasn't high on

Cutter's list of favorite people right now. What if he wouldn't listen to her? She reached the paved walkway in front of the motel and slowed down.

Her first tentative knock went unanswered. She tried again, feeling an odd mixture of relief and disappointment at the silence. He wasn't home.

The partially opened curtains caught her eye. One cautious look into the murky room told her she'd been wrong. He *was* home. Leaning against the doorjamb of the room's small hallway, he held the telephone receiver to his ear with a fist. He looked angry. A half-filled highball glass sat on the dresser top next to an open bottle of Scotch.

Cutter shook his head, gestured, apparently arguing with the caller. She winced as the receiver slammed down and he whisked up the glass. He took a long swallow.

Bad timing, she realized, ready to slip away.

A gasp hovered in her throat as the curtains jerked open. God, he was right there on the other side of the pane—glowering at her! She froze as the door banged open and he loomed in the doorway.

"What do you want?" he asked, his voice low and rough, the glass in his hand.

"I wanted to—" *Incredibly bad timing.* "To apologize," she said quickly. As his glower began to fade, she rushed on. "It was rude of me to be so—well, there's no other word for it—so nosy this morning. It's just that—"

The apology lodged in her throat. Why was he suddenly looking at her like that, with such rapt concentration as if he'd noticed something for the first time?

"Now I know who you remind me of," he said thickly.

"Who?" she breathed, edging a look at his glass. How much had he drunk?

"A woman—" He drained the Scotch and began walking toward her. "No, not a woman, a temptress...from an old Welsh myth."

"Myth?" She exhaled the word and cut it off in a flash of anger. That was twice he'd made her think he knew who she was. Was he purposely baiting her? "I'm not interested in poetry or myths, Mr. Cutter, I'm—"

His empty glass hit the concrete and shattered.

She veered back, screaming as he caught her wrist and dragged her out of the path of the broken fragments.

"Maybe you *should* be interested," he breathed, "because this fable's about a woman who wouldn't listen to warning."

Her heart hammering, she looked up into eyes so perilously dark they held her pinned in place.

"Her name was Blodeuwcdd," he went on, his voice lowering, laced with menace. "And she was irresistible to men."

He released her wrist, and she took a startled, jerky step back, but couldn't go any farther. His eyes were hypnotic, his voice breathtakingly sensual.

"Perfection," he was saying, a cynical grate to the words. "A woman made of flowers...oak, meadowsweet and broom. She should have been Gwydion's finest creation. But he'd made a fatal mistake. He'd forgotten to ask himself one question: Where is the heart of a woman made of flowers?"

"Gwydion?"

"A wizard, a master enchanter." With cold irony, he added, "The name, Gwydion, means 'to speak poetry.'

His words were said to hold sway over the things of the world."

Inexplicably Chloe's heart rate began to climb. "And the fatal mistake?"

His gaze touched hers then, connecting with an almost physical impact. After a moment it drifted to her breasts. "With all that loveliness and no heart, his creation, Blodeuwedd, became a temptress. She took the soul of every man who knew her."

A strange and irresistible sensation moved through Chloe, a quiver of near-pleasure drawn up by his eyes. "And Gwydion?" she asked faintly. "His soul, too?"

"Undoubtedly...if he'd had a soul to lose." The darkness whispered through his features again. "But Gwydion resisted. He was fated to resist. *He had to stop her.*"

*How?* her mind asked.

"A master enchanter and a temptress," he said as though she'd spoken. "Can you imagine what Gwydion did?" Mercifully then, his gaze moved to the ocean, releasing her. "It should have been simple enough. He created her; he could solve the problem by destroying her."

"And did he—" Anxiety closed off her throat. Why was she letting him tell her this? Why was she letting him distract her from what she'd come for?

"No...he didn't destroy her." He glanced back at her, and a low, nerve-shattering timbre edged his voice. "Shall I tell you what he did do?"

The message in his eyes brought a lightning flash of sensation, a painful thrill that nearly took her breath away. "No," she said, shaking her head, averting her eyes. "*No.*" Refusing to look up at him, she blurted, "I told you, I didn't come here to hear myths and poetry.

I came here to talk to you about something important."
She forced her head up. "Please, I have—"

He was watching her, silent and expectant.

Something made her hesitate, a cluster of doubts
pushing up to the surface. In her rush to tell him everything had she overlooked the obvious? If he was
Joshua—and if he *had* done something wrong—she
would be a threat to him. If he wasn't, she'd be telling
a stranger the Guthries' secrets. Her stepfather's hatred
of notoriety had made him one of the media's favorite
prey.

Cutter had moved to the shingled wall of the motel
and settled up against it. "Okay, I'll bite," he said, a
mild cynicism still shading his features. "Let's hear this
important revelation."

She met his eyes and a full-scale war erupted inside
her. Beautiful, those eyes...*as black as midnight, Joshua's
eyes.* Suddenly, she knew what she had to do. Make
this good, she thought, her heart pounding.

She moistened her paper-dry lips. "I wasn't telling
you the truth this morning. I'm a partner in a small
consulting firm in New York. I work with writers, actually. And I wanted to talk to you about—" inhaling,
she summoned her courage "—about the possibility of
your attending a symposium, perhaps speaking—"

His glower returned slowly. "Symposium? Are you
serious?"

Ease out of this, she told herself, gracefully if possible, and make your exit. With a light shrug, she said,
"Serious? Well, yes and no—although now that I've
met you I can see a conference wouldn't be your thing.
And you're probably much too busy anyway."

"Much," he assured her dryly, still angled against

the wall. "For starters, I've got a half a bottle of Scotch to finish."

She detected a glimmer in his eyes, more like a twinkle really. After their last encounter, she'd expected an explosion. Relieved, she found herself becoming increasingly aware of his casual stance, and oddly compelled...by the rip in his jeans, of all things, and his still-untucked shirttail. This man needed care, she decided suddenly. He needed a woman. The thought gave her such an unexpected tug of longing she shoved it right out of her head.

"Drinking alone?" she inquired, her voice softer than she'd intended. When he shrugged, an admission of sorts, she added under her breath, "One of the seven symptoms of alcoholism."

Cocking his head, he stared down his nose at her, almost benevolently. "Only six to go? That should keep me busy till Tuesday."

The wry smile she detected almost persuaded her to try to engage him in further conversation...the weather? Politics? His memoirs? Or maybe just a quick rundown of his whereabouts the past fourteen years? But no, she told herself firmly, she'd recovered from the near catastrophe of spilling the whole story, and that was enough progress for the moment.

With great relief she felt the streak of practicality in her nature beginning to reassert itself. The left side of her brain seemed to be swinging some weight for the first time since she'd arrived in this misty, murky place. Oh, thank God for logic. What she needed now was another way to approach this predicament, a sure-fire strategy.

"Well then," she said, backing away, "I shouldn't

keep you from your—" she glanced down at the glass "—pursuits any longer."

She continued backing away, not quite willing to turn around and miss the next phase of the beguiling semi-smile that was beginning to curve his lips. An enigma, this man. And at the moment just about the most gorgeous enigma she'd ever seen.

Swinging an arm behind her, she grasped her own door handle and felt relief wash through her. Her door, her room, *safety*. She looked again at the broken glass, and a daring, almost provocative grin bubbled. "By the way," she said, giving the door handle a brazen little twist. "You've got a mess to clean up."

# 3

"A SUREFIRE PLAN," Chloe murmured, letting her head and shoulders rest against the door she'd just closed behind her. Where in the world was she going to come up with a winning strategy against Nathanial Cutter?

She began to pace, brainstorming ideas, but nothing she came up with had the element of cleverness she'd need to worm information out of a man like Cutter. An hour later she was sprawled in a dinette chair, staring at the ceiling and entertaining thoughts of thumbscrews and Chinese water torture. In the background Frank Sinatra crooned "My Way" from the antique radio she'd switched on while pacing.

"Resume your post," she muttered, dragging the dinette chair to the window. At least she could keep an eye on Cutter's comings and goings while she plotted. She forced the rusty window lock free and eased the window pane up, startled by a breeze of near-tropical warmth. Sunshine? When had that happened?

Behind her, a deejay interrupted Frank to predict the sudden warm snap. "Don't like the weather?" he drawled laconically. "Wait a minute."

Chloe stared with disbelief at the azure skies outside. Not unlike my mercurial neighbor, she thought. Storm clouds one minute, impending sunshine the next.

She sank into the chair and slid down to prop her

feet on the windowsill. She thought better with her feet up, something about alpha waves, or was it blood to the brain? Whatever it was, she needed all the biochemical advantages she could get.

It occurred to her that she might be taking the narrow view of this problem. Where was it written that she had to get her answers from Cutter himself? There might be interesting information to be had from the desk clerk, local merchants, the restaurant down the road—he had to eat somewhere—and why not contact Marsha? Her partner in New York could make a few pertinent telephone calls.

She pushed herself up in the chair, inspired. She'd ask Marsha to send her copies of all Cutter's work, and maybe do a little research on the side—a soft smile quirked—on a Welsh wizard named Gwydion.

And in the meantime, she thought, her confidence building, she'd do some close reconnaissance work on the target himself. Cutter might look invulnerable, but he had a weak spot...somewhere. Feeling pleased with herself, she shimmied lower in the chair and rested her head against the vinyl back to gaze out the window.

Balmy breezes ruffled the curtains and quieted her humming thoughts. Through lowering lashes she saw a bathing suit jog by. A white bathing suit. *His* bathing suit? She scraped her ankle trying to get her legs uncrossed and down from the windowsill. By the time she was vertical he was well down the beach. Oh Lord, she groaned inwardly. *Him.* In a bathing suit! And she'd missed it.

"Ouch," she grumbled, sitting back down to rub her ankle for a moment, then twisting around to catch her reflection in the vanity mirror. How did she look? "You will *not* follow him, Chloe Kates," she threatened the mirror's too bright, too eager image. "You tried that already, remember?"

She sank back down into the chair, her fingers beginning a series of drumrolls on her denim-covered thigh. The direct approach was simply too risky with an unknown quantity like Cutter. The man reacted to questions as though they were lobbed grenades.

Catching her lower lip between her teeth, she contemplated the secret weapons of female spies the world over and began to realize that her strategy had to include a plan for lowering his defenses long enough to gain his confidence.

A glimmer of an idea, half-formed, lurked seductively in a dark corner of her mind. Intrigued, she went after it.

Blodeuwedd, *the woman with no heart*. A shiver whispered through Chloe. Now there was a woman equal to the challenge of a man like Cutter. She'd lower his drawbridge...but how?

Glamour? Cool, luminous self-possession? Maybe even feminine wiles? Smiles, sighs, downcast eyes? Oh God, no. Chloe exhaled a soft moan and shook her head. It wasn't her style.... It couldn't possibly work.... He'd never... She found herself craning again to catch her reflection in the vanity mirror.

Her wide green eyes blinked with apprehension and something much more dangerous—the glitter of a woman challenged. Settle down, Lucretia Borgia, she warned.

Sobering, she regarded her image skeptically, but even as she inventoried her flaws, Cutter's words filtered through her thoughts. "She was irresistible to men...perfection." Tentatively, she touched her finger to her cheek, her lower lip. Had this face inspired such eloquence?

Her senses quickened. If he really saw her that way, then how did she use this bit of leverage to her advantage? Nothing so obvious, or dangerous, as fluttery eyelashes, of course. She might as well dangle stew meat in front of a wolf.

But cool? And luminosity? The cachet that said available, yes, but darn hard to get. She tried out a chin tilt, a smile iced with intrigue. Never her forte to be sure, but there must be some instinct lurking in her somewhere, some subliminal understanding of body language, of eye contact, of—her breath hitched in slightly—*seduction*.

Ten minutes later she'd slipped into a jade-green sundress and brushed some of the wilder kinks out of her hair. One last glance in the mirror told her she looked passably cool. Recklessly, she shrugged a camisole strap off her shoulder. "Dress for success," she murmured, heading for the door.

It took her nearly a half hour to stroll down the beach to the pier. The demands of carrying off a new image and practicing an expression of artless surprise should she run into Cutter precluded walking at a good clip.

But she didn't run into Cutter. Not a sign of him or his white trunks. Standing on the pier, she scanned the beach, hands on her hips, wondering if he might have doubled back and gone the other way toward the rocks.

The force of her disappointment surprised her. Ignoring the tightness in her chest, she started back, her mood darkening. Had he gone out of his way to avoid her? Possibilities burgeoned. Was this some kind of ruse to confuse her, to scatter her forces? Had even the

Welsh-fable business been an elaborate performance staged to scare her off?

She was on her way back, only a couple of minutes from the pier, when an idea snapped her around to squint determinedly at its rickety substructure. A tiny speck dangling from a crossbeam caught her attention. Was it? She began to walk toward the pier, then to trot.

Yes, *his sunglasses.* A plan formulating, she grabbed a handful of her skirt and began to jog. Cutter had wanted those glasses back bad enough to risk life and limb for them. If she had them in her possession...

Each step added fresh resolve. "Mr. Cutter," she promised softly, her bare feet scattering wakes of powdery sand, "you haven't seen the last, or the best, of me yet."

NAT CUTTER sat with his back and shoulders resting against the granite, his face turned to the sun, letting its warmth dry the rivulets of water that leaked from his still-wet hair. A hard run and an icy swim in the Atlantic was one sure way to work the alcohol out of his system.

And now that he was sober, he had no valid reason not to work on the story idea his publisher had been pressuring him for. Drawing up his legs, he propped a notepad on his knees and pulled off the cap of a Scripto with his teeth.

He jotted down some words, playing with a variation of a 1990s hit song. He underlined the phrase, considered it, and then began to rearrange the words. Might make a title, he thought, only mildly interested.

Other ideas came to mind, but nothing cohesive, nothing solid. So what else was new? He didn't have a story, nothing worth writing. Hadn't in years. It hadn't stopped him from churning them out though, had it? Each book more violent and sensational than the last— garbage he damn near hated. He couldn't figure how anybody else could stomach it, either, but they did— his fans. They bought all his books, every one of them, and figured with each book they owned a larger chunk of his soul.

Exhaling, he shook off the mood and drew a hard horizontal slash through the words he'd written. Maybe he'd put too much of himself into those books, his own black moods.

Idly, he began to doodle. Two parallel lines and a circle and he had...what? A funnel, a drainpipe? Or the greased pole to oblivion, he thought ironically. A couple more circles, diagonals and ellipses and he'd created the futuristic chassis of a streamlined car.

An oval, several small graceful curves and he had the delicate workings of a woman's face.... God, *her* face, he acknowledged silently as he went on, adding detail as though her features were controlling the pen, his hand.

His heart began to pound harder and his hand was less steady as he worked a little faster, stroking in a lush, spiky fan of lashes over sea-green eyes. A small smile lifted the tipped-down edges of her mouth....

What in the hell? he thought, staring at the image. Who was this green-eyed woman-child materializing beneath his fingers? Effortlessly, he sketched in her body, pulled back to study the effect...and felt a flash of desire in his groin. She looked like a mermaid shimmering out of the depths come to haunt the land...and its men.

His jaw flexed as he remembered her scent, her taste, so sweet it made him dizzy. Huge eyes, almost too wide-set, full of naked emotions.... Sobering, he recalled the hurt and bewilderment he'd seen in those eyes when he'd turned on her. God, what a ruthless bastard he could be. He knew himself to be a dangerous man, a taker, a destroyer of hope...but she'd almost made him want to feel it all again, the wonder.

He shook his head and grimaced. *What is all this drivel, Cutter? You're sounding like a man who's been without way too long.* Smiling grimly, he thought, *take the cure—get thee to a woman.*

His pen began to trace the line of her lower lip, shading its fullness. *But not this one...not this one.*

The aching in his gut flared, and his jaw tightened. Who was she? Why all the questions? The probing about his name? He wrote two words: *temptation, opportunity.* Circling one of them, he stared pensively at the sketch he'd brought to life and another question formed. Why was she here? *Now?*


WITH THE PAIR of silver-framed Carreras tucked securely in her canvas shoulder bag, Chloe walked briskly through the fading light of dusk toward the small, two-room house that served as an office for the Sunrise motel. She breezed through the opened door and smiled at the elderly desk clerk.

Brows twitching above sharp old eyes, the senior citizen peered over his glasses and then continued reading his paper.

"Good afternoon," Chloe ventured, ignoring his what's-good-about-it expression. She brushed at the skirt of her sundress, her smile becoming more determined with each silent second. "I have something that belongs to one of the guests. He's been gone, all afternoon actually, and I thought—well, I hoped you might have some idea where I could find him."

The clerk remained serenely disinterested.

"It's Mr. Cutter," she said finally, keeping her voice low but distinct, "Nathanial Cutter?"

He blinked then. A sign of recognition, Chloe wondered, or was she being too optimistic?

Frustrated by the man's complete absorption with his paper, she began to speak faster. "I thought perhaps he might have stopped in to get his messages, maybe even mentioned where he was going. It's important that I find him, urgent actually, so if you'd be good enough to—" Her hushed entreaty flicked off like a light switch as the desk clerk regarded her askance, then folded the paper and peered up at her.

"Something you want?" He cupped a hand to his ear. "Hmm? Speak up."

He hadn't heard a word she'd said? Chloe took a breath and projected, "Nathanial Cutter," then cringed as the room became an echo chamber, seeming to ricochet her request off every wall. She looked behind her and found, to her great relief, that she and the clerk were still alone. "I'm trying to locate him."

The man shook his head and went back to his paper. "Can't help ya."

She'd prepared for that answer. "In that case I'd like to leave a message for him."

"Not much point."

"Why not? Surely he picks up his messages?"

"Might, if he had a message to pick up, but he don't. Likely never will. He ain't here."

It took her a moment to follow his logic. When she did, her pulse jumped. "He's checked out?"

"Never checked in. No one by that name staying here."

A blessedly quick idea occurred to her. If Nathanial Cutter was a pseudonym, he might have registered under his real name. "May I see your registration book?" she asked.

The clerk regarded her as one might a fly in a bakery case. "Nope." He jerked the paper high, summarily blotting her from his existence.

Taking advantage of the cover the newspaper provided, Chloe rose on tiptoe and leaned well over the walnut counter to peek at the book. It was nearly blank. There were only two names and dates: hers and—she stretched farther—the other one looked suspiciously like—

The newspaper came down with a crunch. Chloe's head snapped up so fast she was sure she'd flirted with whiplash.

"You still here?" he accused, lips pursed.

"Just leaving," she assured him, easing off the counter with a wan smile. *One inch more and she'd have read that name.*

The clerk flicked his paper meaningfully and continued reading.

She rubbed her neck and deliberated. Had this grandfatherly man just lied to her? She'd bet money he had, but why? She cooked up another question to stall for time. "Excuse me, but the weather's taken such a beautiful turn, I thought I'd get a little sun tomorrow."

His raised eyebrow signaled he was listening.

"And I was wondering—where would you suggest I go to do some sunbathing?"

It seemed such a harmless question she was startled when he looked up and hissed, "Stay away from those

rocks down south." His eyes flashed like tiny warning
strobes. "Tides are real dangerous there."

"Okay," she agreed quickly, nodding. "Thanks."
Still under his scrutiny, she backed through the door,
turned and started for her room. What was going on?
Why the sudden outburst from a man who, from all in-
dications, had probably read his paper through the last
hurricane? Her mind began to whir. Had she uninten-
tionally hit on something?

As she crossed the parking lot and rounded the corner of the motel, she paused to study the magnificent
natural outcroppings of rock that stretched southward
in a jagged, almost cruel silhouette against the skyline.
A sudden chill tingled across her shoulder blades.
Whatever reason the desk clerk had for warning her
against that area, she was sure it had nothing to do
with the tides.

Despite the fear knotting in her stomach, she instantly revised her plans. "I'll find out tomorrow," she
whispered, staring at the rocks' dark hoary beauty.

THE HORIZON was flushed with the soft promise of
morning when Chloe awoke. She readied herself
quickly, slipping on shorts and a halter top and collecting all the paraphernalia of a bona fide sunbather—
oversized beach towel, a paperback mystery, and *his*
sunglasses.

Easing open the door, she looked up and down the
motel walkway and scanned the beach area quickly.
She wanted the element of surprise on her side, and
that meant getting to those rocks unseen. If, as she suspected, Cutter used the area for some secluded sun-
ning or writing, she wanted to be there, pleasantly surprised, when he showed up.

*Pleasantly surprised, Chloe,* she reminded herself several times during her brisk walk down the beach. In the dead of the night she'd awakened with an idea, a stunningly simple way to trick him into revealing himself. The cold-bloodedness of her deception had bothered her, kept her up most of the night, in fact, seeking alternatives…until she realized that in her case the end justified the means. She had reason.

And, in truth, the ethics of deception were the least of her worries this morning. It was carrying her idea off that had her concerned. If it was to work she had to keep her wits about her, stay cool, intrigue him. Once he'd taken the bait—she shivered involuntarily—she'd spring her trap.

A sparkle in the air invigorated Chloe as she continued down the beach. The water, as slick as sheet glass, looked almost walkable, and the wraparound sky stretched so clear, so vibrantly blue that it hurt her eyes. The coming of summer to New England, she mused, breathing in deeply. Even the breeze smelled wonderful, clean and warm, laced with sunshine.

Bathed in daylight, the rocks had lost much of their menace of the night before. Their craggy peaks loomed so magically that by the time she reached them she felt almost giddily optimistic. Yesterday's dank confusion was gone, burned off by a resolute sun and a determined woman. Nat Cutter was a male. She was a female. Once again nature had come through with the basics. Now all she had to do was maximize their potential.

Whistling, she explored the jutting rocks and natural caves for the better part of an hour before her spirits began to wane. She'd expected to find something—a scrap of paper, a forgotten pencil—some clue that he'd been sequestering himself in one of the crannies she'd found.

Discouraged, she settled on a sandy niche with a view of the motel and its stretch of beach to the north. "Patience," she murmured, spreading out her towel. "Didn't somebody once predict that if you stayed in one place long enough the whole world would pass by?"

Twenty-seven sea gulls passed by in the next hour, but the rest of the world stayed put. On the twenty-eighth sea gull, Chloe had a flash of insight. *She'd been duped.* That diabolical little man had sent her off on a wild-goose chase. Lord, reverse psychology. He'd told her to stay away from the rocks knowing that's exactly where she'd go!

She planted a fist in the sand. He and Cutter were undoubtedly in cahoots, probably having a good chuckle at this very moment. Were they now planning where to send her tomorrow?

She swallowed the blasphemy that came to mind. Her outrage knew no bounds, but she wasn't about to let him rattle her again! She'd deal with this rationally even if it meant permanently clenched teeth.

Taking a deep breath, she began a calm assessment of her situation and decided that living well would have to be the best revenge for now. She'd simply stretch out, get herself a good tan and stroll back to the motel as if that's exactly what she'd intended to do all along. She'd be cool, serene, and no one would be the wiser.

She checked her hair to make sure the Carreras were secured in her curls, then lay back, arranged herself on the beach towel and offered her body to the New England sun. She'd be ready for him next time, a veritable bronzed goddess.

Closing her eyes, she envisioned herself strolling right up to him, casually flicking off the sunglasses, and with a silvery laugh, saying...what would she say? "Did you lose something, Mr. Cutter?" Well, she'd think of something devastating. She'd be silky, irresistible—she'd have it all.

Amusing herself with mental snapshots of Cutter's astonishment, she drifted off. "There's something different about you, Chloe," he'd say, visibly awed, "elusive and exciting, something I never noticed before... *Your nose is red.*"

"Nose?" she mumbled.

And then he said it again. "Your nose is red."

Her eyes popped open. Nothing. She stared straight up into azure skies. Was she having auditory hallucinations?

"Better get some sunblock on that fair skin," came the next terse observation.

She jackknifed to a sitting position. He stood at the base of the rocks, no more than six feet away. Her heart soared like a plane at takeoff. Oh God, not now, not yet. She wasn't ready to deal with him yet.

He didn't move, and some instinct told her that he was unsure, too. But he didn't look unsure. He had the white trunks on and he looked—she managed a faint-hearted swallow—magnificent.

His gaze brushed over her shorts and halter top, and she felt the irresistible evidence of male interest.

"You do have a knack for showing up in the strangest places," he muttered softly.

*Pleasantly surprised, Chloe.* "Call it a gift," she murmured.

"There are lots of things I could call it." Irony settled in his features as his gaze flickered over the small, secluded area and finally paused on her. "Gift isn't one of them. Are you by any chance aware that this was my last bastion of privacy?"

*"Really?"*

"I'm curious." A dark eyebrow slanted. "How did you know I'd be here?"

He assumed she'd— Her stomach tightened. What monumental ego! That he'd assumed right was beside the point. "These rocks looked like the perfect place to sunbathe." She flashed him a smile as cool as iced tea. *"Undisturbed."*

"They are," he agreed. "Only they're my perfect place."

*"Your* place?"

Nodding, he moved toward her. *"Mine."*

She jerked in her legs as he neared. "No way! I got here first—*finders keepers.*" Oh Lord, had she really said that? Third-grade playground warfare lingo?

"Finders keepers?" He hesitated near her feet, a wry smile forming. "Where'd you pick up the tough talk? Harvard?"

Harvard? And then she remembered. She'd worn the garage sale T-shirt the day before.

The way he was studying her told her he wanted her to go on, to say something more. This time she knew better.

After a moment he settled his weight on one leg and folded his arms. "Looks like you and I have something in common," he acknowledged, punctuating the admission with a self-deprecatory laugh. "I don't usually admit it, but I'm an ex-Harvard reprobate, too."

"Oh?" Startled that he'd volunteered the information, she found herself smiling and nodding.

In the brief silence that followed her heart began to stir. Something in his eyes belied the quiet cynicism of his words. A softly tempered nostalgia, she realized, as he asked, "What year?"

Oh, God, what tangled webs we weave. She mumbled the year she graduated NYU. So what if I didn't go to Harvard, she argued with her conscience. He thinks I did, and it's got him *interested.* What are a couple of white lies for the cause?

"A good year for redheads," he murmured.

She tried to sustain a smile, but a vague uneasiness stirred through her, hovering just out of reach, like a thought trying to resolve itself.

"Listen, about yesterday," he said, raising a shoulder, "sometimes I forget how the civilized world lives...."

She lost track of his words, lost them completely as a whisper from the past filled her mind. *Sara's run off to be with her young man from college.*

Chloe's thoughts recoiled as though she'd been struck. Nathanial Cutter had gone to Harvard—but Sara'd gone to Elmhurst in Illinois. Her heart began to throb. Either this man was lying...*or he wasn't Joshua.*

She felt the blood drain from her face. Her head jerked up and her eyes fixed on Cutter as though he might instantly disappear.

"What is it?" he asked. "What's wrong?"

"Nothing," she breathed, trying desperately to conceal the emotion that trembled through her. Her head spun with confusion, ached with exploding questions, but out of the chaos one thing was clear. She'd wanted him to be Joshua. *She'd wanted every man she'd ever met to be Joshua.*

"You're white as a sheet," he said, starting toward her.

Maybe the man at the bridge had nothing to do with Sara, she reasoned urgently, maybe he'd come there for some other reason altogether. What did she really know of the Guthries? They'd been so secretive. And she'd only been at Northpointe two years.

*"Chloe."*

Her head came up sharply. "I'm all right," she said, her voice whisper thin. "It's just that I—" Averting her eyes, she got out, "I haven't eaten today, and I felt light-headed for a minute. But I'm fine now, really," she insisted.

Crouching, he scanned her face. "Are you sure?"

She nodded, shoring up her strength and wishing he'd stop looking at her so intently. Her heart didn't work right when he looked at her that way. You can't afford to let him stop talking now, she told herself, *not now*. "I don't think I remember you...in my class," she said, tilting her head, feigning mild skepticism.

His smile was fleeting. "Probably because I graduated a decade before you."

She was nodding again, wanting to believe him and still wondering why he'd brought up Harvard at all. A way of apologizing, of sharing a mutual experience?

As she glanced at him now, her heart responded to his melancholy, to the need she sensed in him. But her mind dragged up another terrible possibility. Was he intentionally leading her astray? Was he feeding her lies to throw her off the track? Even at the thought she felt a soft ache in her chest. Keep going, keep him talking, she told herself. "You were an English major?" she asked.

He nodded. "Yeah, you?"

Before she could answer, a grin transformed his features; a smile so boyish, so vulnerable that she felt a tug at her heart.

"Evans Cole," he murmured. "God, the holy terror of the English department. Was he still teaching when you were there? Did you take his Critical Analysis class?"

His openness was disarming...but hadn't he caught her just this way before—with a trick question? Please God, she thought, don't let this be another one. Smiling, she pretended to remember. "Quite a guy, Evans Cole."

"A wild man," he agreed, laughing. "Used to squint at us through those Coke-bottle glasses. 'Furor scribendi,' he'd rant, 'none of you has the rage to write!'"

His laughter was so low and rich, so genuine she found herself smiling with him...and sobering instantly as he turned to her. "What do you think," he asked, his voice lowering. "Was George Sand right? Are those of us who don't remember the past condemned to relive it?"

As the words registered, her body convulsed with a soft, audible gasp. "What do you mean?"

But he was already looking away at the water, traces of an inner conflict working in his features. "Nothing," he said finally. "I didn't mean anything." Rising, he walked to the water, his back to her.

"I'm keeping you from your sunbathing, boring you with war stories," he said. "I don't know why the hell I brought up Harvard anyway. Some of us never do grasp the social graces." As he turned, his eyes met hers briefly, but with such a burst of intensity she lost a heartbeat. "Once a selfish SOB," he vowed quietly, "always a selfish SOB."

It sounded like a warning. Still, she couldn't help herself. "Wait," she said as he started away.

His head came around.

"I love war stories." She smiled wistfully, foolishly. "Anyway, what's the hurry?" Color seeped into her cheeks. "We don't have to talk about Harvard if you'd rather not. I didn't find the place all that memorable, either."

The conflict in his eyes intensified, and one message came pulsing through. Unless she was wrong, he wanted to stay with her. "You came for some sun," she added softly, "and this is your bastion, after all."

Was he turning back? "There's plenty of room," she pressed shamelessly. "I'll share."

His eyes grazed her face, lingering on her mouth for a second before returning to her eyes. "Sorry, I never learned to share. A selfish SOB, remember?"

Startled, she watched him turn and walk away.

It was an instant before she realized she was springing to her feet, calling after him, "You're right, Cutter. You are devoid of social graces." A flush stained her cheeks. "Can we chalk this one up to bad manners, too? Or is it *me* that brings out the worst in you?"

He was slowing. *He stopped.*

Her heart thudded as he turned around. Fighting off tremors of apprehension, she began to walk toward him. "I don't think you're nearly as socially retarded as you pretend," she said. "It's me, isn't it? I think I threaten you. Is that it? Do I threaten you, Mr. Cutter?"

She saw him stiffen, felt her nervous system jump in

response. She took two more steps, a deliberate challenge, and held her ground. God, but he frightened her.

His eyes began to glitter, lit from some terrifying inner source. "Yes," he said, taking his time as he closed the distance between them. "I suppose you do threaten me."

She tried to look away as he neared, but she couldn't. "I knew it," she breathed. "Why?"

He hesitated imperceptibly, inches from her. "Because you want something from me."

"No—" she started.

He moved in tight then, flush with her body, the implicit threat stunning her to silence. A liquid weakness assailed her legs. "No," she whispered, trying to step back, desperate to free herself from the energy shimmering around her like a live electrical field.

"I don't know what you're after," he said, his voice resonating through her mind, "but be careful. I stopped giving people what they wanted years ago."

His features were angry, his eyes dark, but she felt a soft shimmer along the line of her throat. His fingertips...and they trembled slightly as they touched her.

Thoughts rippled through her mind, her body—thoughts that couldn't be her own. *I don't want much*, a voice was whispering inside her, *not much...just his soul*.

"What did you say?" No longer gentle, his voice was harsh, commanding.

*Nothing*, she tried to tell him, but she could only shake her head...and watch the tumult building in his eyes. Vaguely aware of a pressure lifting, she realized his hand was gone from the column of her throat.

"Why are you here?" he exhaled, shifting back. "Why the hell aren't you running the other way?"

A flush of color warmed her face. "I never was any good at track," she declared softly. At his grimace, she pulled a breath, steeling herself. "I'm not going anywhere, Cutter. I'll stay and take my chances."

She saw immediately that she'd made a tactical error. He'd taken it as a challenge. Catching her arm, he urged her closer, his breath cooling the dampness at her temples. "How much of a gambler have we got here?"

Her heart began to thump erratically. *He's teasing,* she told herself, *trying to frighten me.* "I guess that depends on what I want, doesn't it?"

"And you're not going to tell me, are you?" His eyes glinted. "Yesterday I was wondering about the difference between temptation and opportunity. Today, I know. You, redhead, are temptation." The muscles in his hand flexed and contracted around her arm; his eyes burned with a light that made her shiver. "And that," he grated softly, "makes me vulnerable to you."

She met his eyes and felt a shock of awareness. "It does?" The implications of this windfall took her breath away. And after a moment so did its obvious drawbacks. "And you're not a man who likes to feel vulnerable."

"Hate it," he admitted, releasing her arm to brush a stray tendril of hair from her cheek. His features moved with the darkness that made her forget how to breathe. "But I can't resist temptation."

His lips parted slightly, an almost irresistible moistness to them, and her stomach clutched in anticipation. Closing her eyes, she felt a sharp ache in the back of her throat as she remembered the sweetness of his mouth.

"God, you are dangerous," he breathed.

A sensation was unfurling inside her, the soft swirl of pain that comes with needing something so badly you ache for it. *Touch me*, she heard the voice inside her whispering to him, the words repeating until they filled her like the shiver of tiny bells. *I need you to touch me.*

She gasped as she felt his hands sliding up her shoulders to rest at the curve of her neck. As his fingers spread, enclosing her throat, she surrendered to the sweet riot of emotion inside her.

He bent to take her lips, his whispering darkness moving over her, hesitating. His mouth touched hers with a tiny, almost audible cry of sensation.

Her inner world dissolved into chaos. It was beautiful, endless. And all she could remember next was being gathered up in the hard crush of his arms, absorbed into him until she only existed through the tender, frenzied brushings of his mouth.

She felt him shudder, heard his ragged breathing, and a flushed scent filled her nostrils—heat, the heat of a climbing fever.

A sound rumbled in his chest, the sensual rattling of an animal's growl. Working his hands into her hair, coiling, no longer gentle, he suddenly broke the kiss. "Chloe," he warned, his voice broken, searingly harsh, "don't do this."

With a convulsive tremor, he lifted his head, his eyes shut. "God bless it, *don't do this to me.*" Just a breath away from her lips, a pulse throbbed in his neck.

"What?" she whispered, her fingertips at his jawline.

"*Damn*," he rasped softly, "I knew this would happen." Looking down at her, anger and frustration high in his eyes, he said, "You're killing me, you know that?

Killing me by inches, ripping my willpower to shreds."
His long, rough exhalation bathed her face. "I want to
see you again, no—I *have* to see you again...tonight?"

"Tonight?" she echoed, dazed. "Like a...do you
mean...a date?"

"Oh God," he groaned, shaking his head, "yes, a
date—if that's what you want, a date."

He pulled back, releasing her, still shaking his head.
"Turn me down," he exhaled. "Say no while you can."

"Never."

"Okay," he said, gazing at her with such intensity
she felt weak, "but don't say I didn't warn you." He
turned away and began to jog toward the motel.

"What time?" she called after him.

"Seven," he yelled over his shoulder.

"Seven," she murmured, a shaky grin tugging at her
lips. "I'll have to check my calendar."

# 4

CHLOE HADN'T prepared for a date with such frenetic energy since the sophomore prom. Success *was* sweet, she decided, poring over her limited wardrobe. But fleeting. Her blissful smile turned practical. She had to look good tonight—irresistible, if she could swing it. She finally opted for a white eyelet sundress with an old-fashioned lace-up bodice.

One look in the mirror and she didn't need any blusher. Her small breasts were buoyed up, full and blooming, by the gentle supports of the white cotton bodice. The nipped-in waist and swirling ruffled skirt further sensualized her petite figure. And her hair, freshly shampooed and brushed at length to loosen the curl, swirled around her shoulders like the mane of a glossy, red-gold animal. Green eyes shimmered against tawny, sunbrushed skin, and a touch of powder quieted the dappling of freckles that decorated the narrow bridge of her nose.

"Chloe," she whispered, stunned at the effect. "He's a goner. The woman you see before you is living proof of the miracle of modern cosmetology. One bat of these Fabulashes, and he'll give away the farm!"

A faint tap at the door made her stiffen nervously. She glanced at the clock. Six-fifteen? He was forty-five minutes early. "He must be even more anxious than I am," she murmured.

She reached for the doorknob gingerly, eased the door open and registered the blink of huge faded blue eyes beneath thick wire-rimmed glasses. The desk clerk.

Her unexpected visitor looked as surprised as she felt. "Did you want something?" she asked.

"Nope," he said, clipping the word off even more closely than usual.

"You didn't?" She blinked. "But you knocked."

He shook his head and held up a well-worn broom. "Sweepin' the walk. Mighta bumped your door by mistake." With a surprisingly polite nod, he added, "Sorry."

Suspicion prickled in Chloe's brain. Much too chummy. Was he trying to smile his way out of something? Like...listening at her door, perhaps?

She glanced toward Cutter's room and saw the clerk following her gaze. Their eyes flicked back and locked for an instant.

With a twitch of self-consciousness, the clerk looked off at the horizon. "Gonna be a warm one," he said, speaking apparently of the impending evening.

Down the beach a flock of gulls swooped and darted in a raucous display of daredeviltry.

"Umm," Chloe conceded, trying to decide whether or not to tell him she had a date with his missing motel guest, Nathanial Cutter. As he wandered away, whistling tunelessly and sweeping, she called out, "By the way—"

His wise-old-owl expression as he turned back made her hesitate.

"How long you staying?" he asked, out of the blue, his head tilted down, his eyes dead level, very much the judge asking the defendant, "How do you plead?"

"I don't know." The halting inflection in her voice made her add defensively, "Does it matter?"

"Might," he said, "might not."

She refused to acknowledge the cold tickle of anxiety in her stomach. "What does that mean?"

"Means you been here longer than most already." He hiked the broom up under his arm, holding it horizontal, the handle end pointed at her like a shotgun barrel.

"Three days is longer than most?" She tried to smile. "Must be difficult to make a living with such a turn-over."

"Living," he muttered obliquely, "ain't difficult if a body uses the sense God gave him." His eyes drifted south, beyond her, toward the rocks. "Now animals, they got sense. Hunted animals got an instinct. Something tells 'em when to run, when to hold still. Humans, they've lost it. Most of 'em don't even know they're being stalked." Without moving his head, just his eyes, he looked at her. "Easy targets, humans, fish in a barrel."

He wheeled around, made his slow-gaited, deliberate way to the end of the walkway and disappeared around the side of the building.

Chloe closed her eyes in frustration. The tickle of anxiety was now a soft throb. *He'd frightened her again.* That strange little man could frighten a rock!

In the next forty minutes, she successfully convinced herself that she had a latent talent for turning slightly morbid senior citizens into Alfred Hitchcock characters. He's probably alone too much, she decided. A golden-agers club would do him wonders.

She forced her mind to dwell on bigger and better things. It was five to seven and she had the evening of her life ahead of her. Where would "tall, dark and handsome" take her tonight? Dinner? Dancing? Anticipation expanded in her chest like a bubble. *Would she find out who he was tonight?* The fact that he'd admitted his vulnerability to her, even given in to it for a moment, gave her a measure of confidence, perhaps more than she deserved to feel. Were tamed wolves ever safe? Weren't they known to turn feral unexpectedly— and usually just when their human captor succumbed to overconfidence? Or that other human failing, trust?

By seven-ten, her confidence was already on the wane.

At seven-thirty, she heard footsteps and rushed to the door, her hand poised on the doorknob. Let him knock first, then count to ten, she cautioned. He's thirty minutes late; he can darn well wait thirty seconds more. And *please*, Chloe, stay cool, unruffled. Think luminous.

She kicked off her shoes, a last-minute inspiration. Oh, was he late? Really? She hadn't noticed. She wasn't quite ready, either.

The tap was so faint she barely heard it. She pulled the door open and searched empty air. It took her longer than it should have to realize she hadn't heard a knock. There hadn't been one.

With creeping chagrin, she stepped outside her door and looked down at his, afraid any minute he'd come out and catch her craning her neck like a ninny. He wants to look good and he's taking extra time to get ready, she decided. That's why he's late.

By eight o'clock, she'd flattened herself against the thin wall that connected their rooms, listening, hearing nothing. An hour late? What was he doing? No one needed to look that good. Should she casually wander over? No, she'd wait him out. This was obviously a test. He wanted to be *pursued*!

By nine she'd run out of excuses for him. The Carreras she'd forgotten to return that afternoon were staring at her from the bureau top. Pretty flimsy, she realized, but better than no reason at all.

Sunglasses in hand, she approached his room and hesitated. The dark windows signaled her that something was wrong.

Her knock went unanswered. She knocked louder, then again. Nothing.

He'd gone, she realized, stepping back from the door. It came upon her all at once, the stunned disappointment, like an accidental elbow to the ribs. Halting, sighing softly, she said it aloud, "He's gone," and the whispered statement made it irrefutably true. He'd stood her up, *run out on her*.

She didn't know how long she stood there, staring at the darkened room before she began to back away. A soft aching filled her throat as she turned and hurried back to her own room.

THE PLASTIC wall clock above the dinette told Chloe she'd been sitting, staring at a crack in the flowered wallpaper and listening to the old radio play mood music for more than an hour. She hadn't even changed her dress.

She glanced around, noticed the Carreras on the tabletop where she'd tossed them. "I hate those glasses," she whispered suddenly, a catch in her voice. "Almost as much as their owner."

A small flame burned near her heart. Never in her life had she felt so many emotions in the course of an hour: piercing disappointment, and then hurt out of all proportion to her predicament. And finally, the soft ache in her throat had tightened into a knot that was hard to swallow over. Now she was angry. *I know nothing about him—and that probably includes his name—and still I care enough to want to hate him for running out on me*, she thought, furious. *How did he do that? Make me care? I hate him for that.*

She came out of the chair, pacing randomly, changing directions like a broken compass needle. Yes, she was angry, and she wanted to be angrier, because the flame hadn't yet burned all the hurt from her heart; the blue mists of disappointment weren't completely dissipated.

"Pull yourself together," she muttered under her breath, not because she meant it, but because after her emotional roller coaster of an hour some gesture of self-control seemed called for. "You've been stood up before."

It took awhile, but the words finally worked. Gradually almost in spite of herself, she felt the emotions giving way to a kind of detachment. Go to bed, get some sleep, she told herself, but vague stirrings of purpose kept her pacing. By the time she'd undone her bodice ties and left her dress in a heap on the floor, a clear, almost ruthless sense of direction had cut through her turmoil.

Okay, Cutter, she thought, if this is how you want to play, you're on. You want to play games, I can play games. You want to play hardball, I can play hardball.

Riffling through her suitcase for her nightgown, she came upon the two tiny bottles of vodka that she'd purchased on the plane flight, thinking she'd need sedation. It wasn't sedation she needed now, but somehow a belt of booze seemed like the right gesture, considering her mood.

"Hard liquor, hardball and a hard-hearted woman," she said, a dry smile tightening her lips. It felt good not to care. It felt even better knowing she was damn well going to get what she came here for. Answers. She wouldn't leave this place until she knew whether or not he was Joshua. And Sara, she thought resolutely, pulling out her nightgown and slipping it over her head. One way or another, she intended to find out what had happened to her stepsister.

Gritting her teeth, she gripped one of the little bottles firmly, unscrewed the cap and took a swig. With a choking sound she swallowed it, then gasped for air as it seared her throat and stung her eyes. She'd forgotten how thoroughly she disliked the taste of alcohol. Stubbornly, she took another drink.

Not bothering to pull down the quilt, she sank onto the bed, propped herself up with pillows and finished the bottle. First thing in the morning she'd start with the desk clerk. A shakedown, she thought, savoring the words. That little bugger knew plenty, and if he wouldn't cough it up, she'd—

When nothing came immediately to mind, she opened the second bottle, took a drink, and decided the taste had possibilities. Sort of warm and sweet, like mouthwash. Maybe she'd offer the clerk money. Everybody had a price.

Everyone but *him*, her fuzzying mind declared.

Settling down into the pillows, her eyelids drooping a little, she decided to case the area once she'd finished with the desk clerk. Someone must know Cutter. And where were those books Marsha was supposed to send her? And that mini-investigation her partner had promised to run on Cutter? She'd call New York first thing in the morning.

The next inspiration swept into her mind from out of nowhere. *She could search his room.* There had to be clues among his personal things, mementos, letters. An address book? A personal journal?

Like a stop-action photograph, her eyes blinked open by degrees. *Break* into his room? She was scheming like a seasoned sociopath. Focusing in on the half-empty bottle she was clutching, she decided it must be the alcohol talking. She relegated the vodka to the bedside table and switched out the light.

Rolling over, she curled up and burrowed into the quilt as she drew it over herself. Grateful for the liquor's soporific effect, she heard herself murmuring, "He'll never know what hit him," as she drifted into sleep.

WRENCHING UP, still dazed with sleep, Chloe listened, all her senses alerted. What had awakened her?

She scanned the room, searching its corners, seeing wraiths in each flickering shadow. The stillness assured her that no one was there...but something had awakened her.

Sounds. She heard them again.

A muffled noise came from somewhere. And again.

The bedside clock said 3:00 a.m. Twisting around in the direction of Cutter's room, she listened. Voices, muted but somehow strained, indistinguishable words, the bang of something dropped...or thrown? Someone was there.

Him? He's back! Leaping from the bed, she stumbled through the darkness to the wall and pressed herself against it. He was talking—no, arguing—with someone.

She strained to hear the other voice, to make out the muffled high-pitched sounds vibrating in her ears. "No," she said and stepped back. A woman, she realized, continuing to back away from the wall. *He was with a woman.*

Faltering to the bed, she sat, paralyzed with disbelief, her brain refusing to assimilate what she'd just heard.

The sounds carried through the wall again. The blurred voices of a man and woman in rapt conversation. The acrid taste of shock was rising inside Chloe, swimming in her throat. "Oh, my God," she repeated, her hand flying to her mouth.

The sounds quieted, and Chloe's head jerked up. She wanted to listen; she couldn't bear to listen. It was only as she lay back on the bed, still clutching her hand to her mouth that she experienced a wrench of awareness. *The woman with him could be Sara.*

She got up fast. Her arms and legs felt like lead as she struggled out of her nightgown and pulled on jeans and a T-shirt. She had to know—but what if it *was* her stepsister?

Joshua and Sara. The image of an intense young man and a fragile blond woman sent Chloe's thoughts hurtling back fourteen years. She knew instinctively that the truth would be more painful if the woman was Sara. Faced with the dilemma she'd suppressed all these years, Chloe's fears suddenly became clear: finding Sara meant losing Joshua.

Her throat tightened. He was never mine to lose, she told herself, he was just a lonely child's fantasy. But she knew it was more than that. Joshua was a beckoning dream she'd never been free of since the first moment she'd seen him. She shook her head. How could a dream hold such power over the human heart?

One part of her wanted to run, to avoid the pain of reality, whatever it might be. Another part of her wouldn't rest until she knew.

Sinking to the floor, she forced on her tennis shoes, struggled back to her feet and walked to the door. She gripped the knob hard to stop her hand from shaking. "Open it," she ordered.

Outside, the still night air heightened her sense of caution as she approached his door. Confused, she slowed and halted. The room was as dark as before. At first she thought she must be going crazy, and then an odd sensation passed through her, almost relief, and she began to shake. They've left, she thought, slumping against the shingled wall for support.

As the shaking subsided another possibility occurred to her. What if he'd taken the woman, whoever she was, to bed? Chloe's heart constricted. Fighting to catch her breath, she rushed to her room, slammed the door and walked blindly across to the bed. The second bottle of vodka sat on the bedside table where she'd left it.

She drank it all, the hot stream of alcohol scoring her throat and backing up into her nasal passages. Again, the urge to run away, to escape, overtook her.

She caught hold of the bedpost and hung on until the shaking eased. All her life she'd been running from the emotional debris of her past. As a child she'd lost herself in daydreams to avoid the pain of her parents' divorce and later her mother's death. As an adult she'd lost herself in work to forget the years at Northpointe.

Staring down at the empty bottle in her hand, she realized the race was over. She could never run far enough or fast enough. The past had caught up with her.

SHIVERING in the early-morning dampness, Chloe walked toward the motel office. One way or the other that desk clerk was going to answer her questions this time, she resolved. This place had become her Holy Grail.

She tried the door of the motel office and found it locked. A dim halo reflected in the window caught her attention. The office itself was dark, but a vertical ribbon of light filtered through the partially opened door of the back room where the clerk lived.

She considered knocking and then discarded the idea, realizing the empty office might be an unexpected opportunity. Hardly believing what she was about to do, she searched her purse for a credit card.

The card buckled several times as she tried to work it into the doorjamb. It all looked so easy on television! Expecting to be caught at any moment, she glanced through the window and then over her shoulder. "Breaking and entering," she reminded herself under her breath, "is a felony in every state in the union."

As she nursed the card in farther and angled it up, a faint click sounded and the knob gave. Her stomach knotted with anxiety.

She slipped into the office. From the next room she heard the slow-gaited shuffle of slippers on hardwood, and then a faucet creaked on and water began to pour. *Now,* she told herself, letting out a taut breath.

She moved to the counter and saw the registration book lying closed on the desk. Rising on tiptoes, she grasped for it when a shrill ring stopped her hand in midair. Her heart surged so chaotically she wasn't sure what she'd heard. And then it shrilled again. The phone.

Lunging for the book, she flipped it open, riffling pages until she found her own name. The other entry on that page, the one she'd tried to see two days before, was Nathanial Cutter.

Nearing footsteps brought her up. Scanning the room frantically, she saw a door at the far end and ran for it, slipping inside as the phone shrilled again.

Crouched in what appeared to be a storage room, she realized she'd learned little beyond the fact that the clerk had lied. *Cutter was registered*—under his own name—and the clerk had denied it. But what did that mean? Probably nothing, she reasoned through rising disappointment, other than the fact that he'd been trying to protect Cutter's privacy.

Her heart was hammering so wildly that she almost missed the name Cutter when the clerk mumbled it. Her senses alerted, she strained to pick up more of the brief conversation. One other name registered—White Rock. The rest was indistinguishable.

The instant she heard the click of the phone receiver, Chloe remembered she'd left the registration book open. Would the clerk notice it? Would he check and find the front door unlocked?

For an interminable moment there was only silence. And then the sound of footsteps receding and the creak of a faucet signaled that she was safe. She crept from the office and sprinted through the patchy, low-lying mist to her room.

WHITE ROCK, she learned through a phone call to the Belmont Chamber of Commerce, was one of several small populated islands off the coast of Maine. An hour's drive would take her to the ferry landing in Belmont, and another thirty-minute boat crossing would take her to the island.

She reinforced her decision to go with a mental nod, tossed her weekender on the bed, opened it and began packing for the eventuality of an overnight stay. Not that she planned an overnight stay, but if she was on to something...

She was in the bathroom, trying to force a traveler-size tube of Colgate into an overstuffed makeup bag, when the creak of a door opening caught her attention. It was such a faint noise she thought she'd imagined it—or that it was someone else's door.

A cool breeze flowed past her ankles, a tangy whiff of ocean air. Had the wind blown the door open?

She caught the hushed sound of something moving, approaching; it pricked at her senses more than her ears. Staring at her frozen reflection in the medicine-cabinet mirror, she waited. Her knuckles white on the makeup case, she listened for footsteps.

The quiet had a paralyzing effect.

"Who's there?" she called.

Clutching her makeup case, stiff-armed, she came around and cautiously entered the living room.

The motel doorway hung wide open, filled by a gold-fringed silhouette.

Her heart jerked. *"You,"* she breathed.

His eyes purple-shadowed, his hair softly mussed, Nat Cutter assumed his favorite stance—shoulder propped against the doorframe, weight casually distributed along the diagonal line of his body.

"Am I late?" he asked quietly.

She hesitated, then realized he meant last night. *"Late?"* The word hung in the air precariously. A twitch of pain bit at her mouth. "No—I'd call it a clean miss."

"Sorry," he said, his voice so low she had to read his lips to understand him, and then he asked, "You going somewhere?"

She turned her back on him and tossed the makeup case into the weekender. "Yes," she hissed softly. With two brisk strides, she reached the bed, snapped the suitcase shut and pulled it to the floor. How *dare* he show up this way? The bastard! Leaning on her door as though he held a lease on the threshold.

"Where?" he said.

Name, rank and serial number, she told herself bitterly. The Geneva Convention required no more information than that to be given to the enemy. She came around, prepared to deliver a withering look and order him out of her doorway and her life...but instead she caught her foot on the weekender and tipped it over on her toes.

The pain made her face go white.

He grinned slightly. "Is this another ploy for emergency medical care?" He started toward her.

With a furious shake of her head she held him at bay. "Don't you touch me." *Don't even think about touching me.* A tear of sheer frustration rolled down her cheek. She had to get him out of here. She should hate him. *She did hate him,* enough to murder him. But not— Her stomach wrenched brutally. Not enough to stop him if he tried to—

"Hey," he said, sobering. "Does it hurt that bad?"

*"Yes."* Yes, it hurt that bad.

She picked up the suitcase and stared fixedly

through him at the door. "I'm leaving, Cutter. Get out of my way."

"Not until you tell me where you're going."

"I'd rather die first," she muttered, her fingers tightening on the handle.

"I don't think we have to go that far," he said, his voice lowering. "But you're not leaving."

Anger flared inside her throat. And then she made the mistake of looking at him, at his features with their shadowed and conflicting needs, at his eyes as he neared, black magic, beautiful...terrible.

# 5

PANIC FLASHED through Chloe. She thrust out an arm, her palm a vertical barrier. "Stay away from me, Cutter, I mean it."

He hesitated, a question in his eyes. "I don't get it. You're leaving because of last night?"

She realized then that he thought she was returning to New York, and in her fury, she hadn't the slightest inclination to set him straight. The disquiet in his features brought a flicker of satisfaction.

"Why?" he asked, moving toward her.

"Why not?" Warning him off with her hand, she stepped back and lost her grip on the suitcase. It hit the floor with a jarring clatter, popped open and spewed out clothes and makeup everywhere.

Staring down at the hopeless mess, Chloe felt a surge of frustration out of all proportion to the situation. *"Damn,"* she moaned, fighting back the threat of tears.

Static burst from the old radio, interrupting a medley of Tony Bennett hits. Each discharge sent a tense crackle through the room.

Nat Cutter's brows furrowed in confusion as he watched Chloe struggle to repack the bag. She was muttering, throwing clothes into the suitcase and hastily wiping her cheek, but not quickly enough to hide the tears he saw quivering in her lower lashes.

Crying? "Chloe, what's—"

"I dropped my suitcase," she snapped as though that event were an unspeakable tragedy. "My clothes, they're—" The words broke off with a choked sound.

"Hey," he said, his voice gentling. "It's not the end of the world. I'll help you."

"*No.*" Her body stiffened, her hands worked faster.

Conflict stemmed high in his chest. He'd come to tell her he was sorry, to explain about last night—why he hadn't shown up, all the reasons he couldn't see her again. He'd expected anger, but not this. She looked like a small cornered animal crouching there, full of sadness and spirit, trying for all she was worth to pull off a dignified exit.

"Chloe," he said, controlling his voice against the unexpected tightening in his chest. "Tell me what's going on."

She shook her head and fumbled to close the suitcase, shuddering when the lock snapped shut. As she rose and picked up the bag, another unexpected impulse hit him. He wanted to stop her. What the hell's wrong with you, man? he questioned, almost violently. She's leaving. She's solving the problem for you. Let her go. *It's better this way.*

But he knew he was blocking her exit. And he didn't move.

She walked to within two feet of him and came to a stiff stop, avoiding his eyes, obviously building her courage to walk around him. Drawing in a breath, he remembered the way she'd come sprinting down that dock two days before, a redheaded, one-woman rescue squad, determined to save him from himself.

Watching her now, her eyes downcast, her lashes a spiky silhouette against her pale cheeks, he felt a wrench of something alien inside him. Need. The need to kiss away the dampness that still clung to her lashes. An almost savage need to soothe her hurt and feel the softness of her mouth beneath his.

An incredible mouth, he thought, mesmerized by its vulnerability. Sensual, full...the lower lip pouting slightly when she wasn't smiling, like now.

*Let her go,* he told himself. She's got trouble written all over her. If you ever needed to stay clear of a woman it's this one. She's impulsive, romantic, always on the verge of something half-crazy. You know the type, man. Wide-eyed, and breathless, an infectious spirit that wants to take up residence in your soul—he felt a wrench of desire in his gut—*the kind you can't make love to and ever hope to walk away from.*

Maybe that was it, he thought, grasping at anything. Hell, yes, that was it. He wanted to get her into bed. He'd been obsessed with the thought of making love to her since he'd sketched her picture two days before.

His eyes moved over her body involuntarily, aware of the rebellious pride in her carriage. Almost as though she sensed his gaze, she stiffened her spine, and the result was a defiant arch that pulled the thin cotton fabric of her Harvard T-shirt tight over her breasts.

Before he could block it out, his memory was replaying their encounter on the beach the day before. The fine quiver that had moved through her when he touched her. Her starry-eyed sensuality as she looked up at him, as though he was the man she'd been waiting for all her life. Why had she looked at him like that? *What in the hell did she want from him, anyway?*

The sound of her throat clearing brought him back.

"Move out of the way," she said, still not looking at him.

Her body was rigid with determination, her will, awesome...but she was tiny compared to him, a foot smaller, easily managed. He could stop her without half trying; he could stop her, hold her— A flash of desire nearly cut off his breathing. You're losing it, he warned savagely, *get out of her way.*

"Move aside, Cutter," she insisted, her voice wire-taut as she raised her face to his. *"Now."*

Her mouth was soft, defiant. Let her go, he argued with his hot-blooded impulses. She's trouble, man. She's been asking questions. *She wants something.*

But it wasn't his own warning that made him step aside. It was the light in her eyes; he'd never seen such fierceness of will in a woman. This one had been through some kind of hell and survived it, he realized instantly. And whatever she was going through now, she'd survive that, too.

He gave her plenty of room, and felt the constriction in his throat as she walked past him with unsteady pride.

"Chloe," he heard himself say as she approached the open door. "Why?"

She hesitated, a shudder moving her shoulders.

In the distance, sea gulls keened, counterpoint to the soft crash of the incoming tide.

"At least tell me why you're leaving."

Poised on the threshold, Chloe felt the rasp in his voice caress her like raw silk. She gripped her suitcase so tight her knuckles stung. If she stopped now, if she even attempted to answer his question, she would never make it out the door—that was the extent of his effect on her. And he knew it. She was sure now that he knew the power he had over her even if he didn't understand it.

"If this is about last night, look, I'm sorry, I—"

A muscle spasmed in her cheek. *"Don't,"* she cut in, swinging around to face him. "Don't explain. I don't want to hear it."

"I had an emergency—"

"Emergency?" she cut him off bitterly. "Is that what they're calling it nowadays?"

His one-shouldered shrug brought her simmering hurt and fury to full boil. He dared to stand there and act perplexed? "I heard the woman, Cutter."

"You heard— When?"

"Last night," she bit out. "Late, in your room."

Stunned, he stared at her for a moment, his features slowly mobilizing with awareness, and then he began to shake his head and walk toward her. "No," he said, "you didn't hear a woman."

Incredulity left her speechless. Now he was going to tell her what she'd heard? She felt the suitcase slipping from her fingers and set it down.

"You couldn't have heard a woman," he insisted, an odd intensity in the voice. Before she could think to stop him he was standing in front of her, staring down at her, paralyzingly near. "It was something else, the television maybe." His shoulder lifted again. "I couldn't sleep last night, I had it on—"

"Television?" She pulled back, her voice taut with disbelief. "Oh Cutter, do you expect me to believe that? I heard her, I heard her."

*"No."* His breath fanned over her face. "It was something else, Chloe...maybe you had a dream."

His closeness was dizzying; his warm male scent permeated her senses. And when his fingers grazed down her arm she felt a fine spray of sparks that drew every cell of her attention to the hand that was closing around her wrist.

"You had a dream," he was telling her with such conviction she almost believed him. "It frightened you, woke you up. We all think we hear things in the middle of the night."

She shook her head, determined to hold out against the irresistible pull in his voice. "No, I heard you—arguing with her. I heard something drop. I—"

She broke off as he glanced at her mouth, just the way he had the day before at the beach. *Just before he'd kissed her.* Her hand flew up to cover the vulnerable area. She couldn't let him kiss her now. That would be the end of her.

Startled, he almost smiled, and then his eyes narrowed, lit with inner flickerings of regret. "Chloe," he insisted, exhaling, tugging her wrist. "I'm sorry I couldn't make our date last night. I wanted to, but I had an emergency. There wasn't time to tell you, and I got back too late to wake you."

He cradled her hand in his, and with gentle unconscious strokes of his thumb, he began to caress the icy coldness from her fingers. "I couldn't sleep so I turned on the televison. That must be what you heard."

"The television..." Looking into his eyes, she felt a dull thud of pain in her chest. Why was he lying to her?

His hand came up to cup her jawline, and she felt the slight unsteadiness in his fingers. "I wanted to be with you last night." His voice was so husky with sincerity that despite her skepticism, she wanted to close her eyes and try to capture its resonance.

"Do you believe me?" he asked.

"Yes...I believe you wanted to be with me."

She saw the slight tremor in his jaw, saw the muscle

catch as he searched her features. His mouth moved, tautening sensually, and a thrill built deep inside her.

"There is no other woman, Chloe."

Staring up at him, she realized what he'd just said. *Other* woman. What did that mean? In that abrupt starburst of a moment, she had no inkling of understanding other than that he was sincere. He was trying to tell her something, and for him, it was the truth.

His gaze held hers until she felt lights darting inside her, primitive messages rushing through her senses. The waver of his forefinger along her lip line sparked a run of electricity, and she reacted instantaneously, her body starting as though a live current had arched through her.

He bent toward her, and it happened again. Just as before when his lips had touched hers, she felt that infinitesimal jolt of sensation, the burst of light behind her eyelids. Deep inside her a warm glow fanned out like a sunrise, and then fell in on itself, gathering energy to expand in another wave of radiance.

Sweet chaos rushed up like a spring tide as he broke the kiss, his hands framing her face in a hovering caress, his thumbs at the corners of her mouth. After a moment, the muscles of his face relaxed, and a slight smile creased his lips. "Tell me the truth. Were you really going to leave?"

"No," she assured him, barely able to talk. "No, just a day trip." And then she added without thinking, "To White Rock."

His fingers contracted. "What?"

Awareness exploded in her brain. What had she done?

In the horrible moment that followed, she would have given anything to take the words back, but it was too late, she'd said it...and the conflict was already rising in his eyes.

He released her, shifting back, searching her face. "The island? What do you want there?"

"Nothing in particular," she said, the lie tangling in her throat. "I—I heard it's beautiful, a must-see for tourists. There's a ferry from Belmont." She glanced down at the suitcase. "I thought I might stay over." It sounded so lame, she couldn't imagine anyone believing it, especially him.

He stared at her for silent, stretching moments. Several times she thought he was on the verge of speaking. But he didn't. He nodded, simply nodded and turned away, his face unreadable.

She suppressed a shiver as a cold rush of ocean air chased the residual heat of his body from her skin. He looked more guarded than angry as he walked to the open doorway and stared out. Dr. Jekyll and Mr. Hyde, this man. Which one was he becoming now?

The desire they'd aroused in each other had flicked off as though he'd hit a circuit breaker. What was he thinking? she wondered. Conflicting messages flooded her, such as: how beautiful he was to her, even now, in his splendid isolation of mind, and how she could still taste the wonder of his mouth. And how much she wanted him back, touching, holding, loving her, all of it, she thought, her eyes flashing shut, *all of it.*

She found herself leaning against the door when the opposing arguments began to lay siege to her fantasies. Taking in his stormy profile, she realized he'd done it again. She was supposed to be ruthlessly investigating Nathanial Cutter—and what was she doing? Gazing at him as if he were Michelangelo's *David.* Once again, he'd waylaid her.

"How are you getting there?"

His question startled her. "To Belmont? I have a rental car. It's parked out front."

"It's going to rain," he said, leaning against the door-jamb. "The roads—they'll be bad."

He sounded so matter-of-fact, it was hard to tell if he was expressing polite concern or dabbling in sabotage. And it did look like rain. The skies were gunmetal gray. But then, around here the skies were almost always gunmetal gray. "I can handle it."

He swung around, and she could see by his expression that he'd made a decision. "I'm going with you. We'll take my car."

"Go with me? Why?"

"I know the way, the roads and the island."

Worried about her safety, was he? More likely he didn't want her on that island alone. Whatever his reasons, he didn't look like he could be talked out of them. A flat refusal on the tip of her tongue, she cocked her head and weighed her options. All things considered, it might be to her benefit to have him along.

CUTTER'S low-slung black Corvette ground gravel for twenty feet before he wheeled it out onto the two-lane highway to Belmont.

Chloe tightened her seat belt to keep from swaying toward her silent chauffeur. "I'm surprised you didn't have something better to do," she said, making conversation.

"As a matter of fact," he said, his eyes on the road ahead, "I had a date with one of the Dallas Cowboys' cheerleaders. I'm throwing her over to take you sightseeing."

"The team will be grateful." Chloe smiled, breathing

a mental sigh of relief that his sense of humor was still intact.

Through the path the highway cut between spiraling evergreens, Chloe saw storm clouds roiling toward them. Black and full-bellied, they dominated the horizon, pierced by intermittent shafts of light that looked breathtakingly like pathways. To heaven or hell? she wondered nervously.

The building turbulence outside spiked the tension in the car as they roared down the highway. Acutely aware of their tight quarters, Chloe distracted herself with the problem of dealing with this unexpected turn of events.

She flinched at a sudden crack of thunder, and before she'd fully recovered, a solid sheet of rain encased them.

Cutter swore and slowed. "I'm turning back."

"No," she said with unusual force. She shook her head as he looked at her. "No—it'll blow over." A less determined woman would have agreed, but his tense behavior had confirmed her earlier hunch. This was no pleasure trip for him. He'd agreed to drive her for his own reasons, and she was sure she'd read the major reason accurately: he didn't want her on the island alone.

He's tripped himself up this time, she thought. If anyone on White Rock recognizes him, I'll know exactly who to question later.

She saw him gear down, felt the car slowing, swinging wide, and realized he was about to negotiate a U-turn. "No, Cutter," she cried, seizing his forearm. "I want to see that island. If you won't take me, I'll drive myself."

The moment of tension broke like a bowstring as he

popped the gearshift into second, hit the gas pedal and swung the car back into the lane. "Why do you have to see island today?" he asked, his voice low as he accelerated into a wall of rain.

"I might not get another chance," she said, adding as he glanced at her, "I'll be going back soon, to New York." Hating the lies, but feeling an urgent need to stir his goodwill, she went on. "I'm a history buff." She recalled the tiny island museum the Chamber of Commerce rep had recommended, and she casually tossed out the name. "The place is loaded with artifacts and memorabilia—the sort of thing we history nuts can't resist."

He geared up suddenly, and she felt the movement of his muscles beneath her fingers. Startled at the sight of her hand still curled around his forearm, she withdrew it instantly, her fingers alive with the feel of him.

As they drove on, silenced by claps of thunder and wild rainfall, her sensitized nerves made her increasingly aware of the space that separated them—the half foot of charged air where his body left off and hers began.

She felt the restlessness in him; it was tangible. And other things, deeper, less physically evident, but even more implicit in his nature: loneliness, hunger and denial.

A guarded glance at him revealed emotions she hadn't expected. She saw vulnerability in the set of his jaw; she saw pride and a lonely kind of beauty. Her heart stirred with the desire to touch him.

Don't, she warned silently, knowing it wouldn't take much more than a touch to spark the tension between them.

Forcing her concentration back to the trip ahead, she

caught the glint of eyes in her peripheral vision. Animal eyes, paralyzed, iced white by fear.

Cutter flinched and hit the brakes.

Slammed against the door by the force of the skidding car, Chloe heard the roar and whine of locked tires. She cringed, buffeted by the Corvette's tortured shimmying as it veered and spun in a half circle.

Nat's hands frantically worked the wheel. The car wrenched back, tires squealing, before he brought it to a stop on the shoulder. He gripped the wheel reflexively, hard enough to snap it in half, and emitted a low curse.

The engine shuddered and died.

"What happened?" Chloe breathed.

"A deer." He exhaled again, audibly. "On the road. I hit the brakes too hard and the tires locked." He released the wheel and looked at her. After a moment he touched her shoulder, then ran his fingers along her cheek. "You okay?"

She nodded, and still he continued touching her as though to assure himself.

"We're going back," he stated flatly. But when he tried to start the car, the engine growled and died with each twist of the ignition key. Swearing softly, he got out and lifted the hood. After several moments, he was back, soaked to the skin. "It's the carburetor. You stay here. I'll go get help."

Watching his solitary stride as he headed back in the direction they'd come, Chloe felt a stab of guilt. He'd warned her about the weather. She hurriedly unfastened her seat belt, struggled out of the car and called his name. When he turned, she began to run.

"I'm coming with you," she said as she reached him. Drenched and gasping, she overrode his obviously pleased protests with an uncompromising shake of her head. "I got us into this," she said, walking beside him, "the least I can do is help get us out."

"God loves a persistent woman," he conceded finally, a smile touching his lips.

He slowed his pace as they walked, urging her along with him at the same time. The deluge worsened, soaking them through to the skin, weighting their clothing, blinding them.

It seemed as though they'd walked all the way to the Maine–New Hampshire border when Chloe spotted a small sign telling them the Sunrise motel was half a mile down the road. They picked up the pace, and the last leg of their journey became a half-running, breathless rush for shelter.

The motel came into sight, its shingles bleached white by a simultaneous crack of thunder and lightning. The skies opened and roared. Instinctively, they began to sprint.

Spluttering water, panting like winded animals, they burst into her room and fell against the door. Chloe's lungs burned with each breath. Her heart throbbed in her ears.

They acknowledged each other's condition breathlessly, water running through their hair, streaming down their faces. "It'll blow over?" Nat said, his voice cracking with disbelief. They began to laugh until, spurred by the sight of each other, they lost control. Chloe doubled, gurgling helplessly. Nat fell on the couch.

"I'll get some towels," she said finally, mustering some control as she headed for the bathroom. Barry Manilow was singing "Even Now" as she passed the dinette on her way and switched off the radio they'd forgotten all about.

She shed her sodden zip-up sweatshirt in the claw-footed bathtub, grabbed two large fluffy bathsheets and returned to the living room, still wearing a damp T-shirt and wet jeans.

She tossed him a towel and began vigorously to dry her own hair, still chuckling, only subliminally aware of his eyes on her. She had the chore nearly done before her subconscious snuck up on her. A spark of recognition ran along her spine. He wasn't moving; he was watching her. Not moving...watching.

Her hands stilled, poised above her head, her fingers entangled in the towel. She raised her eyes, saw where his gaze was fixed, and felt a hot flush of surprise.

Following his eyes, she looked down. Her damp T-shirt clung wantonly to the fullness of her breasts, revealing creamy flesh in patches, catching every movement. She lowered her arms with exaggerated care, dropped the towel and finally, her heart fluttering in her throat, she raised her eyes to his.

His features were taut, expectant, his eyes as black as passion itself.

"I'd better get these wet clothes off," she said, aware of the throaty swell in her voice.

He nodded, hesitating where he stood.

As she started for the bathroom, he called her name with such low force that she shuddered to a stop.

"Stay here," he said, the undercurrent in his words holding her like a physical restraint. She felt a crazy siphoning off of energy, felt the muscles in her legs quiver.

His voice vibrated through her. "Stay here, Chloe... where I can see you."

"Cutter," she rasped, her voice tightening as she realized what he wanted. "I can't."

She stared at the door to the bathroom and knew she had to get there somehow, but she couldn't move. With a sharp intake of air she tried to block out what was happening inside her—the climbing excitement, the breathless whispers.

She felt his eyes on her back, saw them in her mind. Dark and haunting, they drew her irresistibly. Convulsing with an exquisite shiver, she felt it begin... *surrender*.

"Chloe."

"I can't," she heard herself say, and yet she came around, still shaking her head, her arms spontaneously crossing in front of her, her fingers grasping the bottom of her T-shirt. I can't, she thought, her body racked with sweet pain. A cry caught in her throat as she gathered the material up with trembling fingers and lifted....

Nat Cutter watched her tug her T-shirt up and felt a spasm lock his throat. The soft freefall of her breasts as the damp material cleared sent a knifelike pain through him.

She pulled the shirt free of her head and let it drop. Her breath caught; it sounded like a soft sob.

"My God," he whispered, watching her.

Her skin was a shade paler than English cream, her breasts were swollen. Even the fanning delicacy of her lifting eyelashes entranced him. They were dark and as lush as a rain forest. She looked up at him, and his heart bucked.

He reached her in two strides, groaning as he touched her. "You're beautiful," he said, his voice husky, "so beautiful."

The faintest quiver of a smile touched her lips.

He gathered her in his arms, acutely aware of the pressure of her breasts against his rib cage. A sound broke inside him, low, serrated with need. Working his fingers deep into the wild red halo of curls, he breathed kisses over her eyes, cheeks, lips.

He drew his hand around to cup a breast, and its heat sparked nerve endings that ran clear up his arm. "You feel like a dream," he said, soft and harsh against her lips.

His other hand found the waistband of her jeans. Hearing her soft gasp, he began to whisper to her, soothingly, low and seductive, ignoring the rigidity building in her body.

"Wait," she pleaded as he freed the snap.

Caught up in a mindless rush, he began to lower the zipper.

"*Wait*," she said, pulling back.

He scanned her face. She was rigid, trembling like a leaf beneath his hands. "What is it?"

Her head jerked in mute denial.

She was frightened, he could see that in the way she held herself. Not the kind of fear a woman might feel with a new man, this was something stronger. Mixed with it he saw other emotions: confusion, embarrassment, anger...even some shame?

The realization, when it came to him, was sudden and incredulous. A blow to his gut. "*This is your first time, isn't it?*"

"No," she said, looking away. "Of course not."

He caught her chin and drew her back. "Listen to me, Chloe, I need to know." Ease up, Cutter, he told himself. "You've never been with a man before, have you?" he asked more gently.

Her eyes were huge. Their soft desperation cut into him. She dropped her head finally, shook it slowly. "Almost," she said, as though to herself, "in college."

"Almost?" He groaned, shutting his eyes. *Almost didn't count.* "Why didn't you tell me?"

She broke from him and half turned away. "I didn't think it would matter."

"Didn't think— My God, Chloe, it *does*."

He barely heard her whispered "Why?"

"Because—" He riffled his hands through his hair, swung around, walking to the window. "Because I can't be the one to—" He'd never felt such agonizing confusion. The words weren't there. "The first time has to be right," he told her, his voice taut, "the right man."

"And if I want it to be with you?"

Desire beat inside him, but he couldn't. *He couldn't.*

Fighting to control the ache in his gut the only way he knew how, he walked to her and brought her face up, his hands framing her throat in a roughened caress. "You don't know me. You don't know what I am." His heart hardened against the soft pull of her eyes. "I'm the kind of man your mother warned you against."

Feeling the quiver of her jaw beneath his fingers, he added heartlessly, "You're no match for me, Chloe. You and I are like a predator and its prey."

She tried to pull away, but he jerked her back. "Have you ever seen a cat with a moth? The cat watches, fascinated with the moth's quivering movement...and then it strikes. It has to," he grated softly. "Predators are fated to destroy soft, vulnerable things."

He saw the dull shock of fear in her eyes and knew that he'd won. Or had he lost? His heart a stone in his chest, he swung around and strode toward the door.

# 6

CHLOE SKIPPED a stone across the nearly placid water. Above her a magnificent barrier of cloud cover, fluffy and shock-white, blocked off the deepening indigo of the early-evening sky. Oddly, the serenity intensified her restlessness.

The harsh jangling of a telephone climbed her spine.

Him? She turned and started back to her room. The way he'd stormed out that morning, she'd never expected to hear from him again.

Giving her door a quick nudge shut as she passed it, she picked up the receiver, held it in both hands for a minute, then brought it to her ear. "Hello," she said, aware of her own breath against the mouthpiece.

"Ms. Kates?" a masculine voice asked.

Confusion and disappointment flooded her. "Yes?"

"Gordon Browne calling, your stepfather's assistant."

"Oh...yes." She'd detected something familiar in the stilted style. "What is it, Mr. Browne?" In the years since she'd left Northpointe, she and the formidable Gordon Browne had never even come close to a first-name basis relationship. Not that she'd wanted one—his vigilant features had always put her off—but still, it was curious. "Is everything all right?" she asked, suddenly concerned that her stepfather's condition had worsened.

"Fine, Ms. Kates. Mr. Guthrie's made some progress since your visit to the hospital. He might be able to return home soon."

"Oh, that's good," she said, relieved.

"Not to Northpointe, of course. He's taken a suite at a hotel near the hospital. Actually, it's something else I've called you about. I was wondering if anything had changed since we talked. Regarding Sara, that is."

A fundamental question pushed through Chloe's surprise. How had Browne tracked her down? The only person she'd told about Maine was Marsha, and even her partner didn't know the real reason for the trip.

"Sara?" she murmured, stalling. She wasn't sure why she still felt the need to keep a lid on her investigation of Cutter. It was a hunch, but such a strong one she went with it. "Why do you ask, Mr. Browne? And I'm curious. How did you find me?"

For the first time ever, she thought she heard him falter. "I—well, I called your office, of course. Your partner was good enough to tell me how to reach you."

"I see." The awkward silence that followed stirred an idea. "I'd like very much to help find Sara. Perhaps if you told me what you know about her disappearance." The subtle challenge had been on her mind ever since the hospital visit when she began to suspect Guthrie and Browne of holding something back. She'd always assumed it was Guthrie's paranoia about the press that led him to hush up the incident at Northpointe. But maybe...

"Ms. Kates," Browne chastised, ignoring her questions, "Mr. Guthrie's health and advanced years made it imperative that we locate his daughter without delay. He was hoping you might have been in touch with her."

The flicker of passion in his voice increased Chloe's wariness. "I haven't, really. I would have told you." At least the first part of the answer was true.

"You're sure? If there's anything you know, anything you could do—"

"I'd do it," she assured him quickly.

"We thought your trip—" he pressed stiffly. "Well, Maine this time of year is hardly a vacation spot. We thought you had some other reason for going."

Cat and mouse, she thought, frustrated. We're both playing it. Why? And why didn't she trust him? A ripple crossed her shoulder blades as it occurred to her that he and Guthrie might be using her somehow, might even be shadowing her. Lord, that was farfetched. Now *she* was getting paranoid. "It's quiet here," she said, "and I needed some R and R."

"You're vacationing alone, Ms. Kates?"

"Yes," she said instantly—and then wished she'd told him to mind his own business. "I'll be in touch, Mr. Browne," she informed him briskly, "if I should have anything to tell you." Cutting off his attempt to detain her with a polite goodbye, she hung up the phone.

A half hour later, she'd nearly worn a path in the linoleum, pacing, wondering if she'd done the right thing. Fourteen years ago she'd held back the truth about Joshua, now she was doing the same thing with Cutter. And all because of some nagging intuition?

Reasons pushed through her rising disquiet. She was protecting Cutter because he was her only link to Sara...and because if she admitted her suspicions to Browne, he would almost certainly sic detectives on

Cutter. And that would make Cutter murderous. And what if he wasn't Joshua? Or if he *had* done something wrong...?

Anxiety high in her chest, she closed her eyes and saw Nat Cutter's features there, indistinct at first, coming into focus like a photograph developing. With sudden and stunning clarity, she saw the taut, expectant lines, the blinding flash of passion in his eyes. "Sweet heaven," she breathed, crossing her arms to subside her heart's burst of speed.

Eyes blinking open, she glimpsed herself in the vanity across the room and walked slowly toward the image. Is that me? she questioned, astonished by the strained and tousled figure she saw reflected in the mirror. Her clothes awry, her hair as wild as Cutter's hands had left it, she felt as though she were staring at someone else, a woman out of control. *Is that me?*

Huge green eyes stared back at her, full of conflicting needs and confusion. That woman in the mirror looked caught—on the verge of something crazy.

Releasing a breath, Chloe turned away. "It's time to get honest," she told herself unsteadily, putting some distance between herself and the vanity. "You're not handling this well. You're not handling it at *all*. You came here to find Sara, but this thing with Cutter, this *obsession*—" she purposely emphasized the word to shock some sense into that woman in the mirror "—it's taking over."

She went on, merciless now. "You've fouled up plan after plan, bungled almost every opportunity. You haven't got the vaguest idea what to do next—" A knot drew tight in her stomach as she realized how true it was. Cutter had some kind of hold on her, almost hypnotic, a power she couldn't fight. He blunted her natural instincts, continually had her at cross-purposes with herself, and worst of all—her eyes returned irresistibly to the mirror—he aroused her.

The morning's encounter played through her mind in shocking detail: the whispering impulses that had compelled her to undress, the thrill of his hands on her body, the breathless touch of his lips. If he hadn't backed off what would she have done?

You couldn't have stopped him, the mirror image warned. He's in your blood, has taken possession of your senses. You would have done anything, *anything he wanted*.

"I'm in over my head," she whispered, a tremor in her voice. As the realization that she was truly out of control registered in every nerve ending, a drastic solution came to her. "Browne...call Browne back...*tell him the truth*."

The green eyes flashed no, unequivocally, *no*.

"Why not?" Chloe whispered, turning away. Gordon Browne was a competent man; he'd been loyal to Guthrie. He'd never actually done anything to confirm her suspicions. The distrust she felt might be nothing more than her imagination working overtime again. She had Sara to think of—and Guthrie. How could she justify holding back what she knew under the circumstances?

The more she considered the idea, the less desperate it seemed. She turned away, her eyes fixing on the phone. I'll tell him to be discreet, hire the best, she thought. Cutter mustn't know he's being investigated. Exhaling, she walked toward the table. And if Browne learns something, *anything*, he's to report to me first, before he takes any action. "If he doesn't agree to those terms," she resolved aloud, "I won't do it."

Her fingers touched the receiver, and a shock ran up her arm. She froze in place as a vivid snapshot from the past rushed at her: a frightened twelve-year-old confronted by the police, Guthrie foaming with rage, savage dogs that tore people apart. *Joshua. Was she turning the dogs loose on him?*

She forced the images from her mind and stared at the phone, startled at how sinister its bulky, old-fashioned lines suddenly seemed.

"All right," she said finally, exhaling as she turned to face her mirror image. "All right—you win. One more day. Twenty-four hours. But that's all. If I haven't turned anything up by then, I'm going to call Gordon Browne."

MUFFLED VOICES touched Chloe's sleep-hazed mind, registering somewhere in her subconscious. She opened her eyes with some effort, gradually aware that she'd drifted off. Blinking to bring the wall clock into focus, she realized it was nearly midnight. The moment she'd taken to rest and recharge had stretched to two or three hours.

Barefoot, but still fully dressed, she pushed herself up, groaning as she slid off the bed. Her eyes burned; her throat felt scratchy. Chalking it up to that morning's run in the rain, she focused in on the radio's soft blare. That's what she'd heard, she realized, starting for it.

As her fingers touched the switch, a distant clicking sound caught her ear. *The sound of a door opening.* Her senses sharpened, cutting through the last residues of sleep. The noise came from her left—Cutter's room. She opened her own door and edged out, squinting to see in the damp, nearly opaque air.

A quiver of movement, a scuffling sound drew her focus.

Her eyes strained for definition, and abruptly, as they adjusted to the darkness, she saw him. A silhouette, black on black, pulled Cutter's door shut noiselessly. Chloe slipped back into the shadows of her own doorway where he couldn't see her.

Cutter? she questioned as the man darted past, his head angled away, his jet hair flying. She suppressed an impulse to call out the name and watched him stride up the pathway that edged the bluffs.

As the darkness swallowed him, she shook off her uncertainty and bolted in pursuit. Frigid onshore gusts blew her hair and burned her cheeks as she reached the bluffs and continued on, her breath coming faster. Tiny pebbles cut into her bare soles. The sickle moon, shrouded by mists, provided so little light that she blundered off the path constantly.

He came into her sights around the next turn, and she slowed immediately. The path's ultimate destination was Johnson's Cove, a quiet little harbor she'd seen pictures of on the wall of the office the day she registered. Why would he be heading there?

He picked up his pace, and she broke into a trot, increasing her speed steadily to keep up. Suddenly he was running as though he'd heard her. She sprinted in pursuit.

He glanced back, and she feinted aside, snagging something with her foot. Suddenly she was off balance, reeling forward. Her hands and knees hit the ground first, jarring her whole body.

"Damn," she gasped, fighting dizziness as she pushed herself up. Watching him disappear around a curve ahead, she fought to quiet the roaring in her head.

In the hair's-breadth silence between shock and action, a sound pricked her ears. The sickening crackle of leaves underfoot. It came from behind. Her heart rocketing, she heard it again and turned, gasping as shadows dropped down, as dark and shivery as living things.

*The wind, the trees,* she realized.

Five feet in front of her she saw a jagged cavity in the rocks and froze in a panicky examination of its black depths. A claustrophobic feeling engulfed her, the premonition of something unseen, drawing near. Tiny prickles raised the hair on her nape. He'd seen her, whoever he was. Had he doubled back?

Chloe's stomach spasmed with fear. "Who's there?"

The movement of something human, *the glint of eyes, milk white in the darkness*, shocked her senses. A memory pierced the night. She'd seen those eyes before—when she'd been a child, lost in the woods, terrified by the image of a hovering demon. The old terror moved through her, paralyzing her legs as she tried to back away. "Who's there?"

As he stepped out of the shadows, the moon flared to a silver brightness, its light running in his hair.

*"Joshua?"*

Lightheadedness swept her senses.

She saw him coming toward her through a veil of time-blurred space. Dancing phantoms, shot through with oblique light, revealed haunting glimpses of his features. At the last minute, she looked away.

A hand bracketed her jaw, brought her face up. "What did you call me?" His harsh inquiry broke the spell.

"Cutter?" she whispered, staring up at him. Not Joshua, Nat Cutter, of course, *of course*. What in God's name was happening to her? "But you—?" She broke off, looking up the path, seeing only empty space. Her head snapped back. "What are you doing here?"

He took hold of her shoulders as though he meant to shake some sense into her. "Me? What are *you* doing here? Half frozen, shivering." He looked down. "And barefoot?"

"I heard something, someone. I just wanted to—"

His narrowing eyes silenced her. "What did you call me?"

"Call you?" Had she said the name out loud? "I don't...remember," she hedged. "I was frightened."

He studied her face for a moment, or it could have been several; she lost track of time in the wake of his searching inquiry. If he saw the lie, he didn't acknowledge it. Touching a finger to her cheek, he thrilled her gently with a caress. A spark that could have been pain, or passion, glinted in his eyes.

She felt the jerk of his hand as he pulled away, saw his features tighten into a grimace. "Do you have any idea what you're getting into?" he said, the question laced with threat.

"What do you mean?"

He shook his head. "You really don't know, do you?"

"I know I won't be frightened off by your threats," she said, her spine stiffening at the "hopeless child" tone in his voice. "And I also know I can take care of myself."

"No, dammit, you can't." His hand came up, raked through his hair in a gesture that twitched with controlled violence. "You're headed for more trouble than you could ever imagine."

She met his eyes and defied him. "Meaning yourself?"

"Meaning *trouble* in the larger sense—meaning those who play with fire get burned. You're playing with fire, Chloe. You're going to get hurt, and I don't mean a broken heart."

They stared at each other, eyes flashing. Deadlocked.

"I don't know why you're here," he said finally. "But if it's because of me, then please—give it up. I'm not what you need, I never will be—"

"*Stop* telling me what I need," she cut back, her voice low. "And stop presuming that it's *you*."

As she pulled free of his grasp and shouldered away, he caught her wrist and whipped her around. "I'm doing you a favor, dammit. I'm telling you to get out of here. Go home."

"Save the favors."

Steel fingers stung her wrist and then released. "What's with you? A self-destructive streak? A death wish?"

A hot spark of anger and a crazy need to best him, *just once*, spurred her on. "You want me to leave Maine, Cutter? Give me a reason. Come on," she challenged, swiping at him, crooking a finger, "a real reason. Tell me why I should go, and none of this broken heart business, because I'm not the soft touch you think I am. I can play hardball, Cutter. Try me."

"I don't know what you're talking about," he said, so low she could barely hear him. "But I'm not talking any more, I'm telling you. Catch a flight to New York tomorrow. If you don't, I'll—"

"What?" she said, fighting the tremor of fear that assaulted her. "You'll what?"

His eyes deflected moonlight like a cat's. "Be on that plane," was all he said. Wheeling around, he started up the path to Johnson's Cove.

"Where are you going?" she called after him.

"You said you saw somebody. I'm going to check it out." Halting midstride, he jerked around, each word a whip crack. "Get out of here, Chloe. Go home."

It wasn't him she'd been following? Watching him disappear, she felt a delayed reaction of trembling wash her body like the hot chill of a fever. *Go home?* Not on your sweet life, mister, she thought, shivering violently. Instinct told her she was close to what she'd come for, *very close.*

HEAT BURNED Chloe's cheeks and stung at her closed eyelids. She turned restively, opened her eyes and saw pale morning sunshine filtering through the dust-streaked window.

Awareness came gradually. She'd made a valiant effort to stay awake last night, intending to be up when Cutter returned, but racking chills and exhaustion had drugged her into a restless sleep. Pressing a palm to her forehead, she felt the shock of cool skin against hot.

The telephone clanged impatiently.

Cutter, she supposed, not at all sure she had the strength to face him.

"I'm coming," she grumbled, as the merciless clanging continued. Swaying dizzily, she made it to the table and picked up the phone.

"Get on a plane, Chloe," her partner, Marsha, was yelling. "Come back to New York. Come back immediately!"

"Marsha? What's wrong?"

"Nothing's wrong, everything's *right*. This proves it, Chloe. This proves there is a God."

Chloe sat down heavily, her legs unsteady. "Slow down. What's happened?"

"You know how long we've been struggling to make it as publicists? To get this agency out of the red?"

"Yes..."

"And how I've tried to talk you into asking your stepfather for a loan, but you wouldn't do it because you've always felt like a charity case? And how determined you are to prove you can make it on your own?"

"Marsha," she coaxed weakly, knowing how her partner loved a big buildup, "please—get to the point."

"And how we've been waiting for the phone to ring, for that big break?"

"*Marsha.*"

"Our big break just called."

"Who? Who called?" Ignoring her shaky legs, Chloe grabbed up the telephone and walked until the short cord jerked her back.

"Syd Reinhardt. You know—the agent—the one who's organizing the writers' conference this weekend. Sit down, Chloe, you're not going to believe this. They want a speaker from our agency."

Astonished, Chloe returned to the chair and collapsed. Yes, she knew Syd Reinhardt. His agency was fast becoming one of the largest and most prestigious in New York. His authors were big names, bestsellers, but like all shrewd agents, Syd had a warmup bullpen of brilliant rookies, future stars who needed plenty of publicity to build name recognition. What a source of referrals! The Reinhardt logo was *gold*. Just to be able to say they were associated with that agency could put them on the map!

"Chloe? You there?"

She hugged the phone to her stomach. "Marsha, are you sure?"

"Absolutely. One of Syd's people called today. Said he was sorry about the last-minute notice, but somebody got sick and left a hole in their conference schedule."

A delighted smile and sigh of relief welled at the same time. "You're going to be terrific, Marsha. I wish I could be there to hear you."

"Me? Chloe, they want *you*!"

"What? Why?"

"Darned if I know, but they want you and only you. Syd's personal request."

"Personal request?" Chloe's heart began to thump. What did that mean? She tried to stand up and couldn't.

"Sorry about your R and R," Marsha was saying, "but you've got to get the first plane back. You're the opening speaker."

First plane back? Opening speaker? No, not now. She couldn't leave *now*. The chair scraped across the floor as she finally made it to her feet. "I can't, Marsha."

"Can't? What do you mean can't?"

"I can't do it. I can't come home right now, there's a problem here. Listen, you cover for me. You're a better speaker than I am, anyway."

She heard an uncharacteristic gasp at the other end of the line. "What's got into you? I told you—they don't want me, they want *you*." Building up steam, her partner added in typical Marsha, lay-'em-out-flat style,

"If you care anything about me, about this agency, about staying *alive*, you'll get back here, Chloe. Pronto!"

Holding the phone away, her hand over the mouthpiece, Chloe tried to clear her fevered brain and consider her options. It only took her a moment to come to grips with the fact that she had to go. The agency meant everything to her. Not only was it her shot at independence and security, but she and Marsha had put heart and soul into building it into a viable business.

Yes, she had to go, but dammit, *she couldn't leave*. Lord, she groaned, a rock and a hard place would be heaven compared to this.

Ignoring Marsha's repeated "Chloe!" which filtered through her fingers, she finally hit on the only possible solution. "Okay, I'll be there, Marsha," she promised. "I'll catch the first flight back."

Pressing the disconnect button over her partner's moans of relief, she began to dial the airlines. Feverish chills forced her to concentrate. Cutter would think he'd scared her off, and maybe that was just as well. He'd never expect her to catch a plane back to Maine tomorrow, and if she was careful, he'd never know she'd returned.

She still had twelve hours left of the twenty-four hours she'd promised herself. Without Cutter running interference, that should be more than enough time for a thorough casing of White Rock Island.

# 7

CHLOE STOOD OFFSTAGE, hovering in the wings, while Syd Reinhardt welcomed the packed auditorium to the Tenth Annual Atlantic States Writers' Conference. "A record crowd," she heard the prematurely graying superagent tell his audience.

Listening to him introduce some of the more sterling members of the literary community—publishers, editors and writers of note—Chloe closed her eyes and prayed for strength. In a few minutes he'd be introducing her. Chloe Kates, virtually unknown publicist, untested public speaker, owner of watery knees and a fevered brow. Her throat felt like rusty steel wool. Even two industrial strength aspirin hadn't dulled the five-foot-three-inch toothache her body had become. Why hadn't Syd asked Marsha? Marsha loved to talk. Marsha never stopped talking!

Last night was a good example, Chloe thought ironically. From the moment her partner had picked her up at the airport, Marsha'd barely stopped for a breath until they reached the two bedroom sublet flat they shared in the Grammercy Park area. Besides giving Chloe a running commentary on the events of the past few days, she'd repeatedly pointed out what Chloe already knew—that Reinhardt's conference was their "ticket to ride."

"Wipe that glazed expression from your face," she'd

urged desperately. "You've got to impress Syd Reinhardt even if that means cartwheeling onto the stage. Energy, Chloe, *energy*."

Chloe hadn't found the right moment to tell her partner that the speech she'd prepared on the plane was certain to "impress" Syd, whether favorably or not was the question!

"Our first speaker," Syd was saying, "represents an innovative new agency here in New York. Not content with being 'just a publicist,' this woman is a creative strategist, a risk taker, and a businesswoman on the cutting edge of change. With a finger on current trends and a focus on the future, she and her partner are turning their agency into a high-velocity publicity machine...."

Chloe listened, stunned. Having only met Syd Reinhardt in the most casual sense at mutual business functions, she couldn't imagine where he'd come up with those superlatives...unless he'd been talking to Marsha, too. She took a deep breath and held her hand to her forehead. *What doesn't kill me makes me stronger.*

"How about a big welcome for Chloe Katherine Kates!"

He even knew her middle name?

The audience thundered out applause. Adrenaline spurred Chloe into action. She walked onto the stage, rubbery-legged, an overlarge smile on her face.

"Thank you," she gushed nervously. "Any chance you're looking for work?" she quipped as she took the mike from Syd. "After that intro, I'd like to sign you up."

The audience tittered and went silent as she turned to face them, a thousand eyes trained on her. "What does it take to be a best-selling author in the nineties?"

she asked, wishing she didn't sound so short of breath. "Talent? Persistence? Luck?"

Seeing heads begin to nod, she raised a hand. "If your answer is none of the above, you're right." She looked around the room and saw what she expected— surprise, skepticism. "Talent and persistence still count for a lot, of course, but this is the media decade, the television generation is coming of age and today's formula *and* shortcut to success is 'hype.' Not a pretty word, but if you're in a hurry—and who isn't in the nineties—it works and it's fast."

Stopping to clear her throat, she realized her hushed voice had them straining to hear. "With the right book—and by 'right' I don't mean good, there are plenty of bad bestsellers out there—I'm talking about a workable concept, an idea that captures the public's imagination. With that kind of a concept and a full-tilt ad campaign, you can guarantee yourself a bestseller."

She had them. Some eyes were wider, some narrower, but she had them. Now, all she had to do was back up her extravagant claim. Her voice getting huskier by the minute, she explained how a clever publicity campaign could put any book on the bestseller list, even a distinctly bad one. "You've all read them," she said, "the books that are so marginal you wonder why one copy sold, much less the one hundred thousand or so it took to put them on a bestseller list. Why do you buy them? The same reason everyone else does. Because you saw a flashy television spot or a full-page print ad. You were drawn in by a big money ad campaign."

Aches and pains forgotten, she went on, talking with more energy and animation as she explained how the right combination of packaging and promotion could make even a dull read sound dazzling. Seeing the heads begin to nod as she backed up her claims with cost-comparison data and industry statistics, she realized how good it felt to be back on her own turf, *sane again*, and effective.

She went on to warn them that even though "bestsellerdom" could be bought once, or maybe even twice, a series of terrible books could ruin even the most highly-financed career.

"The most important bit of advice I can give you today," she told them sincerely, "is to put heart and soul into your work. *Don't shortchange your readers.* Write the best book you know how, and then promote it. If you can't afford to hire a professional, do it on your own, and don't be bashful. If you love the story, that's reason enough to promote it."

High on a wave of audience approval, she went on to outline a step-by-step course of self-promotion and finally summed up her talk with a brief rundown of the services her agency provided.

The applause was loud, long and deeply gratifying.

Breathing out a sigh of relief, Chloe asked for questions. As hands went up, she saw Syd Reinhardt at the back of the hall standing near the entrance.

Her heart nearly stopped. Was the man next to him a trick of her overstimulated brain? Nat Cutter glanced up from his conversation with Syd, and his dark gaze brushed over her—lightly, but with enough force to make her feel like she'd been zapped by a live wire.

Shock brought a wave of feverish light-headedness. She grabbed for the podium and held on, aware that hands were waving at her. What was he doing here?

"Yes," she said, responding to a man in the front row who called out, "Ms. Kates?" to get her attention.

She tried to muster the presence of mind to answer his question, but the words kept trailing off. Even in a packed auditorium, Nat Cutter drew her like a negative charge attracts a positive one.

She wrenched her eyes away from Cutter and nodded at a woman waving several rows back. "Next question."

"You look so young," the woman remarked. "How long have you been a publicist, and how did you get your start?"

"Three years—or has it been—uh, no, yeah, three years." Aware that she was stumbling, Chloe compensated with an energetic smile. "My journalism professor convinced me I had a flair for public relations and volunteered me for the staff of the university yearbook. The rest," she said, her attention darting back to Cutter, "is history."

Leaning against the back wall, no longer talking to Syd, Cutter looked like a figure out of time—as though he might always have been there, all his life, all eternity, just waiting for her to look his way. Their gaze touched, and for an instant everything stopped.

He acknowledged her, not with a smile or a nod, but with his eyes. An energy connected them, penetrating her so deeply she felt it like a physical tug.

"Ms. *Kates*," someone called out. Chloe jerked in the direction of the voice and saw a heavyset man coming to his feet. "Has your agency ever promoted a book that made the bestseller list?"

With Cutter hovering in the background, Chloe described promotional campaigns for a pop psychology text and a science-fiction series. "And we're currently working on several—" she stopped midsentence to watch as Cutter straightened and began to walk toward the door "—other projects," she said faintly. *Don't leave.*

His hand hit the door and she heard herself whispering "Wait." The impulse to break away and follow him moved through her like physical pain. Explaining that her time was up, she began to back away from the podium, thanking the audience several times through a last wave of applause.

A short flight of steps backstage took her down to the auditorium. She hurried up the aisle, acknowledged a scattering of compliments, and pushed through the auditorium doors. It only took moments to confirm her fear that he'd left. Finding no sign of him anywhere in the marble halls, she returned, spotted Syd Reinhardt in the midst of a cluster of conferees and headed for him.

"Could I speak to you a minute?" she asked, standing on her tiptoes and signaling to him.

"Sure," he called back, working his way through the crowds. "Great speech," he said as he reached her.

"Thanks." Smiling, she urged him away from the confusion. "And thank you for making it possible," she added when they found a quiet spot. "While I was talking I saw a man standing next to you. I wanted to speak with him but it looks like he's already left."

"You mean Nat Cutter?"

"Yes, do you know him?"

"Know him?" Syd grimaced in mock despair. "Cutter's responsible for most of my misspent youth. We went to Harvard together, Nat and I, both bent on becoming the great American novelist. He did it, and I did the next best thing. I represent him."

"Really?" was all she could say.

Reinhardt's steel blue eyes regarded her. "You a friend, too?"

"Yes," she said hesitantly. Misspent youth? She was staring at a storehouse of information! "Actually, I'm Harvard, too—" As soon as she said it, she realized Marsha had probably provided him with a bio that declared her an NYU alumnus.

"That right?" Syd smiled. "One of the walking wounded?"

"Just flesh wounds," she clarified quickly. "I only took a graduate class or two."

They both laughed, and Reinhardt folded his arms, adding, "Yeah, Nat's quite a character. We go way back, fraternity brothers."

Chloe nodded subtle encouragement. "Then you probably remember Evans Cole?"

"Oh God, yeah," he chuckled. "Cole nearly flunked me out of his class. Great days those were. Nat and I and two other guys from the frat took off right after graduation, toured Europe, rode the trains, slept in flophouses."

"I always wanted to do that," she said sincerely. "Were you there long?"

"Me?" He shook his head. "Three months. Nat stayed on though. He met his wife there, of course."

Chloe nearly staggered. "Wife?"

"Yeah, Elena." He looked at her oddly. "Hasn't he ever told you about her? But you must know the story of Nat and Elena. It was in all the papers."

"I—yes, of course."

"God, what a tragedy that was." Sadness briefly touched Syd's features. "She was so young."

Fighting to hold herself steady, Chloe tried to assimilate what she'd just heard. Nat had been married? Her brain refused to accept the information.

"They'd only been together three or four years. Police never did figure out whether it was an accident or a suicide."

Chloe's head snapped up. "She's dead?"

"Yeah, of course. Ten years ago." He considered her, questions in his eyes. "How long have you known Nat?"

"Elena Fiori?" she whispered, remembering suddenly.

As Syd nodded, the newspaper accounts of the drowning of the young Italian film ingenue who'd been married to an American writer began to surface in Chloe's mind. "Yes, of course, Elena." Despite her shock, some lowest common denominator of logic kept her talking. "I guess he—Nat—doesn't like to talk about her, or that time."

"No, he doesn't, you're right," Syd agreed. "I think the scars are still there. He held himself responsible."

"But he *wasn't*, of course."

"No," Syd affirmed. "Only in that he never should have married her in the first place. Elena had deep problems, but Nat wouldn't be talked out of her. He was into rescuing people in those days, and she was a beautiful girl, lonely despite all her fame. She had that wounded animal quality so irresistible to a man like him."

Half listening, Chloe managed to ask over the dull thud of her heart, "You said you and Nat left for Europe right after graduation?"

At his nod, Chloe felt a slow, cold realization taking hold, a kind of psychic numbing as her mind registered each successive bit of information. Nat Cutter was in

Europe when Sara disappeared. In Europe and either married, or about to be married to another woman. He couldn't have been at Northpointe. And then came the final jolt to her nervous system. *He wasn't the man she'd seen.*

She stepped back, and Syd reached out to steady her. "Are you all right?"

Through a rush of heat and lassitude, she shook her head. "No, no, I don't think so. I've been sick the past few days, and all this excitement—I think I'd better go."

"Sure, I'll come with you, get you a cab," he said, taking hold of her arm and walking her out of the auditorium. "You sure you're going to be okay?"

She nodded, and when they reached the street, she thanked him again for everything.

"I should be thanking you," he told her, "for getting the conference off to a good start." He hailed a cab and turned back to her as it sped on by. "And by the way, your agency intrigues me. I've taken on a couple of new writers who'll need some PR. You interested?"

"Yes," she said, without a second's hesitation.

"Good. I'll be in touch, then. Actually, my Manhattan office uses Dillon and Paine, but I'm in the process of opening up a second office near Grammercy Park, not too far from you. We'll be signing up new talent every week." He shrugged, smiled pleasantly. "Who knows, maybe we can work something out."

At last her heart began to beat normally again. "I hope so," she said, thanking him with a valiant smile.

A taxi roared up to the curb. Opening the door, he helped her inside. "Take care of that fever," he said, shutting the door and waving.

She waved back, wondering briefly as the taxi pulled away how he'd known she had a fever.

THE EXCITEMENT of Syd Reinhardt's offer evaporated like steam in the first few minutes of the trip back to the office Chloe shared with her partner. Alone, and feeling oddly isolated in the back seat of the cab, she worked to make sense of what she'd learned. "I believed he was Joshua," she said, wondering how her own instincts could have betrayed her so totally, "I really did." She felt as though she'd been told her green eyes were brown, looked in a mirror and discovered it true.

Disbelief welled up. "I couldn't have been that wrong," she mumbled, numbed by indisputable facts. Nat Cutter was in Europe when Sara disappeared...in Europe and in love with another woman.

"We're here, lady," the cabbie informed her.

She found a bill in her purse, handed it to him unsteadily and got out of the cab.

"Lady? Your change?" he called after her.

"Keep it," she said, not quite sure how much she'd given him. Moving more out of habit than conscious intention, she walked to the elevator and pressed the fourth-floor button.

Marsha was there, talking on the phone and pacing as Chloe entered their tiny two-room suite of offices. "I've got him booked on The Today Show and I'm working on Oprah," she said, talking into the receiver tucked under her chin as she leafed through a file.

The familiar chaos jarred Chloe momentarily. This was the real world, her office, where she belonged. Yet, looking around the room, she took in the cluttered desk and stuffed file cabinets with a sense of alienation, as though something fundamental had changed. She felt as if she'd come out of a dark dream...and into a waking world that wasn't the way she'd left it.

It's me, this damn fever, she thought, a dizzying throb setting in just above her eyes.

Forcing herself to wave and wink as Marsha looked up, she continued on through the front office, entered her own work area and set her briefcase on the floor. Everything looked exactly as she'd left it, with the exception of several haphazardly stacked piles of mail on her desk.

She began to sort through the first stack, her fingers working, her mind held by a question lurking in its shadows. Was she going back to Maine?

"Tell me everything!" a voice squealed from behind. Her partner rushed into the room. "How'd you do? What happened?"

"Did great," Chloe said, looking up with a nod and a tight-lipped smile.

"Great?" Marsha breathed, bubbling with excitement. "What does that mean in round figures?"

"Two referrals now, more to come if we hustle. Reinhardt's opening a new office. He implied he might use our agency exclusively."

"Oh my Gawd!" Marsha twirled and dropped into the chair opposite Chloe's desk. "I'm overcome."

Chloe felt a grin flicker. Thank God for Marsha, she thought, her mood easing a little. Her partner's enthusiasm was as infectious as ever. "I was hoping for speechless," she said dryly.

"What did you *do*?" Marsha's tone implied Chloe might have bargained with the devil or something equally unspeakable to make this deal.

"Darned if I know," Chloe said truthfully. "Maybe I was in the right place at the right time."

The telephone shrilled on the desk behind Chloe. Startled, she jerked around and stared at it, her face draining of color.

Marsha jumped up to answer it. "Order's ready? Thanks," she said and hung up. "That was the printer about our new brochures." She stared at Chloe curiously. "What's wrong with you?"

The throb above Chloe's eyes flared, pulsating in her temples. "It startled me, that's all. I'm not feeling well—"

Marsha took hold of Chloe's shoulders and inspected her like a concerned mother. "Look at me," she insisted. When Chloe did, Marsha clucked softly. "Uhoh—I see unrequited love in those eyes.... It's a man, isn't it?"

"Marsha, let go of me."

"Who is it?" Marsha pressed. "That writer? Nathanial Cutter?"

"How did you know that?" Chloe wriggled from her grasp.

"Give me a minute," Marsha said, darting from the room and returning with an armload of books. "These. You asked me to hunt down and send you a copy of everything he's ever written."

"Yes," Chloe said, sighing. "So I did. And you never sent them."

"It's next on my list of things to do," Marsha said, piling the books on Chloe's already overloaded desk. "How serious is it with this guy? You going back?"

Chloe dropped into the chair Marsha had vacated and let her head fall back against the seat. She had no good reason to go. Whatever had motivated Nat Cutter's strange behavior, it had nothing to do with Sara. And she had several very good reasons not to return. He'd threatened her, frightened her, put her sanity to the test on a regular basis and had her half crazy with desire just by his presence. He'd come *that* close to compromising her virtue and now that he knew she was a publicist, he'd probably shoot her on sight.

"Listen, if you care about this guy," Marsha was saying, her tone softening, "get back there and straighten things out. I'll cover for you here."

Care about him? Why should she care about him? And why couldn't she swallow? "No, I'm not going back."

"Kiddo," her partner chided, coming to sit on the arm of the chair, "I don't know what's going on with you, but I can see you're hurting. You've got that 'little girl lost' look in your eyes. Hey—" she patted Chloe's arm "—if you want to talk, I'm here to listen."

Chloe shook her head and tried to smile. "Not just yet. Thanks, though."

A look of concern lingered in Marsha's eyes, but she nodded. "Okay, you're the boss." She stood up, stretched and grinned. "Problems of the heart always make me hungry. How about an early lunch?"

"No, you go ahead, I—"

"I know," Marsha said, starting for the door, "you've got some thinking to do." She disappeared, then stuck her head back in the doorway just long enough to say, "By the way, Gordon Browne called this morning. He knew you were back in town and was asking lots of questions. Weird man," she commented, and disappeared again.

Gordon Browne? What was he up to? Add another item to the list of reasons not to return to Maine, Chloe thought, Gordon Browne, a.k.a. The Shadow. She might as well call him and get it over with. There was no reason to protect Cutter anymore, or even to mention his name under the circumstances. It was going to be damn awkward though, she realized, trying to explain to Browne why she'd never mentioned the man she saw on the estate fourteen years ago, but if it helped in any way to locate Sara...

She rose and walked to the desk, a dull ache welling in her chest as her eyes were drawn to the books piled there. The volume on top was half the size of the others. His poetry? she wondered, catching herself as her fingers touched the book jacket. Her heart began to beat faster. Leave it alone, she warned instinctively.

But she couldn't. Like a woman obsessed, she picked up the small book and began to leaf through it. The poems were so starkly personal, Chloe's fingers shook as she read one after another. A ferociously angry work about injustice made her gasp, and a poignant ballad about the loss of love brought tears to her eyes. These aren't words, she realized, this isn't even poetry, this is a man's psyche laid bare.

At the back of the book, a poem entitled "Innocence of Heart" drew her attention. Only four stanzas long, it concerned the inevitable losses and disillusionments a child experiences in the journey to adulthood. She read it slowly, and then her eyes returned to the title. Suddenly she remembered where she'd heard those three words before.

"Oh no," she breathed, staggering backward, her hand flying to her mouth. *"Oh, my God."*

# 8

NAT CUTTER STOOD in the doorway of the motel room, one arm propped up against the doorjamb. He took a long drink from a glass half-full of Scotch and stared out at the encroaching dusk.

An unseen sea gull cried.

He glanced at the room next to his, empty now, dark. Staring at the liquor left in his glass, he set the tumbler on the table by the door and walked back into the clutter of his room. Wads of paper dotted the cracked linoleum, the discarded efforts of his attempts to write. A laptop computer would have been more efficient—and less messy—but he'd never liked the damn things.

He sat down at the portable typewriter, leaned back in the dinette chair and focused on a blank sheet of paper. You're losing your touch, he told himself sarcastically. Killing off your characters in new and different ways used to be a snap.

The sea gull cried again, distant now, a plaintive sound.

It echoed in his mind. Shut up, he thought, pulling the paper from the typewriter, crumpling it in his fist. I had to get her out of here. She was about to blow everything wide open.

He sat forward in the chair, determined to leach the last traces of her from his nervous system. The room, the whole damn state of Maine, was alive with her. In his mind, he could still see her out on those bluffs, burning with fever, trembling, *barefoot*. What kind of obsession was driving her? She wasn't a reporter out to break a big story. Syd's conference had confirmed that. But a publicist? How the hell did that connect?

When no answer came, his mind flicked irresistibly to her soaked and breathless body after the storm. He'd been with plenty of women, sexy women, but he'd never seen anything so erotic as the way she'd stripped off that T-shirt, her arms above her head, hands tangled in wet material, breasts freed, trembling.

His fingers ached, remembering. He hadn't even touched her. Now, he never would.

Exhaling, he rolled a sheet of blank paper into the machine and forced himself to concentrate on the murder scene he had to finish. He'd already had his deadline extended once....

The sea gull's faint keen drifted in with the evening breeze, and through it he heard his own name, a whisper, "Cutter."

God, now he was hearing her voice. You're getting maudlin, Cutter, he warned.

"Nat, I—"

He whipped around and came out of the chair, knocking it over with a deafening crash.

She hovered in the doorway, a small book clutched in her hand. "I have to talk to you." Her voice shook, but her jaw was set like stone.

His eyes swept over her. She had on the same herringbone suit she'd worn at the conference, but the blouse was unbuttoned at the neckline, the skirt wrinkled. Her hair was a tangle of flames. "Why did you come back?"

Her eyes veered up to his. "To tell you who I am."

"I know who you are."

"No...you don't. But you will when I've finished. You'll know everything. Why I followed you here five days ago, why I'm here now. And when I'm done—" her mouth drew taut "—I want the same from you."

"I told you once. I rarely give people what they want."

"This time you will."

His instincts told him to stop her while he still could. Get her out of here. Put her on a plane to New York, then call Syd and tell him to make damn sure she stayed there.

"Unless you're afraid to hear what I have to say. Is that it, Cutter?"

"Damn," he exhaled, turning away, slamming his open palm against the wall and leaning into it.

Chloe winced at the sound, but held her ground, calculating the risk of entering the room. When he didn't turn around, she stepped inside and began, talking hurriedly to his bowed head. "Fourteen years ago, I lived in upstate New York with my stepfather and his daughter. She—my stepsister—disappeared one night and was never found. Her name is Sara Guthrie." Cutting off, hushed, she watched for a sign, some indication of recognition.

Cutter remained motionless.

She went on, unable to stop herself, spilling out the events from the beginning: Joshua's appearance at Northpointe, her own encounter with him on the bridge, Sara's disappearance, the police, the dogs, all of it.

She hesitated toward the end, wishing he'd move, say something. She'd prepared herself for a strong reaction, even an explosion, anything but this. "James Guthrie's been ill," she said. "He nearly died a few weeks ago, and now he wants to find his daughter and make amends. That's all he wants, Cutter. No retribution or legalities, just Sara. And that's why I'm here." Her fingers tightened around the book. "Because you look like...him."

He turned around slowly.

"Like Joshua," she said, the words catching in her throat.

She felt a wave of shock and confusion as Nat Cutter faced her full on. His features were immobile, his expression unreadable, etched in stone. For a moment, in the room's murky lamplight, he didn't even resemble Joshua. Disoriented, she felt like she was seeing this man for the first time.

He shook his head, slowly, and doubts piled up inside her. Syd Reinhardt, Harvard, Europe, *Elena*. She'd seen it in the papers—the evidence that he wasn't Joshua. She couldn't deny it, any of it, *but the book*. It was Cutter's book, but they were Joshua's words. How could that be unless— Her eyes glanced from the volume pressed between her whitened fingers to him. "You wrote this, didn't you?"

He considered it a moment. "Yeah, I'll take the blame."

"And this?" She leafed through the book with trembling fingers until she found the poem. "This poem— did you write it? 'Innocence of Heart'? Are those your words?"

He exhaled and nodded. "Yes, I wrote it, and yes, those are my words, but I can't claim they're very original, or even very good—"

"He said these words to me. *He* said them, don't you

understand?" She searched his face, hating the desperate ache in her chest. "I was twelve years old and terrified. He carried me out of the forest. He whispered things, beautiful things, and then he said three words to me, *innocence of heart*." She looked away from his shaking head, her voice dropping to a rasp. "How could you have written this...unless you were him?"

A painful silence followed until his voice, gentler, filled it. "Any number of people could have written those words, Chloe. And probably have."

His huskiness made her look up. And then she saw it, the dull light in his eyes, like something tortured.

"What is it?"

He shook his head and turned away, raking a hand through his hair. "God, how I wish you'd never come back here." His voice lowered, taut. "Do you have any idea what havoc you're wreaking in my life? I don't know what the hell I'm doing anymore. I can't even write, that's how crazy—" He broke off abruptly, reining himself in. When he came around finally, he looked almost haggard.

Studying her, he grimaced as though he had finally reached some painful understanding. "You said his name like he was some kind of god. You loved him, didn't you?"

The book slipped from her fingers and clattered to the floor. "I was a young girl."

"Young girls can love."

The darkness gathering in his eyes threatened to draw off all her energy. "Yes," she said, barely able to speak. "I may have—"

"Why?"

"I don't know. For the same reason I couldn't tell the police about him. Because I'd lost everyone I loved. Because he said my name and touched me, and no one had done that in so long."

Her eyes welled with unshed tears, and through the blur of moisture she saw a look of near anguish cross his face. As she stared at him everything came together at once for Chloe, past and present, radiating through her in soft waves. The final realization, when it came, felt oddly like freedom. "You're not him, are you?" She wasn't asking him, she knew.

He shut his eyes briefly, shook his head and exhaled. "I wish I could tell you what you want to hear."

"No, it's all right. It's easier this way." She picked the book up from the floor and gripped it so tightly against her chest that its edges cut into her fingers. "I'm sorry for all of this. I know I've caused you all kinds of grief. I should never have come back here."

His jaw flexed and hardened.

In the brief connection their eyes made, she saw what she'd done to this stormy, private man who'd only asked to be left alone. "I'm sorry," she said, her voice aching. "I'll get out of your life."

Nat watched her turn for the door, and the words that could stop her locked in his chest. A blunt force assaulted him, like the thrust of a dull knife through his ribs. "*Wait.*"

She stopped on the threshold, her back to him.

"You and I," he grated softly. "We're killing each other, aren't we?"

She jerked around, tears sparkling in her eyes.

The sight of her mouth, sensual and trembling, made him seize up inside. He wanted her more than he'd ever wanted anyone, anything in his life. He knew he had to let her go, that anything else would be insanity, but the flush transforming her pale face to radiance extinguished all thought of consequences.

Her breasts trembled beneath her blouse. His hands curled, aching. Insanity.

He turned away, an oath on his breath.

Chloe pressed a hand against the edge of the table, steadying herself. She searched for words that might ease the tension. "Cutter, I know I should go, but—"

He glanced back, his eyes grazing her with such ferocity she felt faint. They flicked to her breasts and she started as though he'd touched her there. An alarm sparked her nerves; a sudden flush aroused her skin.

Seeing his hands close into fists and release, she knew he meant to throw her out. She also knew he wanted her, badly, enough to tighten his jaw muscles to bands.

It would be so easy to break his control, she realized. And God help her, so dangerous! But if she left now she would never see him again, never feel that dizzying rush when his lips touched hers. Never know what it could be like with a man, with this man.

He turned back to her, his dark torment stunning.

*It had to be this man.*

"I know I should leave," she told him brokenly, "but I can't. Do you understand? Do you?"

Silent, he moved toward her.

"Cutter," she whispered. "I'm frightened."

He reached her, and his hands, fingers splayed, found her throat. Her breath caught hard as she imagined what he might do, but his hands lay still, exquisitely still, as he bent toward her.

The sensation of his mouth touching hers drew a shattering response, like a crystal falling through space and exploding on impact. Through the chaos, she heard her own body's soft cries of longing. They penetrated her to the bone marrow. All she could do was whimper.

Nat's hands tightened reflexively on her throat. Hearing her sob, he pulled back, hesitating, his breath harsh against her face. "Chloe...do you know what you're doing? Are you sure?"

Her stricken features were agonizingly beautiful to him. Her eyes were huge with fear, her mouth slightly swollen from his kiss. He ran his thumb along her jawline, then followed its path with his fingers. "Shall I stop?"

A moment passed while he caressed her, experiencing the textured silk of her skin beneath his unsteady fingertips.

Her eyes never left him and gradually the sensual flush returned to her face. He felt his heart surge as she began to shake her head. "No," she said, rising on her tiptoes, pressing her mouth to his. "Don't stop."

The excruciating softness of her drove him wild with longing. He slid his hand to the back of her neck, worked his fingers into her hair and without thinking closed his fist possessively.

The movement jerked her head back, and her startled cry sent his heart rocketing with excitement. Like a trainer with a frightened, unpredictable animal, he knew he had to slow down, gentle her. But the wild green pulse in her eyes devastated his control. God, she was *irresistible*.

His groin tightened painfully. Taking hold of her hips, he urged her into the fit of his thighs. As she softened against his hardness, another gasp, like a sharply drawn-in breath, shook her.

An urgent grace seemed to control her movements

as she looked up and met his eyes. Her fingers touched his face, everywhere, more unsteady with each new discovery, and he felt a wrench of emotion that went beyond desire, beyond passion. I need her, he realized savagely. Like fire needs oxygen, I need her to survive.

Picking her up in his arms, he swung around, kicked the door shut and carried her to the bed.

Chloe felt an uncontrollable tremor of excitement as he began to unbutton her blouse. She'd never been undressed by a man before, and every brush of his fingertips against her skin made her heart quicken painfully. This was all new to her, this breathtaking intensity. His knuckles grazed her breasts repeatedly, each touch eliciting sensations that threatened to engulf her.

She reached up as though to stop him, but he caught her hand and turned it over, kissing her palm. "I know," he said, his breath flooding her skin, "I know." He met her eyes. "This is too fast for you, too new. We can take it slower if you want, *whatever you want*." The husky edge in his voice caressed her senses. "But if you're not ready, Chloe, if you can't go through with this, then say so now, before we're both beyond—"

"I can," she broke in, knowing it wasn't quite true. At his hesitation, she brought his fingers to her lips. "I am—ready." She felt him tremble and her heart surged.

He was swift and sure and stirringly gentle as he removed everything but her ivory satin slip.

Her inner world sharpened, honed with a new awareness as he paused to look at her. His magic still confounded her. He was a mesmerizing man...a spellbinder. But he was real. Not a fantasy, *real*.

His gaze stroked her body like radiant energy. Trembling, she felt the strap of her slip drop off her shoulder, seemingly of its own accord, and her breath came faster.

"If I could describe the way you look right now," he said, sitting opposite her, "I'd be a very rich poet."

He caressed her face and, at the same time, drew the remaining strap off her shoulder. As the satin fabric slid down her flushed skin, leaving her breasts naked, an exquisite shiver crossed her skin.

"You are devastating," he said, each word a groan from somewhere inside him.

His dark gaze brushed over her, stirring her nerves, tingling her breasts to taut, acutely sensitive peaks. Soft and swollen, they ached for the pressure of his hands. "Touch me, Cutter," she heard herself saying. "Now, please, *now.*"

She caught his hand, and he pulled back. "Don't, Chloe," he warned. "You have no idea what you do to me when you say my name like that. I have to fight like hell not to take you—" He broke off, his jaw wrenching.

His admission startled and thrilled Chloe. She knew he was holding back, and for some crazy reason, she re-experienced the desire to test his control. Dangerous, she thought, her heart racing, *playing with fire.* Still, she touched her fingers to his mouth, drawing them along his lips.

He grimaced, as though a physical pain had gone through him. "Chloe, don't."

*"But I want you to take me,"* she whispered.

Her heart caught as he took hold of her arms, pressed her back into the pillows and drew the satin material down to her waist. He loomed over her, the flash of his eyes blinding. Swept with lightheadedness, she felt his hands on her rib cage, moving with a crescendo of sensation to her breasts. "My God," she gasped, as instinctively frightened as a child caught in the ocean's undertow. "*Wait.*"

She felt her senses dissolving into chaos under the sweet roughness of his hands.

A low moan vibrated through him. He caught her by the waist, accentuating the arch of her body, his lips searing her skin. She felt every breath of sensation, even the brush of his teeth as he took her breast in his mouth. Each urgent pull on her nipple aroused a knot of pleasure inside her. "Cutter," she whimpered, a sob in her throat.

His hands drugged her into a quivering state of surrender. She felt the slip being dragged from her body and was helpless to stop him. Awash in sensation, she heard herself sobbing softly, "*Wait.*"

His body shuddered in response, startling her into consciousness. He brought her up by the shoulders, holding her face, raining kisses over her eyes and mouth. "God, I'm sorry," he said. "I'm insane. I'm scaring you half to death."

She gasped softly as he released her, her body quaking, alive with the traces of his mouth and fingers. "No, *no*, I'm not frightened. Cutter," she said as she caught at his shirt, "please, it's all right."

"You're sure?" he said, and as she nodded, he put her hands away, stood up and pulled the shirt off over his head, throwing it aside. Body hair graced his tanned skin in the most sensual pattern she'd ever witnessed. As he unsnapped his jeans, revealing a dark, strategic arrow of hair, she felt a soft throb between her legs.

His pants dropped to the floor, and she looked away, stunned by the sight of him. She knew how men were built, but she hadn't expected— A flush stung her cheeks, and the knot of pleasure in her belly evaporated in fear. And then he was next to her, murmuring words so low and urgent she couldn't distinguish them.

After a moment he caught her chin and brought it around. "Is something wrong?" he asked. She shook her head, but couldn't stop herself from glancing down. His eyes followed hers, and he exhaled a short gust of laughter.

She tried to laugh, too, over the lump in her throat.

His jaw twisted. "Chloe, you know I'll have to hurt you a little."

The tenderness in his voice roused her heart to a deeper beat. She met his eyes and it was like staring into the sun. Yes, he might hurt her, she thought, but her body was already anticipating ecstasy.

She lay across the bed, and he came into her arms with a low groan, gathering her up and whispering kisses over her eyes and cheeks.

When he stretched alongside her, the feel of his body drenched her in sweet desire. He was hard and long and everywhere so gloriously warm.

"I don't care about the pain," she said, running her fingers over the muscles in his shoulders, "I want you, Cutter, *I do want you.*"

"Easy," he warned, catching her wrist, holding it still. "I'm trying my damndest to stay sane, but if you keep touching me like that, *talking* like that."

"All of you," she murmured wickedly.

"*Don't*, Chloe." He covered her mouth with a kiss and then rose over her. "Don't say anything more." His eyes glinted, stunning her with their darkness.

Again the contact of his body drugged her. His arms

were hard and muscled. His hands were ruthlessly sensual as they stroked her nakedness, caressing her breasts with urgent pressure, purling softly across her belly. He touched the mounded triangle, and her body gave out an answering flash.

Soft moans swirled around her. Vaguely aware that they were her own, she felt him opening her legs, trailing his fingers up her innner thigh toward the quickening throb.

She cried out, and he gentled her with murmurs and hushes, caressing her with gradually increasing strokes of intimacy, priming her body slowly, stirring her nerves and senses to a state of sweet torment.

Dazed by the stimulation arcing through her, she pressed against him, only vaguely aware that he'd shifted his weight over her and eased his hips into the juncture of her thighs.

She felt him at the entry to her softness, and she was instantly alert. Her legs closed instinctively, but it was there, as hard as steel, a threatening physical presence lodged against her.

"I need you," he said, drawing her head up. The dark haunted beauty in his face stole the breath from her body. "Do you understand how much? I can't stop now. Don't ask me to stop now."

She reached up to touch his mouth.

"Need me back, Chloe," he whispered against her fingers. "Take me inside you."

A radiance flared up from deep inside her. She arched against him, her fingers digging into his back. The first jolt of penetration brought a choked cry of pleasure.

"Am I hurting you?" he asked.

Amazed by the sweet, aching pressure of his body as

it merged with hers, she could only shake her head. He hesitated halfway, gathering her tightly to him, and then with one quick stab of pain, he thrust deep inside her, filling her. The sudden union sent a wild cry of pleasure reverberating through her senses.

Inexplicably then, he stilled. She urged him to move with her hands and felt a thrilling quiver deep inside her. His whole body tautened. "Not yet," he said, holding her face with his hands. "When your body is used to the feel of me...then I'll move."

He kissed her lips, and she melted around him like warmed wine. In the hot flush of surrender, her body accommodated all of him. "God," he breathed, features contorting with strain. Easing back, he pressed into her again, losing himself in her warmth.

Her softness was too much for him; her heat seared his blood. He began to rock faster, deeper. A soft cry of pleasure came from her, mingling with his, as a brilliant rhythm built.

Their bodies knew each other; their bodies were destined.

Whispers filled the room, erotic, calling from beyond time, from the mists...an enchanter, a temptress who takes men's souls...

Again and again he buried himself inside her and felt his whole body drowning in sweetness. He tried to slow the mindless climb toward ecstasy and failed. The woman beneath him was torment; she was heaven. Her body was a silky glove, holding him in the exquisite grip of a woman aroused.

Moving, thrusting, surging with uncontrollable need, he acknowledged her broken gasps with caresses. She was trying to tell him what strange and wonderful things were happening to her. And then her body fluttered and tightened, and a sensation flicked through him like a whip crack.

She was climaxing and the knowledge snapped the last thin thread of his control. He pushed high into the narrow vault of her, shuddering as the light burst from him in a hot explosion. "No," he rasped, gathering her to him, crushing her in his arms. *"No."*

Someone whispered his name, sweet and shivery as bells.

"Chloe," he said, lost in sensation.

The light burst again, wondrous, and he felt as though his soul was being drawn from his body.

# 9

CHLOE WOKE FIRST...to a world that was a dreamy haze of soft-focus images. Heavy-lidded and languid, she peeked out from under the mountainous folds of the patchwork quilt. Sunlight sprinkled the room, capturing and suspending free-floating particles in its rays like fairy dust.

She turned on her side, elbowing up to consider the man sleeping with his back to her. With his dark hair ruffled against the white pillowcase, he looked like an eighteenth-century ruffian.

His back to her? That troubled her for a moment. When had he turned away? The last she remembered before they'd drifted off, he'd had her pinned in a dreamy wrestling hold—his head nuzzled into the hollow of her neck, an arm across her breasts, his leg entwined with hers.

Watching his back move in rhythm with his breathing, she contemplated this man who'd introduced her to ecstasy. Her heart still hummed with the words he'd whispered—lyrical and eloquent, the stuff of which fantasies are made.

All said in the heat of passion, she reminded herself, sobering. He'd been caught off guard last night. And this was the proverbial morning after. He might not feel so eloquent in the cold light of day.

As he shifted and stretched, dragging the covers farther down his back, Chloe's thoughts took an abrupt turn toward the physical. The wedge-shaped taper of shoulder to hip he'd exposed stirred an errant thought. Perhaps she'd just lift the blankets and take a peek at the rest of him.

Her heart beat a little faster as she argued against such silliness. A mature woman wouldn't, she thought, slipping a finger under the blankets and lifting. "Oh my," she breathed, her eyes straying to never-never land.

As though he'd heard, he swung around and rolled to his back. Chloe froze, her eyes darting to his face. Assured he was still asleep, she took another peek. "Oh *my*." She'd read an article about male hormones raging to their peak level in the morning. That author definitely knew her subject.

He opened his eyes. Chloe dropped the blanket.

"Lost something?" he inquired, a sleepy grin on his face.

"Just my mind." She was considering hiding under the covers for several hours, maybe the rest of her life, but then she'd be face-to-face with those hormones!

His smile deepened. "You're spectacular when you blush," he said, reaching up to caress her cheek. "Like a bowl of strawberries and cream."

She breathed a sigh of relief. He was still eloquent.

"You're pretty spectacular, too," she admitted, feeling the color deepen and tingle across her skin.

"Oh lady," he said, pulling her down beside him. "Don't make me lose my head again."

She snuggled into the muscular warmth of him, careful where she put her hands. "Why not? Then there'd be two of us."

Rolling to his side, his gaze intent on her features, he

drew her into the circle of his arms. She sensed the passion in him, felt it in his aroused body. "I had a dream about you," he said.

His voice caressed her. It was tender and rough, the soft scratch of wool across sensitive skin. He didn't have to tell her what the dream was about.

An impulse, sweet and wicked, stirred her. Her hands whispered down to touch that forbidden part of him. "Want to make it come true?" The look in his eyes as she touched him sent the blood rushing and tumbling in her veins.

"Yes," he said, his face tautening. Foregoing the preliminaries, he lifted her leg and drew it up over his hip.

The abruptness of it all thrilled her. His hardness found its target, and her stomach spasmed with excitement. "In a hurry, Cutter?" she breathed, feigning nonchalance.

He caught her hips, his fingers biting into the soft flesh of her buttocks, and drew her down onto him. "*Yes,*" he said, a half smile flickering. "And under the circumstances, maybe you'd better call me Nat."

She let out a soft shriek of excitement as he simultaneously thrust up and eased her down. The tingling blush that had started earlier spread like wildfire, scorching her entire body. "Oh, yes, Nat," she gasped, melting around him just as she had the night before. "*Hurry.*"

His swift strokes brought them to the peak of the mountain in moments. Chloe's body screamed for release and when it came, sudden and breathtaking, she felt as though she'd been flung off the summit and was free-falling to earth.

It was a long while afterward before she could rouse herself. When she finally did, he awoke, too. Still entangled, their heads on the pillow, they stared into each other's eyes for a time before he managed a husky, "Good morning."

"You poet you," she said, unable to keep herself from grinning like an imbecile. She'd never felt this wonderful—she'd never been this happy in her life. It occurred to her then, in a tiny, frightening explosion of insight, that she was in love. Flat-out, fall-on-your-face in love. "Oh no," she whimpered.

His face narrowed with concern. "Did I hurt you?"

No, but you will, she thought, anticipating the agony of being hopelessly in love with such a man. She raised a shoulder in answer. "Just a twinge. I'm new at this, remember."

An emotion she didn't understand whispered through his features. With a slight shudder, he combed his fingers into her hair and brought her face to his. "You're good for this sinner's soul," he said, kissing her with such tender ferocity she felt her senses swim.

They came into each other's arms then, spontaneously, holding tight, neither quite understanding the other's urgency, and yet communicating with such intimacy through the mute language of their bodies that they couldn't speak when they parted.

The room grew silent, except for their breathing. Awkward and intense, they lay apart, fingertips touching...until the silence was so painfully alive that Chloe had to break it.

Gratefully, she remembered some unfinished business. "Speaking of souls," she said, her voice unsteady as she drew back her hand and turned to stare at the ceiling, "what about that Welsh myth? Gwydion and the woman made of flowers?" She lifted herself up on an elbow to look at him. "You never told me the ending."

Nat rolled his eyes. "The elephants would kill for your memory." Sliding a hand from her waist to her breast, he cupped it and sent a warm shiver through her. His eyes told her that he wasn't interested in myths. The warm throb of his body told her exactly what he was interested in.

She held him off with a bawdy wink. "Right after you tell me the ending."

He tried his black magic on her—a penetrating look, a startling nip on her bare shoulder, but she, a thoroughly satisfied woman, wasn't having any of it.

"Okay then," he acquiesced, sitting up and bringing her with him. "But first some coffee. I'm dangerous before my first cup."

"Umm, now he tells me." Her stomach rumbled. "And nourishment," she said. "I'm starving."

They dressed quickly, percolated coffee in a thin metal pot with a lid that didn't fit and found some stale doughnuts tucked away in a cupboard.

"A picnic," Chloe decided, grabbing a blanket and starting for the door. "Come on," she coaxed. "It's such a beautiful morning." Nat followed, grumbling, coffeepot and doughnuts in hand. While they were spreading out the blanket, the desk clerk appeared around the corner of the motel, gawked at them and shook his head before disappearing.

"What's with him?" Chloe asked, smoothing the last lumps from the blanket before she sat down.

"Walt?" Nat chuckled, joining her. "I slip him some money and he makes sure I'm undisturbed. We writers need our sanctuary."

"Walt—is that his name?" She paused long enough

to breathe in a long draft of sea air. "Well, I hope you're paying him enough because he's worth it. The man is inscrutable. I had to break into the office and steal a look at the registration book to find out that you were a registered guest here."

Nat looked at her curiously.

"On my honor." She raised a hand. "I couldn't pry a word out of the man."

"Really? Maybe I'll give him a bonus." He laughed, handing her a foam cup of coffee. "Now, do you want to hear the myth or don't you?"

She fished a doughnut out of the box and sank it into the steaming black brew. "I can't wait."

He took a gulp of coffee, grimaced and poured it out on the sand. "This stuff would strip paint."

Thinking better of eating her doughnut, Chloe set it and the coffee aside. "The myth," she prompted.

"It's not much of an ending," he admitted, scratching his forehead in a gesture that was almost sheepish. "Gwydion turned her into an owl."

"An *owl*?"

"Hold on," he said, "there's a certain poetic justice involved here. Gwydion created her from daylight and flowers, and he wanted an appropriate punishment. What could be more appropriate than a life of darkness?"

"But as an *owl*?" she complained. "It's just not—I don't know—romantic."

"Oh?" He surveyed her provocatively. "You thought it was going to be something sexy? Hoping for some debauchery, were you?" Catching her arm, he tugged her to him. "Come here, you little fire-breather."

He chastened her with a "take that" kiss, whispered

further kisses along her cheekbones and caught the tip of her chin off guard with a soft nip. "Sexy enough?"

He looked a little smug as they settled back to stare out at the ocean, so she murmured "For starters," and caught both her hands around his waist. Laying her cheek against his chest, she let the emotions run rampant inside her. Did every woman in love for the first time feel this way? Little flurries of excitement, the sweet ache of anticipation around the heart? Probably their stomachs didn't rumble, she thought, hearing hers. But other than hunger pangs, her immediate world felt like newborn bliss. Having no idea how long it might last, she savored it.

A blazing ball of sunshine spun heavenward, its ascent much too grand to signal just another morning making its debut. Not a cloud marred the blue sky. It's going to be a day of days, Chloe prophesied, drinking in a scene that seemed almost too beautiful to view.

After a time, Nat's hand ruffled her hair. "Chloe...I was married once."

Anxiety tapped at her. "I know. Syd told me, and I remember reading about it in the papers."

"Then you know how she died?"

"Yes." If he told her he was still in love with that woman, it would kill her.

"Maybe you should hear my version." He was quiet for a while, his chest rising and falling more noticeably. "I was just out of college," he said finally. "Full of ideas about truth and beauty—you know the type—a young turk out to right an off-center world. Elena was a beautiful, long-legged waif just begging for rescue. Nobody could talk me out of her, that's how sure I was that I could make a difference in her life."

He expelled some air. "Her death wasn't an accident. She killed herself over a part she didn't get. It was an absurd waste of life and beauty and talent, of everything that's meaningful."

"And you felt responsible?"

"I didn't love her. I thought I did, but afterward I realized that all I wanted was to save her. For the glory, I guess. I think she knew." He dropped his arms from around Chloe's shoulders and distanced himself a little. "No, I don't blame myself anymore."

But he did, she realized, and probably always would. "Would she have blamed you?"

He thought about that for a while. "She told me once she believed she was fated, pulled by some self-destructive siren's call."

"Sounds dramatic," Chloe observed, trying to keep her voice casual. Was it possible, she wondered, that Elena had unconsciously used Nat in some way—a self-fulfilling prophecy? "Maybe she didn't want to be saved," she suggested quietly. "Maybe that wasn't the role she auditioned you for...."

His head came around slowly. "What is this, no-wait psychoanalysis? Is there a bill in the mail?"

"Umm, at several times the going rate. I'm quick, but I'm expensive."

"Really?" His eyes twinkled, dark memories apparently set aside. He ran his thumb along the base of her throat and looked point-blank into her eyes. "How much?"

She felt a delicious flutter in her stomach. "For you? A repeat customer?" She could hardly believe the provocative things that came to mind. "Depends on what you need. Talk therapy has its moments, but in your case, I think some behavior modification—"

He emitted a throaty chuckle. "Behavior modification? Sounds rigorous." A glance at his watch sobered him. He looked up, apologetic. "I'm going to have to take a rain check. I've got an appointment with Syd and my publisher this afternoon."

"Today?" She caught at his arm.

"What's wrong?"

She shook her head, shivering as he put a hand to her forehead. "Are you running a temperature?" he asked.

"No, I'm all right. How long will you be gone?"

Rising, he helped her to her feet. "I'll cut it short and get a flight back tonight if I can."

"I'm going, too."

"No way, lady." His hand at her elbow, he urged her toward the room. "The only place you're going is to bed with two aspirin. You've been flirting with pneumonia since that morning we got caught in the rain."

She protested all the way to the four-poster, but his solicitous concern eventually won over her unease. She knew she didn't want him to leave, but no reasons came, just premonitions so vague and free-floating she couldn't express them.

He seemed to guess what she couldn't say, and in his reassuring ministrations, she glimpsed another side of Nat Cutter, unselfish and gentle—the man who rescued waifs and painlessly removed splinters from wounded hands. Propped up by pillows and feeling very much the pampered princess, she watched him throw some things together.

As he started for the door, a feeling of fear caught at her. "Wait, Nat, I'm better." She felt her head. "See, warm, not hot. And I need to go back anyway, to see Marsha. Business," she added emphatically.

He blew her a kiss from the door. "You'd have to

hang on to the wing. I'm taking the shuttle and the flight's booked solid." Sun flooded the room when he opened the door. Squinting, he shaded his eyes with his hands. "Why didn't I pick up some sunglasses?"

Chloe threw back the covers. She knew those Carreras would come in handy. Her purse lay at the bottom of the bed. She found the sunglasses exactly where she'd been keeping them, in the zippered compartment. "Will these do?"

Nat's brows lifted in amazement. "How'd you—"

She thought about how she'd almost killed herself, hanging out over the ocean by a splintered railing. If she'd been one ounce heavier... She shrugged. "Piece of cake, actually."

At his laughing admiration, she allowed herself a momentary puff of pride, but she held the glasses back as he reached for them.

"Chloe, I'm in a hurry."

She took them with her under the quilt, shaking her head as he approached the bed. "I want you to come back, Cutter, whatever it takes. I don't know why these glasses are so important to you, but I'm hanging on to them until—"

A slightly exasperated grin adorned his gorgeous face. "I'll be back, lady, but not for the glasses." Scrutinizing her, he said, "But you don't believe that, do you?"

"Sure I do." Her fingers tightened on the metal frames.

"Trust me. I'm coming back." He closed in, knelt and kissed her. "Rest, hear? Don't get out of this bed. Don't even answer the phone." Touching her face, he added, "But do wait up for me, okay? We have some things to talk about when I get back."

She watched him open the door and stride into the sunshine, his words lingering in the air.

"Things to talk about?" she murmured. "Does that sound promising, or does that sound *promising*?"

She set the Carreras on the bedside table and rolled over to his pillow. Snuggling her head in the imprint, she luxuriated in the traces of him...remembered scents, sounds and textures. Nat Cutter was wildly sexy and impossibly difficult. Not a safe or sane choice for any woman. But he was her first man, her first love. She closed her eyes and smiled, triumphant. Nothing could change that.

CHLOE'S PROMISE not to set foot out of bed held until noon. The day was glorious, her spirits high. And she'd seen almost nothing of the Pine Tree State of Maine except the four walls of the Sunrise motel.

Ignoring a pang of guilt, she dressed hurriedly. She'd go for a walk, or better yet, take the rental car out for a spin, all the windows down. Maybe she'd drive up the coast.

Another place lingered in the back of her mind: White Rock Island. No, she thought, squinting as she opened the door, no more sneaking around behind Nat's back. She slipped on his way-too-large sunglasses and started for the car. I'll ask him about the island when he gets back. "We'll talk," she murmured aloud, *"intimately."*

The breathtaking drive up Route 1 conspired against serious thinking. Euphoric, Chloe dispatched her remaining concerns one by one with almost ruthless ease. *Sara:* Well, there was little else Chloe could do about her stepsister now except call Gordon Browne and tell him what she knew. *Joshua:* A memory, still poignant, yet oddly neutral. *The new Nat versus the old Nat:* Chloe looked at herself in the rearview mirror and winked. Never underestimate the curative powers of a good woman.

Her drive took her through several small, clustered communities before she reached Belmont, the first major coastal harbor. She might have continued on to Camden had she not noticed the large white clapboard house alongside the road. "The Midcoast Historical Society?" she murmured, pulling in.

She spent a half hour atoning for her history buff lie by browsing through artifacts dating back to the earliest settlements of the area. Steeped in New England pioneer heritage, she walked to the nearby harbor on foot, taking in the industrial seaport's architecture—austere, but somehow reassuring—and its locals, purposeful merchants and fishermen who seemed slightly startled when she smiled.

She had lunch on the waterfront, staving off starvation with half a Maine lobster and lots of crusty French bread. Afterward, she wandered at whim, perusing local shops and seashore museums along the city's main street, her senses pleasantly attuned to the briny smells and the noisy hiss and chug of the working harbor.

Coming out of a gift shop, she noticed the Belmont ferry pulling into its slip. A short line of cars and people waited to board. With rising interest, she realized it must be the shuttle that ran between Belmont and White Rock.

On impulse, she walked to the terminal, entered, approached the ticket counter and inquired about the ferry's schedule.

The clerk, a thin young man, began a painstaking recital of the entire day's schedule. "If you left now," he advised, summing up, "and caught the last ferry back at four-thirty, you'd have an hour and a half on the island."

"Thanks," Chloe said, mentally calculating. Adding on the hour's drive back to the motel, she figured she'd arrive somewhere between six and six-thirty. Nat hadn't said when he'd be back, but she was sure he'd be late, assuming he could arrange a return flight at all.

The clerk was regarding her expectantly. She glanced out the window at the boarding passengers and was sorely tempted. "Not today," she said finally. "Thanks anyway."

Her conviction a little shaky, she made for the door quickly, barely aware of the woman and adolescent boy who entered as she left.

Chloe was a quarter-block up the street when the ferry's horn sounded, a mournful blast that reverberated through her nerves. She turned around, her eyes drawn to the terminal as the woman and boy came out and hurried toward the boat.

Something about the woman struck her, the slender frame in motion, the cascade of white-gold hair. The ferry horn sounded again, a horrible wail. The woman said something to the boy and they began to run.

Perspiration sheened Chloe's forehead, her upper lip. No thoughts came to her whirring brain, just a constant jamming signal. She began to follow them, jerky, her legs surging and halting.

As they ran up the ramp, the ferry gave out one last howl, and the bulwarks closed behind them. Lurching forward unsteadily, Chloe felt a mute cry building.

A cluster of departing passengers blocked her path. She tried to avoid them, hit someone's shoulder and staggered.

"You're too late, miss," a man called as she reached the gate that spanned the road. "Next one leaves at two-thirty."

"I know," she said, watching the ferry pull away. Her hands froze on the railing as the woman turned around slowly to look back. The blond hair lifted and fluttered in the wind like corn silk. Her blue eyes caught light from the sun. She was the most beautiful woman Chloe had ever seen.

*She was Sara Guthrie.*

A low roar exploded in Chloe's head. Gripping the metal gate dizzily, she saw the boy join Sara at the railing. His dark hair and eyes were a direct contrast to Sara's fairness, and his adolescent features had that look of a young male in transition.

He looked directly at Chloe, and their eyes connected for an instant before he disappeared among the other passengers.

"No," she whispered, shaking her head, backing away. Her chest was a vise, cutting off her wind. Her legs felt weighted and trembling. *"His eyes. Dear God, he has Nat's eyes."*

# 10

THE DRIVE BACK to the Sunrise motel was a blind journey through time and space. Everything beyond the highway lane Chloe occupied spun away like refracted light and dissolved into pale streams. When she pulled into the motel parking lot, she had no idea whether she'd been on the road minutes or hours. The clock in the room told her it was nearly 5:00 p.m.

With her purse in her lap, she sat on the bed wondering why she was there, in his room, sitting on his bed...and why she felt nothing.

She looked around the room, her sense of detachment growing. None of it seemed real—last night's dreamlike intimacy, today's nightmare. The emptiness inside her felt as though it might expand until she disappeared. She touched her own face, her fingertips icy against her skin. If she could think, talk, she could fight off the numbing shock.

Ask yourself a question, she thought, any question. One gradually materialized. Why hadn't they condemned that old pier at the beach? Someone could be hurt there. Another question, quickly. Why can't we live without lies?

She stood up, her purse sliding to the floor, her voice hushed. "Is that where she's been hidden all this time? On the island with the boy?" Dark eyes flashed at her from a young curious face. "His son?"

She let out a broken sob and caught hold of the bed-post to steady herself. *Some things to talk about when I get back,* that's what he'd said. She'd thought he meant them, their relationship. Now she knew he was going to tell her about Sara and the boy.

She closed her eyes, her mind racing ahead of her with the ruthless efficiency of a machine fueled by pain. It was all beginning to make sense, his anguish the night before, his behavior since the beginning, the secrecy, the intimidation.

She'd told Nat everything, and now that he knew Sara had nothing to fear from Guthrie, he could make a clean breast of it. He'd undoubtedly planned to tell her when he got back from New York. And along with his confession, he'd explain why it was impossible for them to see each other again. Or maybe he'd want an affair? *Oh, God.* Her heart wavered, a painful hesitation. Her eyes came open. "No—he's not like that, not purposely cruel."

Another soft thud of awareness rocked her. He *is* Joshua. She dragged in a breath. *My* Joshua.

In the blur that followed, time reached out its unforgiving hand and swept her back. Rapid brush strokes painted the past in deep-stained hues of red and blue. Defenseless against the slashes of color, Chloe relived her losses—her mother, a father she'd barely known and Joshua—and felt again the heartache that only an abandoned child can feel.

Her jaw clenched, trembling. "Stop it," she whispered. "That was so long ago. Don't do this to yourself."

Drawing in a quick, fierce breath she bent to pick up her purse. Go home, she told herself brutally, leave the three of them to their life. You've done what you came to do, you've found Sara. Nat will tell her about her father. They'll be all right now...all of them.

She had the motel door half open when a rattling burst of sound stopped her. The telephone. Her body froze; her heartbeat accelerated. She prayed the phone would stop ringing, and then, afraid it had stopped, she rushed to pick it up.

"Chloe?" Nat's voice called. "Is that you? How's the patient?"

Mercifully, a spray of static cut him off.

"Are you there?" he asked. "We've got a bad connection."

"Yes, I'm h—" Her throat convulsed, swallowing the words.

"I can't hear you. Let me call you back," he suggested.

"*No.*"

"Okay, then listen to me, Chloe. I can't get back tonight. Syd's got a big deal cooking, several books, and he wants me to stick around until tomorrow to finalize it—"

As she listened to him describe the seven-figure contract Syd was negotiating, an impulse moved through her, a wrenching need to cut through the impersonal conversation and silence him with the truth. He'd hurt her, God, how he'd hurt her. How could he talk about finalizing deals and contracts? How could he be so casual when he knew he was coming back to tell her about Sara? And if he was going to tell her the truth anyway, why not last night? *Before they had made love?* Hurt swelled to outrage. *Explain yourself,* she wanted to shout at him.

"Wish I could get back there tonight," he added over

the crackling on the line, "but Syd's wound up like a clock spring. Will you be okay?"

Chloe couldn't hear what he'd said over the sharp surge of her heart, but a word, *a name,* spun out at her. *Syd.* Her brain made the connection with a chaotic pop of awareness. Syd, Harvard, Elena. Nat had been married. He'd told her himself. But all those years in Europe. But how could that be? Sara— Confusion swept her.

"Chloe, what's wrong?"

The certainty she'd felt earlier became hazed with doubt. An instinct silenced her. There was something going on here she didn't understand at all.

"Chloe, dammit, talk to me. Are you sick? Do you need a doctor?"

"No, I'm fine," she said slowly, her thought processes beginning to clear. The shock of seeing Sara and the boy had blocked out all conflicting information. The connection had been instant—Nat, Sara, their son. But now she didn't know. There were so many inconsistencies—

"You're not fine. I can hear it in your voice."

His intensity stirred her, but she couldn't give in to it. The possibility that he'd lied to her made everything he'd said, and would say, suspect. Somewhere—was it in her mind?—she heard the faint blast of a departing ferry.

"I am, really," she told him, forcing energy into her voice. If she could get to Sara...her stepsister might have the answers. "I'm taking it easy here, a good rest, so relax and take your time. Don't worry about me, *promise*?"

"Okay." He sounded perplexed "See you tomorrow then."

"Yes."

Neither hung up. "Nat—" Breaking off, she found it almost impossible to speak. "Good luck with the deal."

"Thanks," he said. "And hey, firebreather...I miss you."

She closed her eyes, swallowed painfully and without a sound replaced the receiver. Fumbling for her purse, she anticipated the telephone's next eruption and shuddered when it didn't come.

She couldn't tell him what she was going to do because he might try to stop her. Her chest tightened with conflicting emotions. She had to get out of the room in case he called back. She had to get out of the area in case he *came* back.

Within minutes, she was pulling the rental car out onto Route 1 toward Belmont. Dusk was descending, already dominating the sky. She shivered and switched on the headlights, wondering where she would stay that night.

Think, she ordered silently. Did she have enough gas to make it? Would it rain tonight? Her foot pressed the gas pedal. What was the speed limit? Think, think about what's coming around the next bend in this road. Think about the ferry, the island, Sara.

Intuition told her Sara was the source. With each passing mile, she felt more certain that getting to Sara meant understanding everything.

An energy drove Chloe, but she knew better than to completely trust its momentum. Her instincts were too skewed with emotion. She'd been sure before—and burned each time.

But the energy was there, undeniably. And with it came fear. A resurgence of the premonition, however irrational, that someone didn't want her to get to her stepsister.

In the next half hour, she decided against a motel. She didn't like the idea of registering—even with a false name—or the dread of sitting and waiting. She felt safer with the car's potential for motion and power. But if she stayed in the car, she had to find a place to park. The police would notice her in Belmont, even on a side street.

Twenty minutes from the city, she pulled off Route 1 onto a deserted dirt road and parked alongside a sheltering copse of trees. Assuring herself that she couldn't be seen by passing cars, she settled back, shut her eyes and resolved to wait out the night.

CHLOE'S EYES blinked open. Momentarily disoriented, she sprang up, grazing her thigh on the steering wheel. The first light of dawn filtered through the trees. It was morning. She fell back in the seat and let out a sigh of relief, her worst fear averted. She'd made it through the night. There'd been other fears, born in the darkness, plenty of them. But it was morning now, *daylight*, and she'd survived them all.

The business of getting to Belmont and the ferry terminal preoccupied her. She had an hour if she started now, plenty of time. A quick twist of the ignition key brought the car awake, eliminating another fear.

Back on the road, she considered stopping at a gas station to clean up and decided in favor of the ferry's rest room. She hadn't changed her clothes since Syd's conference, and her slept-in herringbone suit looked it.

A shudder shook her, and then another one, violent. Startled, she realized she was chilled to the bone. She turned the heater on high, and by the time she reached

Belmont she felt as though her blood had begun to circulate normally again.

A sign at the entrance to the ferry terminal parking lot clearly stated that only island residents were allowed cars on the island. The parking lot provided little cover, but Chloe weighed her options and decided an empty corner space with an unobstructed view of the ferry was worth the risk. At least from where she sat she could watch the passengers' comings and goings, and then, at the last minute, buy her ticket and board. It seemed crazy in the clear light of day to be calculating her every move, but she couldn't dismiss the lurking conviction that someone might not want her to find Sara. Possibilities ran through her mind: Nat, Gordon Browne, or someone else unknown to her?

The blast of the ferry's horn jarred her into action. She locked the car hastily and hurried to the terminal. The same clerk helped her, with the same methodical efficiency, and if he was surprised to see her again, he concealed it well.

An excruciatingly long wait in the boarding line increased Chloe's agitation. She glanced over her shoulder repeatedly, and when the attendant finally opened the gate and waved the passengers aboard, she glanced back one last time—into the curious eyes of the people lined up behind her. You're acting like an escapee from somewhere, she warned herself. Stop searching people's faces and calm down.

She found the rest room before they even pulled away from the slip. The cold tap water shocked her senses. Braving its icy bite, she washed her face vigorously, then put on some fresh makeup and brushed her hair.

By the time she emerged, most of the passengers had taken seats in the ferry's small cabin enclosure. She walked the outer deck instead, thinking, planning her search.

The thirty-minute crossing went quickly, too quickly for Chloe as she stood at the railing and watched White Rock's looming silhouette take form. Something about the island's water-bound isolation reminded her of a prison. Was Sara happy there? Was she there of her own will?

Coming from nowhere, the second question jarred Chloe, but she found herself unable to put it aside. Sara wasn't physically imprisoned, of course, because Chloe'd seen her and the boy returning to the island yesterday. But there were other ways to control people, psychological constraints like dependency, intimidation, and even—Chloe's heartbeat quickened... sexuality.

Her mind flashed instantly to Nat Cutter and his effect on her. Such a stark, mesmerizing presence, enough to frighten off any woman, and yet, in just a few days' time, Chloe had surrendered it all to him, everything she held precious, her body, her heart. She caught in a breath, remembering.

She couldn't explain why she'd responded to him in ways she'd never responded to any other man. But Cutter was no ordinary man. Just his voice alone could thrill her into mindlessness. And beyond that, it was something to do with his eyes. Uncanny. They had a hypnotic quality, those eyes, beautiful...and terrible.

Chloe could almost believe he had some kind of hold on Sara. She could almost believe he was the reason Sara hadn't contacted her father in fourteen years.

A low wailing blast jarred her. She grabbed the rail,

her heart racing. Easy, she told herself, it's just the ferry. Feeling the boat slow as it pulled into the dock, she walked along with the other passengers to the exit ramp.

The island was beautiful, rocky and green, and, at first glance, primitive. She saw a few concessions to civilization as she descended the ramp: paved streets, telephone poles and several homes with the rustic weather-beaten charm of Cape Cod cottages.

Looking around the quiet harbor, disproportionately populated with sailboats, she realized she had no idea where to start. The exit road from the ferry branched off in several directions, but most of the cars were turning left at the intersection and heading up a slight incline. Follow the crowd, she thought.

The hill descended into a small village of stores and shops, a real-estate office, a garage and a rambling unnamed block building that had the official look of a town hall. Chloe launched her search at a one-room mom and pop grocery store with a rusty porch swing out front.

Confident that it shouldn't take too long to find a woman who looked as Sara did, she gave the proprietor a cursory description and was surprised when he took his pipe out of his mouth just long enough to say, "Sorry. Can't help ya."

"But you must have seen her," Chloe pressed. "Her name is Sara, and she's in her early thirties." Chloe hadn't planned to say anything more, but now she felt compelled. "There was a boy with her, around thirteen or fourteen, dark hair."

"Nope, don't know either of 'em," he said, pleasantly enough. "Something else I can do for you?" The calm finality in his manner discouraged further questions.

"Yes." Realizing she was starving, she picked up some cheese, hard French rolls and an apple, paid for them and left. When you're starving everything's delicious, she thought, devouring the apple first as she considered the real-estate office across the street. "And when you're looking for something," she observed, remembering a stock line of her mother's, "you can never find it."

She was halfway across the street when she heard a buzzing sound. She glanced around, saw nothing and continued walking, but the drone persisted, swelling into a whining high-pitched roar. Down the street to her left, a bright blue blur wheeled off a side street and bore down on her.

Chloe dashed for the stoop of the real-estate office, reached it and whirled around just as something that looked like a streamlined golf cart pulled its shuddering bulk and full-blown racket up alongside her. Its driver, a husky blue-eyed teenager, grinned at her. "Delivering groceries," he volunteered, with no apologies for lopping ten years off her life. "You going all the way around the island?"

Panting like a winded animal, she nodded. And wondered how he knew.

"Long way. Want a ride?"

She considered the vibrating machine. "I think so. Give me a minute." After a steadying breath, she introduced herself, told him why she was on the island and described Sara.

"Never seen her." His eyes squinted thoughtfully. "And it'd be real hard to miss a lady like that. Sure she lives here?"

Hope plummeting, Chloe realized Sara might not be living on the island. She could have been visiting, sight-seeing, anything. The possibilities were endless and endlessly depressing, especially since they hadn't occurred to her before. "She was here yesterday," she said staunchly. "Someone must have seen her."

Behind the bravado, she knew she had no choice but to go on. The island was all she had. She climbed into the golf cart beside him. "I'll take that ride."

They looped the small island in just under two hours, including stops at the infrequent clustering of homes that dotted the shoreline. Not only did the islanders Chloe spoke to not know Sara, several of them began shaking their heads before she'd finished her stepsister's description. Others didn't even bother to answer their doors. Her mother's line was turning out to be prophetic, Chloe realized, as they chugged up the last hill and the village came into view.

Scanning the nearly deserted main street, she experienced one of those elusive premonitions that all is not right. She was tempted to explain away both the feeling and the aloof treatment she'd received with bromides like typical New England reticence. But another stirring was taking hold, the distinctly crazy feeling that she might be the victim of some kind of conspiracy of silence.

"Too bad you didn't find your friend," her young driver said as they pulled up in front of the general store.

"Yeah," she agreed. "Thanks anyway." Preoccupied with her thoughts, she got out of the cart and smiled at him. What would she do now?

"Maybe she lives on one of the other islands," he suggested, his shoulders lifting.

His answer came so quickly after her silent question it spooked her. This was the second time he'd anticipated her. "Other islands? On this ferry's route?" She didn't remember the clerk at the terminal mentioning other islands.

"Yeah," he said eagerly. "Well, just a couple more, but if you really need to find her, you'd better check 'em out."

Chloe felt her legs and her spirit buckling. The prospect of checking out even one more island overwhelmed her. She shook her head and then another thought occurred to her. "Are there any more homes in the interior of this island?" she inquired hopefully.

"Not...really." Pointing to his diver's watch, he added, "If you're going to catch that ferry, you don't have much time. Next one leaves in twenty minutes."

Chloe remembered the exit road from the ferry forking off in several directions. It seemed odd there'd be no homes on those roads. A hunch sparked as she glanced at his expectant face. He wanted her off this island. It was nearly as crazy as the conspiracy of silence idea, but she decided to play it out. "Twenty minutes? Then I'd better get going. Thanks again."

"S'okay," he said, beaming. "Hey—I'll drop you off at the slip."

"No," she said quickly. "I'd like the walk. Do me good." She waved and started off, hoping he didn't follow.

She remembered correctly. The intersection before the harbor forked out in three directions, including the road she'd returned on. The other two roads led into the island, and one of them had a wooden signpost with four surnames branded into the surface.

Chloe got the same response at all four houses, a disapproving look and a single syllable "Nope." On the way back, she noticed an overgrown driveway she'd missed, and tucked back in a dense thicket of trees, a rustic log cabin with an incongruously shiny boy's bike by the front door.

She knocked at the door and hesitated when no one answered, thinking she'd heard someone inside. "Anyone home?" she called, walking around to the back. From all angles the house appeared curtained and silent.

The ferry's horn sounded in the distance. Torn, Chloe circled the house again, knowing she had to catch the ferry if she wanted to make the other islands today. The boat's second wail tugged at her. She broke away, reached the road and began to run the last two hundred or so feet to the intersection. Her strapped, low-heeled shoes slapped against pitted, water-warped pavement.

The attendant saw her as she darted across the empty intersection. "Come on, miss," he called, waving her on.

Breathing heavily, she reached the ramp, climbed it and nearly collided with the man's outstretched arm. "Ticket, miss."

"Oh, yes." Shuddering through the ferry's next blast, she searched her purse, found the ticket and boarded. The gate closed behind her, and the ferry's engines roared in preparation to pull away.

Turning back to look at the island, Chloe formulated a last-ditch question and yelled at the attendant over the din. "Did you notice a blond woman and a dark-haired boy on this ferry yesterday?"

He nodded, and Chloe slumped against the railing. "Where did they go? Which island?"

"Only one island on this route," he told her shrugging. "This here one. Seen that blond lady before, I think. Must live on White Rock somewhere."

"Let me off," she said. The ferry lurched. "Let me off now!"

He opened the gate, and Chloe descended the ramp, stepping off just as it lifted away from the boat. The last house, she thought, it has to be that one. Half running, half stumbling, she retraced her steps to the log cabin.

She avoided the driveway, skirting the crescent of trees and approaching from the side instead. She didn't want to alert whoever might be inside.

Crouched beneath a curtained window, she listened, and after several moments of silence, slipped around to the back of the cabin. Pressing in close, she stopped, her heart jerking. The cabin's back door hung open a crack.

A twig snapped beneath her foot as she stepped forward. Everywhere, sounds magnified. Murmurous breezes rustled the trees, and a dog barked several times and stopped abruptly. The door creaked on its hinges. Chloe shrank back, her heart hammering. The wind?

An uneasy silence resumed. She edged closer, listening at the narrow opening. An empty house sounds different, she thought, no residual traces of human activity, not even the rhythmic breathing of someone asleep.

She entered the darkened kitchen, surprisingly modern for a cabin, and crept noiselessly across shiny vinyl tiles.

It was the flickering shadow at the end of the hallway that caused her to freeze. She stepped back, pressing into a closed doorway. Someone was in the house.

Groping for the doorknob behind her, she felt it twist beneath her fingers. In the same instant the door jerked open, and she fell screaming into the room.

A man's hand caught her arm and pulled her to her feet. Twisting, she got a glimpse of his shadowed face before his arm locked around her neck. "*Nat*, why—?"

A damp rag smothered her cry. She inhaled instinctively, dragging the acrid odor of chloroform deep into her lungs.

# 11

CONSCIOUSNESS came slowly, a glimmer in the murky well of Chloe's mind that expanded until it was a light beneath her eyelids. She saw a coffee table first and then the far arm of a couch and a woman's out-stretched legs, oddly bent and half hanging off the cushions. *My own legs,* she realized as the haze began to clear. A dimly lit room swayed around her.

She tried to think through the dull throb in her temples, but the partial images floating in her mind wouldn't jell...a dog's bark, an open door, a man. It all seemed so recent, so urgent.

Struggling to sit up, she saw him. He stood at the window, his back to her, holding the curtain open just enough to look out. *Nat?*

Her foot snagged the coffee table, and the unexpected contact set off a wave of nausea. Swaying weakly, she fought down the sensation. When she looked up he'd dropped the curtain and was turning around, his body a black outline against the diffuse sunlight penetrating the curtain.

Seeing him brought it back, the struggle, the drop into blackness. She felt panic but she couldn't find any words.

He shifted in the shadows. "Cutter," she whispered as he walked toward her. "Why?"

He paused in a stream of light from the hallway, and

she saw his face. The dark features were strikingly familiar, and yet they collided with the image of Nat Cutter in her mind. This man was tall, lean, dark-haired, but his features... She strained to see facial contours that lacked the angular definition she remembered, a mouth less carved.

The light was fuzzy, her senses still disoriented from the drug. She must be imagining the subtle differences. He moved closer, in and out of the shadows, and for a second she felt as if she were trapped in a house of flashing mirrors, turning, blinking—everywhere she looked another image of Nat Cutter, all different, yet the same.

It was his eyes that halted the whirl. Her disorientation vanished as he hesitated at the edge of the coffee table, close enough for her to see detail, even color. *Hazel eyes, flecked with green.* "You're not—" She pressed back into the couch. *"Who are you?"*

The edge of his mouth curled, hostile. "Who sent you here?"

The voice could have been Nat's, even the inflection. The suspicion surging in his question took her back to that first morning in Nat's room. Even then she'd had the premonition that Nat Cutter was two men. She'd been thinking in terms of psychological complexity, one man with two disparate personalities. But now, as she stared at his eerie replica—

"Who sent you here?" he repeated.

"No one."

"I want the truth," he snapped. "You've been harrassing my neighbors. You broke into my house. Why?"

"Who are you?" she whispered.

"Dammit—" He kicked the table aside and lunged forward to grab her arm. "Answer the question."

Chloe's started cry brought a gasp of alarm from the hallway. A woman appeared, blond hair flowing around her shoulders. "Let her go," she insisted, hovering. "You promised she wouldn't be hurt."

"I'm not going to hurt her." He released Chloe's arm. "I just want the truth."

Chloe stared at the woman, her breath caught in a mix of relief and awe. She was a wraith from the past, moving with the same grace and fragility Chloe remembered as she walked to the man poised by the coffee table and touched his arm.

"Sara?" Chloe murmured.

She turned, startled, staring at Chloe. "What did you call me?"

Chloe tried to stand, but the man's warning glare stopped her. "Sara, I'm Chloe," she said awkwardly. They'd never had a close relationship, rarely seen each other with Sara away at school, but she added without thinking, "Chloe—your sister."

Sara's face drained of color.

Instantly, Chloe regretted having said it. The flare of distrust in the man's eyes was terrifying. Sara tried to stop him, but he moved away from her grasp.

"Did James Guthrie send you?" he demanded.

"No," she said quickly. "I came on my own. No one knows I'm here."

His eyes bore into her, as though he was trying to penetrate to some vulnerable part of her and read the truth. He was so like Nat, she thought, a chill icing her skin. But her eyes were adjusting to the low light, her senses sharpening. This man's hair was a half-shade lighter, his skin tones ruddier, she realized. And the light in his eyes was fueled by a different source than Nat's. Survival. He had the hunted look of a man on the run.

A question sparked in her mind. *Is he Joshua?*

He glanced at the slender woman, and Chloe saw their silent exchange. The air breathed of tension, as though they were waiting for someone to appear. Quickly, Sara walked to the window, eased the curtain open and looked out.

He turned back to Chloe. "What do you want with her?"

"Her father—" She hesitated. "He's been ill."

"Guthrie?" He moved forward. "You said he didn't know you were here."

"He doesn't."

"Wait, Rob." Sara had turned from the window. "My father, ill? What do you mean?" She approached the couch with evident concern.

*Rob?* The name eddied in Chloe's mind, pooling and sliding over impenetrable surfaces like an incoming tide. Maybe Joshua didn't exist, maybe she'd only imagined him.

"Please, Chloe," Sara pressed, sitting next to her. "What's wrong with my father?"

"It was his heart. He's over the crisis now, but it was close." A hand touched her. Looking down, she focused on the pale skin and attenuated bones. Sara's hand. The sister she'd admired from a distance, wanted to know. She looked up. "Your father wants to see you, Sara."

"No—" Rob muttered in the background.

"Let her finish, Rob," Sara intervened. "Chloe, when did you talk to him?"

"In the hospital. It was about two weeks ago." At the

light pressure of Sara's hand, she went on. "He was in intensive care when I saw him, and very ill, but he wanted to know if I'd heard from you—wouldn't let me leave until I convinced him I didn't know where you were. Afterward, his assistant told me how desperate he was to find you." She tried to smile and couldn't quite. "Your father wants to try to make up for whatever's happened between the two of you. He wants to start over."

"Sara," Rob warned, "*it's a trap.*"

Chloe looked up at him, questioning the rancor in his voice. His eyes were fixed on Sara, full of anger, concern and an urgent kind of love. Was he the man at the bridge? she wondered. Confusion eddied again as she realized how much she still didn't understand. "Sara, what happened between you and your father. Why did you run away from Northpointe?"

Sara looked up at Rob, a question in her eyes.

"No," he said, shaking his head.

"But I want to tell her," Sara argued softly. "I'm sure we can trust her, Rob, please."

He walked to the window, looked out. "How can you trust anyone connected with him after what he's put you through?" He grasped the curtain, yanked it closed. "Put *us* through?"

She got up, went to him and after a few whispered words turned back to Chloe. "How did you know I was here? Someone must have told you I was on this island."

"No—no one. I was in Belmont yesterday. I saw you boarding the ferry." Quickly, Chloe relayed her own account of the incident at Northpointe, describing Joshua. "I saw him again, or thought I did, at a writers' conference in Cape Cod a few weeks ago, only his name was Nat Cutter. That was before I knew your father was ill, Sara. After the hospital visit I followed Cutter here, to Maine. I thought he might lead me to you."

Again, she saw them exchange looks. This time Rob nodded.

Sara walked to the couch. "You were right about Nat." She spoke slowly, as though she knew how important it was to Chloe. "He is the man you saw at the bridge. His name is Joshua Whitney, and he's Rob's older brother."

Chloe's throat tightened. She searched Rob's face. Of course, brothers. A poignancy she didn't quite understand brushed her heart.

Rob sighed. "Go ahead, tell her, Sara," he said gently. "Start at the beginning."

Sitting on the couch, staring beyond Chloe at some distant scene, Sara reopened the past reverently, like a cedar chest full of scented treasures. She and Rob had met in college, and the cliché, well, it was true in their case. Love at first sight, love at first breathless glimpse. They'd dated for over a year, but Sara kept it from her father. "He'd disapproved of every boy I'd ever mentioned, even casually," she said, her breath a sigh. "And Rob was too important. I couldn't take the chance that he'd order me not to see him again."

She stopped, staring down at her hands, as though she wanted to stay with those memories and not go on.

"I was happy," she said, a catch in her voice. "In a state bordering on bliss, really. And when I found out I was pregnant it seemed perfect, planned. I believed we were destined to be together, Rob and I. And the baby proved it."

Chloe saw tears sparkling in Sara's eyes and felt a sympathy build within her.

"We were going to run away," Sara said, brushing her cheek. "But my father found out. My father knew everything." She looked up at Rob, remembered pain moving in her features. "And he used everything he knew."

An emotion very near hatred burned in Rob's eyes as Sara went on.

"He sent Gordon Browne to the school to bring me home, and then had one of his men try to buy Rob off. When that didn't work, he resorted to threats. I didn't know until later—" her voice lowered "—that Rob was suspended from school on trumped-up charges and finally expelled."

Sara glanced back at the man by the window, and a wavery smile appeared. "I also didn't know about Rob's plan to rescue me. Sounds a bit Arthurian, doesn't it? Dragon slayers and maidens—"

Rob's voice sliced through Sara's attempt at lightness. "Guthrie told me he was sending Sara out of the country. He said he'd make sure I never saw her or the baby again. I tried everything, even talked to lawyers, but nobody would go up against him.

"Time was running out," he added grimly, "and I was desperate. I knew if I wanted Sara back, I'd have to go and get her myself, so I swiped a gun from my father's collection and got caught. Josh was due to leave for Europe, but my mother called him back, thinking he was the only one who could handle me...."

He means Nat, Chloe realized when the name registered a half beat later. It struck her as odd, since her intuition had once been so strong, that she now found it hard to fathom that Nat and Joshua were the same man.

Sara was talking, finishing the story in her soft, tremulous voice. "Rob convinced Josh to help him. They were two of a kind then, both idealistic and passionate about justice. I don't think it ever occurred to my father that Rob would have the courage to defy him, and he certainly hadn't counted on the formidable Whitney brothers." Her mouth quirked into a shy, charming smile. "The two of them whisked me right out from under his nose."

Rob grinned, and Chloe felt like applauding.

"Unfortunately," Sara continued, "my father doesn't take defeat lightly. We managed to evade his detectives for a while, but they caught up with us in California right after the baby was born. We were married by then and thought foolishly that there was nothing he could do." She stopped, a shadow crossing her face.

Chloe sat forward. "What happened?" She heard her own heart beating in the silence.

"He tried to take our son away from us," Sara said, raising her eyes to Chloe's. "He brought in a team of high-powered lawyers and sued us for custody. He claimed we were child abusers." She shook her head, looked away. "It wasn't true, but we knew he'd win. We had to run."

"You and Rob?"

"All three of us," Rob cut in. "We took the baby and went to Canada, and when they tracked us down, we flew to Europe. It's easier to disappear there. Josh and Elena lived in Italy, and with their financial help and contacts, we got lost—" he emitted a short, cold sound "—so lost even James Guthrie couldn't find us."

"But you came back," Chloe observed.

"Yeah, about a year ago. Josh had been here in the States for several years. When he was sure Sara's father had called off his dogs, he contacted us. He'd scouted the island, found this place." He shrugged as though he felt the need to defend his decision. "We wanted our son to grow up here, in the United States."

"Of course," Chloe acknowledged, hesitating. "But what about Guthrie? Did he know you'd come back?"

He shook his head. "No—we'd changed our names, phony ID. After years of hiding, you pick up some tricks. Even Josh took a pseudonym while he was in Europe so there'd be no connection." He looked at Sara, and his chest moved with a deep breath. "We've been happy here, so happy I guess we got a little careless. Sara even started wearing her hair the way she used to."

"And then I showed up?"

"And then," he said nodding, "you showed up."

Swallowing, Chloe looked at her stepsister. "I didn't know, Sara. I had no idea your father was capable of—"

Sara stopped her with "I know."

"Maybe he's sincere now," Chloe suggested, hope glimmering. "He's been so ill."

"Men like James Guthrie don't change," Rob said bitterly. "He's obsessed with power and control. He can never forget that I took his daughter, and he won't rest until he evens the score. He wants his only grandchild. He wants an heir for the Guthrie dynasty."

Rob's eyes were drawn to the hallway, and Chloe followed them as an adolescent boy appeared, a dark uncertain figure in the pale light. Again, she felt chilled.

"Chloe," Sara said, standing, gesturing for the boy. "This is Evan."

For a moment Chloe could only stare at the dark eyes, young, deep-set, already slightly haunted. "Hello, Evan." She extended her hand. This is *their* son, she told herself. Rob and Sara's.

The strength of his grip surprised her. There was a fierceness, a pride in it. She stepped back, taking in both mother and son, and felt a swell of emotion. The brief look that went between them told her they were united against the world, sharing a bond of love and loyalty beyond anything she'd ever known. The loneliness of her own life struck her, sudden and sharp in contrast. She wanted a beautiful, dark-eyed son like this. She wanted this kind of love.

Evan's tentative voice brought her back. "Sometimes when my mother was homesick she'd tell me about you," he said, sober-eyed, "and about Northpointe." With his mother's shy, serious smile, he added, "She said your hair was fire-red like maple trees in the fall."

Chloe smiled, touched and charmed by his self-consciousness.

As Evan went to stand beside his father, Chloe turned to her sister, her voice softened with emotion. "Sara, I know what you've been through must have been terrible, but it's over now—and you have so much." Tears threatening, she took her sister's hand. "So much to cherish and protect. Please," she whispered, "don't worry. Your father will never find you through me."

Smiling through the tears in her eyes, Sara pressed her cheek to Chloe's and kissed her lightly. "I know, little sister."

The words filled Chloe with gentle waves of pain.

The sweet ache of something longed for and finally received...the sister she'd never had. With a choked sound, Chloe embraced her. "Take care," she whispered. "Take care."

She broke away, managed a trembling smile. "I have to go. There's someone I need to see."

"Is it Nat?" Sara asked. As Chloe nodded, Sara smiled. "Give him our love. And please—tell him we're okay."

CHLOE STOOD at the bow of the ferry, leaning into the railing as though her body weight might propel them forward. "The slow boat to Belmont," she murmured, squinting to see the mainland. "Bet I could swim faster."

Didn't the captain know she had to get back? Didn't he know she needed to be with Nat Cutter again more than she'd ever needed anything in her life? An image took hold in her mind. Looking just the way he always did in her daydreams, she imagined Nat, his hair mussed, eyes shadowed, leaning up against the door frame with that don't-give-a-damn expression on his face.

Just let me at him, she thought, grinning, and I'll make quick work of that cocky look. Riffling through her purse, she found his sunglasses and put them on. A biblical quote came to mind. "'The truth shall make you free,'" she informed the brisk head wind that was stinging her eyes and blowing her hair.

The truth: Nat Cutter was not the man Sara had run away with. He was free, available, *unencumbered*. The urge to sing out loud came over Chloe—love songs, "The Star Spangled Banner"—but she remembered her fellow passengers and thought better of it. If love was a form of insanity, she was definitely over the edge.

She was in her car and well down the road toward the Sunrise motel before she acknowledged the uneasiness in the pit of her stomach. How would Nat react when she told him she'd found Sara? Musing on the best way to break it to him, she realized that if she hadn't seen her stepsister, she might have called Gordon Browne by now and given away something vital.

The thought sobered her. Sara and her family were the one remaining shadow over Chloe's heart. She hoped Sara's Rob was wrong about James Guthrie. He'd been so sure that Guthrie couldn't be trusted.

In her mind, Chloe reviewed the brief hospital meeting with her stepfather and the conversation with Gordon Browne afterward. The uneasiness built, and her thoughts clicked faster, adding up events: Browne's phone call to her room in Maine, his second call to her office in New York, her own vague suspicions she was being followed.

Chloe hit the brake pedal, wheeled right and pulled the car onto the road's shoulder. *Followed?* If that was true, she'd just led them straight to Sara. She flicked off Nat's glasses, dropped them in her lap.

Rob's words to Sara echoed in her mind. *"It's a trap."*

Was it possible she'd been set up? That it had all been staged—even Guthrie's illness—to flush her out and make her act on whatever information she had about Sara?

No, no, that's crazy, she told herself, remembering the frail, desperately ill man she'd visited in the hospital. A man clinging to life isn't driven by revenge. But she remembered Rob's angry words: *He won't rest until he's evened the score.*

She had to get to a phone, call Sara, warn her.

Accelerating down the last winding, deserted stretch of highway, she imagined the horror of trying to tell Cutter what had happened. "If I've ruined everything he's tried so hard to protect," she whispered, "he'll never forgive me."

She saw his black Corvette parked in the motel lot as she drove in. Her heart thudding, she pulled up next to it. In the rush to open the car door and grab for her purse, she hardly noticed the sunglasses as they slipped off her lap.

The car lurched slightly and rolled backward. Instinctively, she wrenched on the hand brake, recoiling from the sickening pop and crack of glass and metal. "Oh, *no*," she rasped, sliding out of the car.

Staring down in mute horror, she saw the sunglasses caught beneath the tire, their grotesquely twisted frames snapped in two.

# 12

NAT STARED AT the empty four-poster and combed a hand through his hair. Where was she? He'd tried to call her several times last night from his hotel room and again from the airport just before his flight back today. Still wearing his raincoat, he looked around the room for a note or some other clue to her whereabouts.

The empty room revealed nothing, no note, no forgotten clothing. He shrugged out of his raincoat, threw it over a chair. She'd shown up night before last with nothing but the clothes she was wearing and her purse. But then, remembering, he turned to the coffee table. *And that book of his poetry.*

The small volume was there, where she'd left it.

He picked it up, leafed through, a hollow sensation in his chest. Something was wrong. He looked around the room again, unable to get the disturbing thought out of his mind. Maybe she'd been called back to New York, he told himself, a business emergency. He picked up the telephone receiver and began to dial. Walt might know.

The desk clerk, with his typical brevity, told Nat he'd seen Chloe pulling out in her rental car the night before. "Ain't seen her since," he added.

Nat's hand tightened on the receiver. "Thanks, Walt." The dial tone buzzed in his head as he stared at the empty bed. She's gone, he thought, finding it hard to breathe. God, *why*? There's so much to tell her.

Muffled sounds caught his attention, the hurried noise of someone approaching. He turned just as the door swung open, and Chloe burst in. His relief at seeing her evaporated as she hesitated on the threshold, her clothes wrinkled and misshapen. A dirt smudge darkened her chin.

"Chloe, what—?"

She moved toward him, her hands cradling something he couldn't see. "Nat," she said, her voice breaking, "I'm sorry."

"What's wrong?" He dropped the phone back into its cradle and went to her. She was holding a pair of shattered glasses that he recognized as his own. Blood oozed from an open cut on her finger. "What happened? An accident? Were you hurt?" Up close, he immediately saw she'd been through some kind of hell. Her eyes were shadowed, her skin waxen.

"No—" she shook her head "—the car—" Swallowing hard, she lost the words, brushed past him to the table and set the glasses down. "I have to call Sara."

He caught her hand as she reached for the phone. "Hold it—what do you mean, call Sara? How do you know about Sara?"

"I found her." She drew herself up as though trying to rein in her emotions. "I found them, Nat—Sara, Rob, Evan, on the island. They told me everything." She stared up into his eyes. "I know."

He searched her ashen face, disbelief mounting. "You found them? How?"

"Nat," she said warningly, her voice trembling, "let me use the phone."

The conflict in her eyes confused him. There was

something she wasn't telling him. "Not until you tell me what's going on. Why do you have to call her?"

Her jaw rigid, she blurted, "I think Guthrie's been having me followed. I think—" she broke off, stiffened "—that he's been using me to find Sara, and I may have played right into his hands." She tried to twist away. "Don't you understand? I left their place nearly two hours ago. It may already be too late!"

She wrenched out of his grip and lunged for the phone, gasping as he blocked her with his arm. "Stop it, Chloe," he warned, catching her wrist as she tried to push him out of the way. In the tangled rush, they jarred up against the table and sent the phone crashing to the floor.

"What's wrong with you?" she snapped, her eyes flashing. "I have to warn her!"

*"No."* He jerked her away from the table and swung her around to face him. "No, you don't. Listen to me. *James Guthrie is telling the truth."*

"What?"

"He's an old man who doesn't want to die alone. He's trying to find Sara and make amends."

Her narrowing eyes said she was fast reaching the point of trusting no one, including him. "I don't understand. How do you know that? How can you possibly know Guthrie's motives? No." She shook her head, still trying to twist away. "No, Rob thinks it's a trap.

"Give me a chance, Chloe, please?" He released her wrist and exhaled hard. This was not the way he'd planned to tell her. "I paid James Guthrie a visit this morning—in his hotel suite at the Plaza."

"Met with Guthrie? Why?"

"To check out your story." He saw her flinch. "It wasn't you I didn't trust, it was Guthrie. When you told me he wanted to reconcile with Sara, I figured he was using you as bait."

"And now you're saying he wasn't?"

"That's right, he wasn't. He had Browne keep tabs on you, but only because he suspected you knew something you weren't telling him. But he's not into retribution this time, Chloe. He's sincere about wanting to make up with his daughter." Nat could see she didn't believe it any more than he had at first.

"How can you be sure of that?"

She was holding her wrist where he'd caught her, his finger imprints still visible. He'd hurt her. His jaw tightening, he resisted the impulse to take her hand and caress away the remaining redness. She clearly wasn't ready to let him touch her yet. "I've got it in writing, witnessed by attorneys. Mine and his."

She released a breath, and he began to see the tension ease out of her as he continued. "I didn't believe anything could change James Guthrie, even a brush with death, so I made the preliminary contact with him anonymously, through my attorney in New York. Once my attorney was convinced Guthrie was telling the truth, we set up a meeting."

"That's what you were doing in New York? What about the negotiations, the book contract?"

"That was all true—"

"But you conveniently left out the part about Guthrie. Why didn't you tell me?"

"I couldn't without giving everything away—my own identity, Sara and Rob's cover. Until I knew what Guthrie was up to, I couldn't take that risk."

Hurt flickered. "Why not?" she said indignantly. "What did you think I would do, call *60 Minutes*? I could have helped you."

The smudge on her chin distracted him. She's a mess, he thought, an adorable mess. With that wild red hair she could be one of the orphans in *Annie*. But her round, serious green eyes meant business. They demanded a full accounting.

He shook his head. "The James Guthrie I knew was a ruthless man. He wouldn't have stopped at anything, including having Gordon Browne, or one of his other goons intimidate the truth out of you. I couldn't take that risk until I'd checked him out." He hesitated, stirred by the same protective urge toward her that had once threatened him. "And I couldn't put you in that kind of jeopardy."

She looked thoughtful, and after a moment softened. "What's going to happen now?"

"That's up to Sara and Rob. Guthrie's agreed to let them make the first move. He understands they'll need time."

"Time?" She glanced down at the broken sunglasses. "I'm not sure it's that easy. There might never be enough time for Rob to forgive him."

"Maybe not," he agreed, resignation and sadness in his voice as he acknowledged that possibility. "But at least they have nothing to fear from him now."

They both lapsed into silence as she stared down at the sunglasses. "Looking pretty bad, aren't they?" she said finally, touching the Carreras' cracked lenses. "The work of a world-class klutz. Sorry." Blinking away what might have been tears, she murmured to herself, "Especially since I nearly killed myself getting them off that piling."

"A klutz, maybe," he said laughing, tenderness in his voice. "But a persistent one." He drew her around and looked into eyes that shimmered like emerald chips. "You found your stepsister. Do you realize that you did in one week what Guthrie and his goons couldn't do in fourteen years?"

She began to brighten, a slow-growing inner radiance that took his breath away.

"I had some help," she admitted, catching back a smile. "You. Nobody else saw you but me. They didn't know they should have been looking for two men—or that one of them was named Joshua." Hesitating, lashes lowering briefly, she emitted a breathy sound that confused and excited him. "What do I call you now?" she asked, looking up. "Nat? Josh?"

"Call me Cutter," he said, a slow grin breaking. "Everybody else does."

In the glance that passed between them, he felt something unexpected and wonderful, an uprush of anticipation.

She reached up to touch his face, startling his heart to a rapid beat. "Cutter," she said, rising up on tiptoes to kiss him. As her mouth moved under his, he felt a sliding sensation in his stomach, a weakness that spread to his thighs. Leaning back into the table, he pulled her up against him and shuddered at her warmth and softness. She was a spring flood of sweetness...and he was a drowning man.

Their kiss went on, gentle, achingly passionate, until she broke it and pulled back. She didn't say a word, just looked at him as no woman had ever looked at him before.

The desire to take her to bed was like a surge of near pain inside him, but he fought it back, unwilling to break the moment. "I missed you," he said finally, when he could manage the words. His hands on her throat, he caressed her jawline with his thumbs. "Truth is, I was scared out of my mind when I got back here and couldn't find you. For one crazy moment, I thought you'd skipped out on me, gone back to New York."

"Really?" she responded, obviously delighted.

"Really." He brushed at the smudge on her chin with his thumb. "What do I call *you* now? Sherlock?"

She smiled and winked. "Firebreather."

He felt a quick rush of stimulation and urged her closer, sliding his fingers into her hair. "Works for me," he said, grinning.

He'd just begun to kiss her, really kiss her when she murmured, "Wait a minute," pushed out of his arms and looked around the room. "Where's the television?"

"The what?"

"It just occurred to me this very minute. The television you claimed you were listening to at three in the morning when I heard a woman in your room. Where is it?"

He grinned and folded his arms. "On second thought, maybe Sherlock *is* more apt."

"Don't mess with me, Cutter." A fierceness sparked in her eyes.

Damn, she's cute, he thought, and knew if he told her she'd go off like a firecracker. "I had an unexpected visit from Sara that night. She and Rob had been arguing about her father. Sara's wanted to contact him ever since they returned to the States. She thought maybe I could help her convince Rob, but when I took my brother's side, well—" he hesitated, raised a shoulder "—you heard it. She got pretty upset."

Chloe was nodding, pacing, putting things together.

"And the man I saw coming out of your room, the one I followed, that was Rob?"

"The FBI could use a good woman like you."

She didn't seem to have heard him. Stopping at the coffee table, she picked up the volume of his poems, hesitated, then turned around to look at him. "'Innocence of Heart'? Did you write it for me?"

She looked so expectant that he sobered. He hadn't, not consciously, but maybe...? "Yeah, it was you."

She nodded, her eyes filling, sparkling. "I knew it." With a long sigh and a heartbreaking smile, she said, "I want to go back there, Cutter. To Northpointe, to the bridge."

The bridge. Joshua Whitney? He'd been afraid of this ever since the night she told him about Sara's disappearance. A flash of pain surrounded his heart. She was clutching the book just as she had that night, like it held some precious, inviolable memory.

I DON'T REMEMBER the old house being this beautiful, Chloe thought, gazing at the red brick of Northpointe through the latticed, sun-drenched bowers of the bridge. She inhaled the nostalgic scent of mossy rocks, gurgling creek water, green trees and sunshine. Her heart full, she could almost believe she'd been happy here.

Turning to see where Nat had gone, she found him standing near the creek bed, staring into the water. A windy gust rustled the tree branches above him and sprinkled him with light and shadows.

Beautiful, she thought, *haunted*. Was she imagining the darkness in him? Watching him turn to stare into the distance, she thought of the myth, and for one enchanted second, she could almost imagine him raising his arms like some marvelous force of nature, splitting the heavens.

She turned away, inexplicably disturbed. Her heart heavy, she realized what must be bothering him. He was trying to find a way to tell her he couldn't continue the relationship. She should have realized that a man like him, a writer, moody and complicated as he was, wouldn't want to be committed. He'd already had one disastrous marriage—

Her thoughts strayed to the day before when she'd asked him to come to Northpointe with her. She thought she'd seen it then, his subtle withdrawal. He'd agreed to go, but said he had to talk with Sara and Rob first. So they'd gone to the island together.

She would never forget the obvious love and surprise in Rob's eyes when he opened the door and embraced his brother. And later, when Nat confirmed what Chloe had already told them about Guthrie, Chloe watched and listened quietly, poignantly aware of the mutual caring and respect the three of them shared.

When Evan entered and went to stand by his uncle, Chloe saw how they were linked, the four of them, by something even more intimate than blood. History, a saga that started at Northpointe. I was there, too, she thought, her heart surging softly. In some way maybe I'm a part of it all.

By the time she and Nat left, Rob had agreed to take Sara and Evan to visit Guthrie. And the healing had begun....

Chloe sighed, a bittersweet sound. A shadow crossed the wooden planks in front of her. She looked up and Nat was there, an arm's length from her. She hadn't imagined the darkness. His features whispered with it.

"Can we talk?" he said.

She leaned into the rail for support. "Yes."

"I think I envy you," he said after a moment. "You've obviously come to terms with your past. You're here, facing it, reexperiencing the good feelings, putting the others to rest."

Awareness came gradually, a heavy thud in her chest. Elena, of course. Was that going to be his reason, that he hadn't resolved the situation with Elena? "And you haven't come to terms with yours?"

"My past?" He hesitated. "No, it's not *my* past that's bothering me, it's yours...or rather, ours."

"I don't understand."

His voice was low and deliberate. "I'm not the man you're remembering, Chloe. The one who carried you to this bridge."

"Joshua? You're not him? Then who—?"

"No—" He raised a hand, his eyes asking her to understand. "I mean I lost Joshua Whitney a long time ago. Too much has happened, too many shattered illusions. Men like him, full of dreams, they don't survive in this world."

He broke off and exhaled. "I know you loved him, but if you came back here hoping you'd rediscover him, that I'd suddenly be him again..."

Whatever it was he said next got lost in the whirling sensation in her brain. "Do you mean that's it?" she whispered through a dizzy, giddy little tornado of insight. "That's what's been bothering you? You thought I was trying to recapture that past, the love I might have felt for Joshua?"

He considered her, puzzled. "Yeah...you weren't?"

"Oh, Cutter," she breathed, sagging against the railing. "I thought you were going to tell me you didn't want a relationship, that the artist in you couldn't be confined—" She broke off, looked up at him. "You weren't coming to that next, were you?"

The glint in his eyes unnerved her. Wicked, she thought, easily the closest approximation of sheer wickedness she'd ever seen in her life. She felt a pulse quicken in her throat. "Don't mess with me, Cutter."

He caught the collar of her blouse, dragged her closer. "No, I wasn't coming to that next. I was just wondering if you've considered what you'd be getting into. You and me, I mean. I'm hell to live with—cynical, stubborn, given to moods—"

"True," she breathed, dizzy from the nearness of him. "But you're also gentle and funny—" she felt her face flushing "—and you make love like a god."

With a husky sound, he pulled her to him. "I leave my clothes lying around," he confessed, breathtakingly near her lips. "I stay up all night writing."

"All true," she agreed again, tidying the hair that curled onto his temples, the thrill of touching him tingling down her arm, "but I think I can train you."

His soft growl of laughter kindled a fire inside her. She pressed her fingers to his mouth, anticipating his protest. "No more excuses. I want you, Nathanial Cutter, I want your dark-eyed babies."

He sobered instantly, a shudder passing through him. Holding her face, he kissed her with such unbridled passion that she saw starbursts in her head. His hunger aroused her; the connection their bodies made thrilled her to her soul.

The kiss deepened, echoing through them, gentling to breathy, nerve-spun tremors. Trembling in its wake they held each other, silenced by emotion. Sunlight poured over them, soft and golden, and Chloe knew in her heart that she'd finally come home.

Through the mist in her eyes, she looked up at him, and tried to smile. "I adore you, Cutter, I always have."

She saw the miracle happening inside him, felt its power. He caressed her face, obviously shaken. "I wish I could tell you what I'm feeling—" his voice caught "—but there aren't words."

"I know," she said. "I know."

And then, suddenly, as though something had broken free inside him, he whispered, "I love you."

He said it again, touched her face, and Chloe felt a moment of inexpressible rapture, like the crescendo of a symphonic chord inside her. Her heart was beating everywhere, in her own hand as she pressed it over his, in the air around them, in the covering bowers of the bridge.

Her world hesitated in its orbit, waiting, shimmering, caught like the hand of a clock between seconds. "I love you," she whispered, hearing the peal of soft chimes. Time had begun again. The world was new.

# Afterword

ON THE LAST morning in June, an unsurpassingly beautiful summer day, Chloe Katherine Kates married Joshua Whitney beneath the sun-drenched bowers of the old bridge at Northpointe. Rob and Sara Whitney were in attendance with their son, Evan.

One year later, Chloe and Joshua had their first child, a boy.

Dear Reader,

A man with secrets in his past and a woman who threatens to expose them. That's the stuff that gothics are made of, and I was thrilled to have the chance to create a gothiclike story for Jenna, Trent and Claymore Mansion.

When Jenna Daniels returns to her hometown in search of a career-making news story, she knows she'll come face-to-face with her teenage crush, Trent Claymore—a man she spent one magic night with. But Jenna encounters more than just passion in the walls of Claymore Mansion. There's danger, too. And if she isn't careful, this may well be her final trip home.

I was so honored to be asked to write a novella to pair with the rerelease of Suzanne Forster's *The Man at Ivy Bridge.* I hope you like Jenna and Trent's story. Please do let me know! You can reach me at www.juliekenner.com or at P.O. Box 151417, Austin, TX 78715-1417. Hope to hear from you!

Happy reading,

*Julie Kenner*

# DANGEROUS DESIRES

## Julie Kenner

# 1

A HEAVY FOG covered the manicured grounds, shrouding the pine trees and blocking the sun that still rose in the eastern sky. Both beautiful and foreboding, the wisps of mist danced like fairies, ephemeral creatures that existed only in dreams.

Even the stone walls of Claymore Mansion, a building that had been erected over a century ago, seemed insubstantial, as if the heavy mist could consume the granite itself, so that when the sun finally did peek through it would see nothing more than a wide meadow where once the stately mansion had stood.

A fog that dense could hide anything....

From the safety of her taxi, Jenna Daniels shivered, her imagination running wild once more. She'd told Winston Claymore, the family's patriarch, that she was writing an article on mansions rumored to be haunted along the Pacific Coast. But that was only part of the truth.

She was here to find a murderer.

"And even a fog has to lift sometime," she whispered.

"Pardon, miss?" the driver said.

Jenna shook her head. "Just talking to myself."

He cast a curious glance toward his rearview mirror, then tapped the brakes, bringing the sedan to a halt. "This is it."

So it was. He'd pulled around the circular drive, and now the entrance to Claymore Mansion loomed before her. She hadn't seen it for about nine years, but still Jenna would have sworn she'd been here only yesterday. There were the heavy stone lions that guarded the entrance. There was the marble fountain, the centerpiece of the manicured drive.

Everything appeared the way it had the last time she'd seen the place. The night of the Claymore family's annual spring fete. The night Trent Claymore had driven her home, and she'd boldly pressed a goodnight kiss to his lips.

Even now she could feel the blush rise on her cheeks. It had seemed like such bravado at the time, but really it was nothing but fear. Fear that he'd return to college and she'd never see him again. Fear that she'd lose the one chance to taste heaven in the arms of the man she'd craved.

She'd been only sixteen, a mere kid, while he was already halfway through college. She hadn't even planned to go to the party that year, but when she'd learned that Trent had come home from Stanford for the event, she'd been compelled. She'd *had* to see him again, and so she spent the entire evening holding up the wall in the Grand Ballroom, watching him drink toast after toast with the other guests, watching his father introduce him to debutante after debutante.

Jenna had watched the other girls in their beautiful dresses, her stomach twisting and her fantasies shattering. Her own dress had been rescued from Goodwill, saved by her mother's excellent seamstress skills. Jenna was no debutante; she'd never catch Trent's eye. And when the clock struck eleven, she'd called her mother, begging for a ride home. At eleven-fifteen the butler had found Jenna in the foyer—her mother had called back. The battery in their run-down Chevy had died once again.

She'd set out walking over the butler's protests, determined to leave, tired of watching Trent flirt with the other girls. She'd had a crush on him for years, but he'd never noticed. Why would he? Except for this one annual party the family threw for the entire town, their paths never crossed. Her mother could barely make ends meet, whereas Trent had more money than God.

Besides, he was four years older than she was. A worldly twenty to her gawky, still-in-a-training-bra sixteen. Her well-endowed mother insisted Jenna was simply a late bloomer. To Jenna, that was mom-speak for homely.

She'd barely reached the end of the private road when the glare of headlights had lit the surrounding bushes. She'd stepped back off the road, fearful of getting hit by someone who'd partied just a little too much, and then was immediately shocked when she recognized Trent's red Mustang convertible. He pulled up, leaned over to open the door, and said, "Get in."

Jenna hadn't argued. She might be homely, but she wasn't stupid.

They'd ridden in silence all the way into town. Once they hit the square, he asked for directions, and she'd told him that the Main Street Café was fine. She could walk from there, and she didn't want him seeing her tiny house where the neighbors still burned trash in barrels in the front yard.

He'd given her a look, as if he wanted to argue, but then he did a U-turn and pulled up in front of the café. "You didn't need to walk, you know. You could have just asked for a ride."

"I'm sorry," she'd mumbled. "It's warm. People were having a good time..." She shrugged. "I didn't want to be a bother."

"*People* were having a good time? But not you."

She shrugged again.

"Now you're going to give me a complex," he teased. "Make me think I've been a bad host."

"Oh, no," she'd protested. "You're wonderful." Immediately, her cheeks had burned. "I mean, you've been a wonderful host. I didn't mean I thought you—I mean..." She closed her eyes. "I'm an idiot."

He chuckled. "No you're not," he said. "You're sweet. If I wasn't heading back to Stanford in the morning, I'd invite you back to the house for dinner tomorrow. We could try again. Maybe see if I can't get you to have a good time, too."

She'd squinted up at him. "Do you mean that?"

"Can't have you thinking I'm a bad host."

"I'd never think that." No, she pretty much thought he hung the moon.

"Thanks, Jenna."

She hadn't even been certain he knew her name, and when he said it, something inside her snapped. She leaned forward, over the gearshift, her hand clutching the emergency brake for balance. She didn't give herself time to think. She just *did*. And what she did was plant a kiss on his mouth. He made a startled noise, and his lips parted. She slipped her tongue inside, bold and daring and just a little bit desperate, and felt him relax under her assault.

And then she experienced the first bit of heaven she'd ever known in her life. His hand had cupped the back of her neck, and he'd pulled her closer. His mouth became firm under hers, and he took control of the kiss, claiming her with his mouth. He tasted of champagne, and the sensation was heady. She wanted to lose herself to the moment, to him. To never come back to Earth.

All in all, it probably lasted less than a minute, but when their lips finally parted, and he looked at her with that crooked smile, Jenna was certain that they'd been holding each other for hours rather than seconds.

A police cruiser slid by in the dark, and Jenna jumped, reality crashing down around her. "I'm sorry," she'd mumbled, even as she'd scrambled backward out of the car, fumbling for the door handle, and practically falling out onto the sidewalk.

Trent had lunged for her, his fingers closing around her arm. "Please," he'd said, his voice raw. "Don't run away."

Even now, so many years later, she could remember the way her stomach felt, all fluttery and hot, as she'd blinked stupidly at him, unable to believe that he meant the words he'd just spoken.

"Stay with me." A grin tugged at his mouth, as if he understood her confusion.

"I…" She shook her head. "I think you've had too much champagne."

"Maybe," he admitted. "But not so much that I don't know what I'm doing."

"Oh." She licked her lips. "What are you doing?"

"I'm inviting you to go have some eggs with me."

*That* got her mouth moving again. "Eggs?" She raised an eyebrow, amused.

"Or whatever. I'd just like to spend some time with you."

Trent Claymore wanted to spend time with *her*. All

those debs flitting around his mansion, and it was her he was inviting out for a midnight breakfast. "I...I..."

"Accept," he finished for her. "Come on. Get back in the car so you don't freeze to death."

"What's wrong with the café?" she'd asked, nodding across the street to the lit up facade of the cozy diner.

His face hardened. "Gossip," he'd said.

She'd understood at once. Trent's father would throw a fit if her son was seen with the likes of Jenna. And Winston Claymore's fits were not something any sane person wanted to experience.

She'd climbed back into the car without comment, and he drove to the next town over, finally stopping at Big Jim's All Night Diner, where they were the only customers in the place who hadn't arrived in an eighteen-wheeler.

They'd stayed the entire night, holding hands and talking, their laugher bridging the four-year, million-dollar gap that loomed between them. They'd talked about everything and nothing. He'd told her about how he was studying business so he could step into the family empire, and she told him about how she wanted to be a journalist like Woodward or Bernstein, and crack important stories.

Their conversation had bounced from light to dark, from frivolous to deep. He told her about life at the Mansion, about his father's aspirations for Trent and how they didn't always jive with what Trent himself wanted. "Family duty," he'd said with a shrug, then asked about her home life. At first, Jenna had balked. But the truth was that Jenna *wanted* to tell Trent. And so, for the first time ever, Jenna had described her life in great detail, her words matter-of-fact instead of em-

barrassed. Her resourceful mother, a struggling waitress who made their clothes. Her father, a drunk who'd
run out on them both.

"I'm sorry," Trent had said. "But try not to judge
him too hard. The pull of the bottle..." He'd trailed off
with a shake of his head. "Well, it's hard to resist."

She'd studied him for a long moment, then changed
the subject. There had been rumors of horrible
drunken rows at Claymore Mansion, Trent railing
against his father's harsh rules. She'd dismissed the rumors at the time, unable to believe anything ugly about
her perfect Trent.

Now, though, she wondered if her perfect Trent
wasn't somewhat flawed. And the truth was, his im-
perfections didn't make him any less attractive. Not
now that she was coming to know the real man and
how he struggled behind the Mansion's stone facade.

Morning had come all too soon, and as the sun rose
in the eastern sky, Trent drove her home, then walked
around the car to open the door for her. He'd pressed a
kiss to her cheek, a silent goodbye. Neither of them
made any comment or pretended that they'd keep in
touch. She hadn't expected it, and she was secretly
happy that he hadn't parted with some sugarcoated lie
about how they'd see each other again. She wanted to
hold on to the memory as it was—*perfect*. And as he
drove off, she pressed her fingertips to her lips as if she
could make the kiss last longer by holding it in place.

That afternoon, he'd left town. One month later,
Jenna and her mother had moved to Philadelphia.

Was he here at the mansion now, she wondered.
Would she see Trent in just a few hours? And if so,
would he remember their one magical night? Had it
meant as much to him as it had to her?

The taxi driver cleared his throat. "Um, miss?"

She jerked upright, a marionette yanked to attention. "I'm sorry?"

"I don't mean to rush you or nothing, but I've got other calls."

"Right. Of course. I'm sorry."

"Do you want help with the bags?"

She shook her head. "I can manage." As the car idled, Jenna passed the fare over the ratty vinyl seat. She'd come from Los Angeles with only her purse and a single suitcase, and now she grabbed both bags, took a deep breath, and slid out of the cab.

She'd barely taken one step toward the mansion when the taxi pulled away, leaving Jenna alone in the mists. She squared her shoulders and examined her destination. The carved wooden door was set back under a stone archway that formed a small alcove. The three gargoyles she remembered vividly from her childhood were perched on the arch, still watching. Still waiting. But for what?

For her to come back? For her to solve the mystery of poor Alicia's death?

Swallowing, Jenna hurried under the archway and out of the gargoyles' line of sight. The space was bathed in shadows, and she took another deep breath before lifting her hand to the knocker. She pounded three times, and the thud of brass on wood echoed in the still air. After that, though, nothing. Not a sound from inside or outside. Just a silence so thick she could almost reach out and stroke it.

Jenna shifted from one foot to the other, wondering what to do now. Winston Claymore expected her today, but she'd been unable to give the elderly man a specific arrival time. She hadn't anticipated taking

such an early flight, but she'd lucked out and managed
to get her reservation changed. She probably shouldn't
have bothered rushing, though. Now that she was
here, it didn't look like anyone else was.

Damn.

She considered using her cell phone to call the taxi
back. She could go back into town and do some background research in Dryer Cove's tiny municipal library. But that seemed like a waste of time. She'd just
come from there, and besides, the library was sadly un-
derfunded. Any serious research would have to wait
for her to make the trek all the way into Portland.

She frowned at the door. Surely if she just waited
someone would be along soon.

Besides, her reporter's instincts were screaming for
her to stay. After all, she might not get another chance
to wander the grounds alone. She'd come back to Claymore Mansion on a mission: to prove to herself and her
boss that she had the mettle of an investigative reporter. And this article—this investigation—had been
all the more appealing since Trent Claymore was right
in the middle of it.

For almost a year, she'd been busting her tail at the
*Los Angeles Times* trying to break into serious reporting,
spinning her wheels writing features and fluff pieces,
never getting the serious assignments.

But then the call had come in from Miriam Farnsworth, and Jenna had smelled a hot story. She shivered, remembering the dowager's hushed tone, the
desolation and loss that had permeated her thin voice.

*Alicia was murdered*, she'd said, her words chilling
Jenna to the bone. *Someone at Claymore Mansion mur-*

*dered my daughter. Find the murderer,* she'd begged. *You're a reporter. Write a story and force the police to do their job.*

Jenna hardly knew Alicia Farnsworth Claymore; they'd been sorority sisters at Stanford, but Alicia had been a senior during Jenna's freshman year, one of the old money types. She'd seen the older girl often enough on Trent's arm, though. Even after so many years, Jenna had still ducked whenever she'd seen Trent, now a grad student, on campus. According to Mrs. Farnsworth, Alicia and Trent had married two days after Trent received his M.B.A.

For three years, Alicia and Trent had been gloriously happy. As expected, he'd taken over the lumber and paper industries that had amassed the Claymore fortune, and Alicia had run the house. But then tragedy struck. And at midnight on Halloween, Alicia Farnsworth Claymore plunged to her death from the cliffs behind Claymore Mansion.

Her body was found the next morning, broken and battered on the rocky shore.

The police had made a few perfunctory inquiries and then ruled the death a suicide. Recent depression, they'd said. Change in behavior, they'd noted. Mrs. Farnsworth had protested, but she'd been living in Boston. Obviously her daughter hadn't shared her depression with her mother, the police had said.

That had been a year and a half ago, and nothing else had been done.

*Please,* Mrs. Farnsworth had begged Jenna. *Please help me.*

Of course Jenna had said yes. There was no down side. Worst-case scenario, she wrote a fluff piece on haunted mansions. Best case, she landed a career-making story. A murderer on the loose and a community who believed one of the brightest flames in society took her own life. That was the kind of story icons like Dominick Dunne wrote, not newbie reporters like Jenna. But if she could nail this story...if she could find out the truth...well, then she'd never have to take another fluff assignment again.

With a little sigh, Jenna ran her fingers through her hair. The truth was, she'd landed a great job at a great paper right out of school. For somebody else, maybe that would have been enough. But Jenna's ambition wouldn't allow her to take the slow and steady course. She needed to make it. To succeed. To prove that despite where she'd started out in life, that she was worthy of the big leagues.

This story could do it for her. And, as an added benefit, she might just get to see Trent one more time. There was no way she was going to turn the opportunity down.

In truth, the prospect made Jenna a little nervous. She knew well enough that the husband was usually the top suspect. But even the fleeting thought seemed disloyal. She knew Trent. He'd never do anything like that. But *someone* had. If Mrs. Farnsworth was right, someone had murdered Alicia. And Jenna intended to figure out who.

It had taken no effort at all to come up with the perfect cover story. It was well-known in the small town that Winston fully believed the mansion housed the Claymore ancestral ghosts, and so Jenna had pitched the haunted mansions story, saying she wanted to feature Claymore Mansion. The ruse had worked like a charm.

That had been only one short week ago. She'd arrived in Portland that morning, taken a shuttle into Dryer and taken a taxi to the mansion. And now here she was, the damp morning air permeating her thin jacket and chilling her to the bone.

Frustrated, she stepped out of the alcove into the drive. She left her suitcase by the door, but slung her purse over her shoulder as she glanced around to get her bearings. The mist was starting to dissipate, and as the wind blew, she caught the faint scent of lilacs. She shivered, suddenly unnerved. Alicia had loved lilacs. She'd filled the sorority house with sprays of the flowers and her specially made cologne captured the subtle scent.

The memory was oddly creepy, and Jenna fought the unwelcome sensation that she was being watched. With a forcible shake of her head, she laughed it off. She was being foolish. Alicia had lived in this house. Most likely there was a garden with lilacs nearby.

At the thought of a garden, she glanced around, noticing the winding stone path snaking toward the back of the building. If she remembered right, it meandered around the house, then forked, one branch heading toward the cliffs and the other disappearing into the topiary garden.

She stepped onto the path, tentative at first, and then with determination. What the heck? She certainly wasn't about to wait on the front stoop twiddling her thumbs. Besides, she wanted to see the cliffs again.

She wanted to see where Alicia had died.

As she walked, she let her mind wander, taking in her surroundings almost subconsciously. A bird here, the scent of dew on the grass there. She looked around for a lilac-filled flowerbed, but saw nothing.

A low rumble caught her attention, and when she

licked her lips she tasted salt. *The sea.* The surf was pounding against the rocky beach at the base of the cliffs. The cliffs were too far ahead to see, but she knew what the view would look like. She'd seen it before, and time hadn't dimmed her memory of the stunning sight.

But she didn't need to rely on memory alone. She'd seen the pictures. Every paper in the area—and quite a few national ones—had covered Alicia's death. And each story had run with a photograph of the cliffs, illustrating just how far the despondent woman had fallen.

*Or had she been pushed?*

Jenna may not have known Alicia well, but she never would have pegged her as suicidal. Neither would Mrs. Farnsworth. And that, of course, was why Jenna was there now—to find out what really happened. And to write the story of her career.

As she walked, the silence was broken by the soft rustle of the wind through the trees and the crunch of gravel beneath her feet. And another sound. A steady, almost rhythmic sound. Oddly familiar and yet she couldn't discern the source.

She quickened her pace, curious, and then stopped short when she saw him—a lone man, shirtless, the muscles of his arms and back rippling as he hefted a mallet and brought it down with pure and clean precision on a wooden stake. Again. And again. And one more time.

A thin sheen of sweat covered his back, glistening in the weak light that permeated the mist. His jeans hugged his rear and thighs, accentuating the muscles in his legs. Dark hair curled at the back of his neck.

From behind, the man was a fine specimen, and she

couldn't help but wonder if the view from the front would be as good.

She watched as the man worked. Time itself seemed to stop, until there was nothing left but this man, the perfect embodiment of a fantasy. The handyman who made every woman's dreams come true. The gardener who seduced the princess behind the gazebo.

What he *wasn't* was the gardener of Claymore Mansion. Jenna remembered Mr. Neely, and the gardener had to be pushing eighty by now. This man couldn't possibly be a day over thirty-five. And he couldn't be Colin Neely, the gardener's son. Not unless Colin had decided to dye his cornhusk blond hair to midnight black.

Just then, the man's head tilted sideways, a quick, wary movement, and Jenna sucked in air, gasping as she realized that he'd sensed her presence. The faint glow of embarrassment burned across her skin, heating her face and chest. She'd been gaping like a teenager. The man had completely mesmerized her, and the temporary loss of control left her feeling shaky and unsettled.

"I...." She trailed off, waiting for him to turn around. When he didn't, she cleared her throat and tried again. "I didn't realize anyone was back here. I...I was just on my way to the cliffs. I'm invited," she added, in case he might be thinking about tossing her over his shoulder and carting her back to the road. "I'm not trespassing."

At that, he turned around. And Jenna felt a gasp rise in her throat, escaping as a startled little "Oh!"

*Trent Claymore.* Right there. In the flesh. Literally.

She couldn't fault herself for not recognizing him. After all, she hadn't seen him in years. And she'd never seen him without his shirt on. Now she was seeing

more than just his back, and she had to say, the view
from the front was just as nice.

He didn't say a word. Instead he just looked at her
with those deep chocolate eyes. No recognition. No reaction. Just taking her in.

Jenna stood there, her stomach fluttering as he continued his appraisal. Gone was the playful gleam of his
youth. These were eyes that had seen passion and pain.
The kind of eyes that could suck a woman in. The kind
of eyes that could watch a woman's every move, that
could caress her with nothing more than a glance. Eyes
that could spark with humor or with anger. Dark eyes.
*Dangerous eyes.* But not the eyes of a murderer. Not
Trent. Surely not.

She shifted her purse, clutching it close in front of
her. Already, the all-too-familiar ache was returning,
undiminished by the years. Hell, just three seconds after seeing him and her palms were sweaty and she
wanted nothing more than to curl up in her bed, close
her eyes, and analyze the way he looked at her. Was
that still attraction she saw? Did the fact that he shifted
his stance just slightly mean he remembered their
night together? That he wanted her?

*God.* She was pathetic. Twenty-five years old, and it
was as if the last nine years hadn't happened at all.

And then he smiled. Slow and charming and a tiny
bit crooked, just like she remembered. "Hello, Jenna."

The wide smile that crossed her face was hardly the
mysterious response of a woman of sophistication, but
at least it was honest. "Hi, Trent," she said. "I, uh, I
wasn't sure you'd remember me."

"Oh, Jenna. How could I forget you?"

She blushed as waves of relief washed over her.
She'd been so afraid that their evening together had

been special only to her. "I just meant..." She looked up, meeting his eyes. "Well, it's just that it's been a long time."

A hint of a shadow darkened his eyes, and he nodded. "Yes. I suppose it has. A lifetime."

She swallowed, thinking of Alicia. Here she was fantasizing about this man, and he'd lost his wife to either suicide or murder. "I'm sorry," she whispered. He didn't respond. "Listen," she continued, needing to fill the heavy silence. "I should probably just keep going." She took a step forward. "I didn't mean to disturb you. I'll...I guess I'll see you inside later."

"Wait."

She complied, her brow furrowing as she looked at him.

"Why are you here, Jenna?" His voice was flat, any sign of welcome in his eyes extinguished.

"Your father invited me. I'm doing a story on the mansion."

"There's no story here," he said. His voice rang flat, holding no room for argument.

Jenna argued anyway. "Your father thinks there is."

"No good will come from publicizing that the founder of Claymore Mills and Claymore Paper thinks he lives in a haunted house. Father's eccentricities hardly need to be shared with the world."

"I'm not going to make him out to be a kook," Jenna promised. "But everyone knows your father's passion for the stories. And besides, he's not eccentric. It *is* haunted." At least, that's what Jenna had always believed. The ghosts at the mansion were common knowledge among the townsfolk. "Isn't it?"

"Does it matter?"

"I think so," she said.

He shook his head. Clearly, they were coming to the end of their conversation. A pity, too, because of all people, Trent could be a huge help to her. Assuming, of course, that she could manage to keep her mind on her stories when she was within five feet of him.

He let go of the mallet's handle. The wooden stick fell to the ground, seemingly in slow motion, as he stepped away. With a slight tilt of his head, he gestured for her to follow. "Come on. I'll get you settled."

She hesitated, her body leaning almost involuntarily in the opposite direction, the direction she'd been walking. "That's okay," she said. "I don't want to take you away from what you're doing." She took another step toward the sea. "I was just going to walk around until someone got back to let me in."

The tiniest hint of a smile played at his face. "I'm someone."

*Oh yes. Yes, you are.* Her cheeks warmed, and Jenna was certain she was blushing. "Yes. But—"

He waved one hand, then leaned down to grab the mallet again, hefting the heavy tool. "Knock yourself out. When you're finished sightseeing, I'll be here." The warmth had left his voice, and he turned, his back to her. In one smooth movement, he swung the mallet, and Jenna jumped as the hard rubber smacked against the wooden post.

She fought the desire to reach out, to explain to him. But what was there to explain? All she'd said was that she wanted to take a walk. And somehow, with those words, she'd managed to disappoint him.

She knew she was being foolish, and so she tightened her grip on her purse and headed down the path, the rhythmic pounding of his mallet hitting the wooden stakes echoing behind her. By now, the fog had entirely lifted, and the once-familiar view took her breath away—a precisely manicured lawn that eased toward the cliff with a gentle rolling motion, the path curving through the center. She moved quickly down the path, her eyes barely noticing the richly colored plants that had bloomed with the spring.

The lawn gave way to a graveled area, peppered with scrub brush and native plants. The area appeared much wilder, but still gave the impression of human intervention. A metal bench nestled between two low, leafy plants, and she headed in that direction. As she did, the ground rose slightly, and Jenna breathed deep, absorbing the stunning view. She'd thought her memories had done the view justice. She'd been wrong.

An endless blue sky seemed to reach down from Heaven to brush the ground. Clouds lay low, almost even with the horizon that appeared to fall off into the sky. She wasn't yet close enough to the edge to see the sea or even to discern the drop-off that she knew was out there, but the air was heavy with the smell of salt and the rhythmic rush of the waves crashing against the rocks below filled her head.

One step, then another; and on like that until finally she was right there. Right at the edge where the world ended and opened up on to the sea below. There was no fence, no rail, and it would be so easy to simply step off into the nothingness. How many people had done just that? Particularly at night, on a still evening when the stars reflected in the sea, and it would almost seem as if you'd be buoyed by the heavens themselves.

The wind rose, and she stepped back automatically, wanting to move away from the edge. To not accidentally follow the siren's call and leap to the rocks below.

Another gust of wind, this one heavy with the scent

of lilac. Frowning, Jenna looked around, once again feeling eyes upon her, but she saw nothing, and as she turned back to stare out toward the sea, the wind caressed her, making her feel warm and safe and welcome. Memories of Alicia filled her head. The times she'd seen the woman on campus. The sorority meetings they'd attended together.

*Alicia's ghost... She was right there!*

The possibility should have scared her, but it didn't. If anything, she felt stronger. And why not? Now she had an ally, because Alicia, more than anyone, would want her murderer caught.

"It's beautiful, isn't it?" Jenna jumped a mile as Trent stepped up beside her.

Her heart pounded against her ribs, and she pressed a hand to her chest. "You startled me."

"Sorry." His voice seemed genuinely contrite. "You looked lost in the view."

"I'd forgotten just how amazing it is," she said. "Almost hypnotic."

He nodded thoughtfully, then took her arm, gently moving her a step back, further from the precipice. "There are no ghosts here," he said.

She turned to look up at him, wanting to ask how he explained the sweet familiar smell, but a shadow fell across his face, silencing her.

"No ghosts," he repeated. "None that we didn't invite in ourselves, anyway."

Jenna nodded, understanding. Trent believed his wife committed suicide. That the ocean had tempted Alicia, the reflected stars beckoning to her until she simply stepped off the cliff to join them.

Jenna drew in a deep breath as she looked up at

Trent. "I'm so sorry about your wife," she said, knowing the words were inadequate.

He released her arm as something unrecognizable fired in his eyes. Sadness? Anger? Loneliness? She couldn't tell, and the firefly of emotion winked out before she could catalog it.

"Thank you," he said, the words sounding stiff and hollow.

Jenna swallowed, the weight of the moment hanging between them. She fought the urge to reach out and touch him, to offer some comfort. She ought to say something else, she knew, but she didn't know what. And in the end, she said nothing at all.

He remained silent as well, watching her, his gaze intense and probing, as if he anticipated that she'd find the right words and speak. She didn't, of course. And when the silence became unbearable, he reached out and took her hand, the sensation of his skin against her own sending a current of electricity shooting straight down to her toes.

"Come on," he said, tugging her gently away from the cliff. "I think it's time I show you to your room."

# 2

TRENT PAUSED outside the door to the guest suite. She was in there. *Jenna.* A woman he'd tried to forget. A girl he'd never quite been able to get out of his blood.

With a low sigh, he pressed his hand against the textured wallpaper, seeking support. He wanted to touch her, to hold her, but instead he was going to have to avoid her. She'd come here as a reporter. It was her job to poke, to pry. To get into the cracks and crevices of life at Claymore Mansion.

He wondered if she had any idea of the secrets she might stumble across—*his* secrets. Even more, he wondered if she had any idea how she still affected him. How she'd always affected him. As far back as high school he'd known that the Daniels girl had a crush on him. But she was just a kid, and his father had had another type of woman in mind for him. And so Trent had never pursued her interest.

Jenna had, though. The girl had more guts at sixteen than he'd had at twenty, that was for sure. She'd been magnetic that night, boldly kissing him and opening the door to one magical night of sharing secrets, hopes and dreams. She'd stirred his heart and his mind. But she was too young and not the "right" kind of woman for a Claymore, and so he'd tucked the memory of their night together into a locked place in his heart and tried to forget about her.

He'd been a fool, of course. Because Jenna was exactly the type of woman he'd always craved. Vibrant and open, she was the kind of woman who would walk barefoot in the grass. Who'd stay up late watching old movies. Who would go into town in jeans and a T-shirt and not give a damn about what the locals might say. She'd come into his life with a single kiss and the force of a tornado, and her memory would stay with him forever.

Alicia, on the other hand, had snuck in when he wasn't looking. They'd met at a school function, and he'd been struck by her beauty, both inner and outer. Moreover, Alicia came from east coast old money and was exactly the type of woman that Trent had been expected to marry. A woman with a family name. With clout and access to the society pages even if the bank roll had run dry.

Alicia wasn't his soul mate, but Trent had truly loved her. Or at least, he'd thought he had. And his father had completely approved of the union.

And then, two days after Trent asked Alicia to marry him, he'd seen Jenna walking across the Stanford campus. He hadn't seen her since that night at the truck stop, and the shock that went through his system upon seeing her again was like ten thousand volts of pure electricity.

He'd battled the urge to go to her, reminding himself that he was engaged. He'd found the perfect wife; his life was all in order.

And so he hadn't said a word, but he'd spent that night alone in his apartment with a bottle of Scotch. It was a terrible habit—turning to alcohol when life at home got confusing or bad. He'd justified it for years, telling himself he deserved the drink for putting up with a father as demanding as Winston, but that night something snapped, and he realized he was using a woman he barely knew—that he'd spent only one night with—as an excuse to get loaded.

He'd thrown the bottle away and slept off the lingering effects of the drink. Less than a year later, he'd married Alicia. Loving her, and yet fighting the fear that there was a tiny place in his heart that she simply couldn't fill.

As it turned out, of course, the joke was on him. Trent and Alicia may have loved each other, but they'd never really been *in* love. That was a reality both of them had recognized too late. Alicia had worked hard to keep up the Claymore family name and to perform all the duties expected of her. She'd respected Trent, and they'd even been friends, but they weren't truly lovers. There'd been no passion. No *oomph*. And in the end, his shortsightedness had cost him everything.

He'd thought that was all behind him; he'd thought that the past was finally really past, and that the dead would stay buried. But now Jenna was in his life again. Only this wasn't the woman of his fantasies. This Jenna was nosing around. Asking questions. And he could tell from the line of her jaw that she was determined to find the answers, too.

In the garden, he'd seen the desire that still burned in her eyes. But that was before she knew the whole story. What, he wondered, would he see reflected in her eyes after she learned the truth?

JENNA TURNED A CIRCLE in her room, breathing in the peach scent emanating from the bowl of potpourri on the small coffee table. She'd been in the public areas of the mansion several times during the annual parties, but she hadn't known what to expect in the private rooms. In this case, at least, she wasn't disappointed. The rooms could not have been more luxurious if she'd been staying in the honeymoon suite of the Four Seasons Hotel. Everything about the suite screamed money and taste, from the crystal and china knick-knacks to the framed Matisse paintings—originals—to the decadent satin sheets.

Trent had left her here, telling her someone would be back to get her as soon as his father returned from breakfast. She'd noted the word and clung to it—*someone*. If she was lucky, that meant somebody other than Trent. Her nerves were too raw, her senses too fragile. She needed a bit of time to build up some backbone if she was going to behave like a rational human being around him. Just by proximity alone, the man tempted and teased her, awakening emotions that had lain dormant for years.

Not that she'd been pining away for almost a decade. She'd dated, even fancied herself in love. *That* had been one of her bigger mistakes. David had dumped Jenna after two years of living together, then married another women just six short months later. The breakup had been bad enough. Watching their mutual friends' excitement over his impending wedding had been torture, and it had cooled her interest in the whole dating scene.

She'd taken a break from romance, instead focusing on her career. She wasn't avoiding men; she just wasn't running across any other than the usual suspects. She had her girl friends and her guy friends, and they did movies and coffee and shopping and brunch, and it all seemed perfectly normal and fine. She was doing great. Or, at least, she thought she was.

Then she'd received the call from Mrs. Farnsworth, and suddenly images of Trent filled her head again. And when she'd seen him, up close and personal, well, every erotic desire came flooding back with a' vengeance. The years hadn't dulled her attraction to him at all. She was still totally smitten by his dark good looks, his strength, and his stalwart manner. He had a certain charisma that could turn her all warm and gooey.

Trent Claymore was one of those people who didn't move *in* the world, he moved through it. And he pulled everything around along with him; he was a force as compelling as gravity. Years ago he'd pulled her in. And the tug hadn't lessened one iota.

In truth, Jenna enjoyed the sensation of being drawn in. Even more, she liked the way he looked at her. Like she was a woman. She'd seen that look in his eyes the night she'd so boldly kissed him, and her persistent fantasy since then had been to see it again. Now, here it was. Here *she* was.

Only this time, those eyes held secrets, too. As if Trent were haunted himself. Frowning, she remembered the shadow that had darkened his features. The man had had a rough time of it, that was for sure. His mother had died when he was only seven. And then Alicia's death...well, no wonder he didn't want her stirring up ghosts.

With a philosophical shrug she eased out of her jacket and tossed it over the back of a chair. Her blouse came next, and she peeled it off, feeling sticky from traveling and the intense humidity. She stifled her automatic reaction to just let it fall to a heap on the floor. Instead, she hung the shirt up, not sure when she'd have the chance to do laundry. She hung her pants up, too, then stood there in only a thin cotton camisole and bikini briefs. The air felt wonderfully cool. A gentle breeze from the slightly open window caressing her heated skin.

She shivered, her thoughts turning back to Trent. In truth, she liked the way she felt around him, even if she did react like a high school girl with a crush. There was something invigorating about the swell of hormones, the rush of awareness.

And while her instinct might be to fight the attraction and run away, she really did have reasons other than lust for staying close to him. Trent was in the unique position of being able to help with both stories. After all, he'd surely have an opinion as to whether the ghosts were real or just tricks of the wind. And as for the murder...well, Trent probably knew more about his wife's death than anybody.

She frowned, her thoughts drifting back to a conversation she'd had before she'd left Los Angeles. She'd called Maryellen Carter, a former waitress who now owned the café on Main Street, and told her she'd be coming into town to write an article on ghosts. "Drop by when you get in, sweetie," Maryellen had said. "I've got an earful for you."

Maryellen hadn't been at the café that morning, but maybe she was there now. Jenna ran her fingers through her hair, still not used to the short cut she'd recently got on a whim, and tried to remember the phone number for the restaurant. No luck; it had been too long. But she clicked on her cell phone and asked for information. Within minutes, she was chatting with Maryellen like it was old times.

"Sugar, I'm so sorry I missed you. You'll have to come into town and let me buy you a meal. I bet you're as skinny as ever."

Jenna grinned, picturing Maryellen holding a pie tin in one hand and a pitcher of iced tea in the other. She was a matronly woman with a solid shelf of breasts and panty hose that *swished* between her thighs. She was also as nice as she could be, and Jenna had always loved her dearly.

"I'll take you up on that," Jenna said. "Even if I will be putting my perfect cholesterol level at risk."

Maryellen snorted.

"So, what did you want to tell me?"

"Are you on the mansion phone?" Maryellen whispered.

Jenna squinted, feeling suddenly very James Bond-ish. "Um, no. I'm on my cell. Why?"

"You never know who might be listening."

"To what?"

"Ghosts," Maryellen said. "That's what you're writing about, isn't it?"

"Well, yes."

"Not that I want to speak ill of the dead, but you mark my words...Alicia's among the ghosts that walk those halls."

Jenna sat up straight, thinking of the mysterious scent of lilacs and feeling vindicated. "Well, I guess that makes sense," she said, measuring her words. "Suicide. A tortured soul."

"Tortured, maybe," Maryellen agreed. "But suicide? That I'm not so sure about."

Jenna leaned forward, concentrating on Maryellen's words, her first real lead. "What do you mean?"

"Aw, now, honey, you know I'm not the type to gossip," she said, when Jenna knew exactly the opposite. "You're actually *staying* at the mansion?"

"That's right. I'm sitting on a bed in the most amazing suite you've ever seen in your life right now."

"Mmm."

Jenna laid back down, the phone cradled at her ear. "Alicia," she prompted.

"Let's just say that there are some folks that don't believe that girl took her own life."

Jenna could practically feel her ears tighten and perk up. "There are rumors that she was murdered?"

"You'll never hear that kind of gossip from my lips."

"Oh, I wouldn't ask you to gossip. I just—"

"But I will say that Mr. Claymore is awfully concerned about appearances, you know? The family name and all that."

"Mr. Claymore—"

"No, no. I've said enough. You need to talk to Mr. Neely."

"The gardener? What on earth does he have to do with this?"

"Right after the suicide, he had some things to say."

"What things?"

But Maryellen wouldn't say. "You talk to him. And Jenna? You be careful at the mansion."

They said their goodbyes, and Jenna shut her eyes, letting Maryellen's words sink in. The truth was, she felt safe at the mansion. Despite the ghosts and the secrets and the buried accusations, she felt safe around Trent. She always had.

But that didn't mean she was going to pull any punches with her article. And this afternoon, she'd find the path to the gardener's cabin and go visit with Mr. Neely.

First, though, she was due to meet with Mr. Claymore. And if what Maryellen said was true, she just might be meeting with a murderer.

THE SHARP KNOCK AT THE door startled her, and Jenna realized she'd dozed off. She twisted on the bed, still lost in the haze of sleep, and peered at the clock—almost noon.

"Coming," she mumbled, then pushed herself up on her elbows.

The door's hinges groaned, and she scrambled sideways, pulling the bedspread up to cover her front, as Trent appeared in the doorway.

"What are you doing?" she demanded. "Get out of here."

Confusion flashed across his face, replaced quickly by amusement. "You said, 'come in.'"

"I most certainly did not." She pressed the spread tighter against her chest, as if the cotton and batting would somehow protect her from him.

He licked his lips, his eyes on hers. He looked like he was about to say something, but she didn't wait to find out what.

"Go," she said, pointing toward the door. "Go now."

"Yes, ma'am," he said, then backed out of the room with a little nod. He paused in the doorway. "My father's ready to see you. I'll wait for you downstairs."

"Thank you," she said, hoping she sounded dignified and businesslike. She'd fantasized about being alone in a bedroom, half-naked with Trent Claymore. But this had definitely *not* been the setup.

"You're welcome." Another step backward and then another pause. "By the way," he said. "I really do think that pink is your color."

He was gone before his words even had time to register. *Pink?* She scooted off the bed, confused, then bent over to unzip her carry-on bag that she'd neglected to unpack earlier. As she did, she caught a glimpse of herself in the dresser mirror on the far side of the room. Pink panties and a pink camisole—and all of it had been reflected back at Trent while she'd so carefully covered her front. *Damn.*

So much for trying to maintain a proper and businesslike facade around him. Scowling, she pulled on a light knit dress. It was bad enough that he'd seen her; did he have to announce it as well?

*Unless...*

With her head cocked slightly to the left, she considered the thought that had tickled her brain. Unless he'd *wanted* the professional facade to drop. Was he flirting with her? The idea thrilled her, and she smiled to herself as she bent to fasten her sandals. She could handle flirting. No problem there, at all.

But then, as she crossed the room to the doorway, another possibility occurred to her. A more nefarious one, and not nearly as flattering. What if he simply wanted to throw her off balance, to distract her? Was he, God forbid, a murderer? Or was he, perhaps, protecting his father?

The possibility both irked and intrigued her. His reticence might as well be a neon sign that something was fishy at the Claymore mansion. And if what Maryellen said was true, then Jenna was about to go meet with the man at the center of it all.

No matter what, her initial chat with the senior Claymore promised to be a pivotal moment, and Jenna didn't intend to let Trent destroy her edge. He might be trying to throw her off-kilter, but he wasn't going to succeed. No matter how attracted she might be to the man himself, she resolved to be the epitome of cool and in control. He could try to steer her off course, but he'd fail. And that, quite simply, was that.

She was pumped up and confident when she pulled the door open. She was still holding strong when she stepped out into the hallway. But when she looked down the expanse of stairs at him, she felt her resolve begin to dwindle.

She hadn't gotten a good look at him when he'd burst into her room, but she got an eyeful now. Gone was the man who'd been working in the yard. This man was the Lord of the Manor; the man she'd remembered from her youth, but all grown up. And oh, how nicely he'd grown. Tall and dark and casually elegant in a starched white button-down shirt and tan slacks. The slight hint of beard was gone, revealing a face drawn in classic lines and angles, with a strong jaw and a wide, firm mouth.

His expression was bland, as if he was thinking about nothing in particular. And then he tilted his head up and saw her—and a smile touched his lips, and a glimmer of light danced in his eyes.

Her stomach twisted, her palms dampening under his steady appraisal. *Off-kilter*. She'd definitely been knocked off-kilter.

She started down the stairs toward him, knowing only one thing for certain. She was going to have to fight to keep control—of herself, and of the situation. Oh yeah. She was going to have to fight hard.

*HE STILL WANTED HER.*

She was trouble. Trent knew that. And yet he craved this woman.

"What?" She squinted at him, her head tilted just slightly to one side as she slipped onto the landing, so close that he could feel the whisper of her breath on his skin.

"I didn't say anything," he said. Without thinking, he pressed his fingertips to her back, silently steering her toward the library. It was a nothing gesture, and yet it seemed to set his fingertips on fire.

The touch affected Jenna, too. He was certain of it. She paused midstep, her posture straightening almost imperceptibly. Time seemed to stop, and it was just the two of them. Just them, alone, and the power of the universe all wrapped up in a touch.

She twisted slightly, breaking contact, and he jumped, realizing just how much his imagination had gotten away from him. She faced him, her eyes accusing. "You don't want me here."

"I don't want a reporter here," he admitted.

She nodded, purely businesslike. "I appreciate your honesty, and I'm sorry if I'm putting you out. But I have to be here. It's an important story for me."

At that, he had to grin. "Haunted mansions?"

Her cheeks bloomed with color. "I'll admit I'm not Bob Woodward, yet," she said, and he remembered her confession of ambition that night in the truck stop. "But this could be a good solid feature. Personality, drama, history. It could really get me noticed by the city editor." She met his eyes. "Trust me, Trent. It's important to me."

"I'm sorry. I didn't mean to laugh. I think it's going to be a fascinating story."

She cocked her head to the side, then licked her lips. "Do you want me to leave?" she asked.

He opened his mouth, but no sound came out. He wanted her there, yes, but he also wanted her a thousand miles away, out of sight and out of mind.

How could he tell her that? How did he tell her that of all the women in the world, she was the only one who truly threatened him? The one woman who had the potential to draw him out, to get under his skin. To discover things he didn't want any living soul to know.

Once he'd wanted her. But not now. He didn't want to disappoint yet another woman. But he couldn't tell her that. Lord, he couldn't even try.

Instead, he just met her eyes, then let his gaze slide down to her toes and back up to her face, wishing his fingers could follow the same path. He'd glimpsed her bare shoulders in the mirror earlier, and could imagine how soft her skin was under her clothes.

When he met her eyes again, he saw that her lips were parted, her cheeks pink. "This isn't personal, Jenna," he said, pretending to not understand that she'd shifted the conversation from her story to them. "I'm only concerned about the family name. I don't want my father looking foolish."

She licked her lips, her chest rising and falling with her quick breaths. For a moment, he thought she would respond, that she'd call his bluff. But then she turned, walking away in the direction they'd been traveling.

He stepped in beside her, oddly disappointed that she didn't fight back, that she'd dismissed his answer so easily. They continued through the gallery in silence, their footsteps echoing off the marble floors. As they walked, her head turned slowly, her eyes wide as she took in the surroundings.

He tried to see the inside of the mansion through her eyes—the antiques brought over from Europe by his ancestors, the tapestries that dated back generations. But he couldn't see anything but his home. The antiques weren't ostentatious, but familiar. The textured wallpaper wasn't gaudy—well, maybe a bit—but soothing. Despite the ghosts that walked these halls, Claymore Mansion was home, and it always would be.

To Jenna it was where the rich family lived. Where the doors opened occasionally for the town folks. The Claymores had always tried to make their parties warm and inviting, but he knew that for some of the guests, the home was cold and sterile. For Jenna, he knew that at least one party had been no fun at all.

He tugged open the ornately carved mahogany door, stepping back to let her enter before him. He heard her surprised intake of breath as she stepped into the one room that never ceased to inspire awe even in him. Smiling, he entered the library after her, his fingers once again lightly pressed against her back. This time, though, the gesture really was chivalrous. Her head was tilted so far back that she could easily have toppled over, her eyes glued to the three stories of bookshelves and the ornate spiral staircases at each angle of the octagonal-shaped room leading up to the second and third level walkways and reading areas. There were over fifty thousand volumes in the Claymore family library, and Trent had spent almost every day of his childhood pouring through the pages.

"Wow," Jenna whispered. "I've never been in here before."

"It is awe-inspiring, isn't it?" The refined voice drifted from the seating area on the far side of the room, and Trent watched as Jenna's attention shifted, her eyes focusing on his father, Winston Claymore.

"Dad, I'm sure you remember Jenna Daniels."

"You look wonderful, my dear. Come here, come here. It's been such a long time." His father waved

Jenna over, his face alight. "Forgive me for not standing," he added, nodding briefly at the large ball of fur in his lap.

Jenna went to the old man without hesitation, her expression clearly delighted. Trent secretly breathed a sigh of relief. Winston Claymore had been intimidating as hell in his youth, and with the locals, that intimidation still lingered. Jenna had left years ago, though. And from what he could tell, she was now immune to his father's reputation. Either that, or she was self-assured as hell.

"She's darling," Jenna said, reaching for the mongrel ball of fur on Winston's lap. "Can I pet her?"

That did it. Trent knew she'd just wrapped the old man right around her little finger.

"Of course." He slid his hands under Shelby, who opened her eyes and blinked sleepily as Winston urged her forward on his lap.

Jenna reached out, tentative at first, and then bolder as she stroked the furry area between the cat's ears. A purr started low, then built like an approaching freight train. Clearly, the cat was in heaven.

"She's a sweetie," Jenna said.

"She likes you, too," Winston answered, managing without words to say, *I* like you, too.

He sat up straighter, reaching idly for his Scotch. "And we're both so glad you're here, aren't we Shelby?" He chucked under the cat's chin, who mewed a soft agreement.

Jenna laughed, turning just enough to pull Trent into the conversation. The simple gesture got him right in the gut, and he found himself smiling back at her. To Trent's horror, his father noticed, his still-shrewd eyes gleaming. Once upon a time, Winston had wanted only a debutante for his son. Now, he simply wanted to see Trent happy again. For that, Trent gave him credit.

"We're *all* pleased you're here, aren't we, Trenton?"

Trent plastered on a host's smile. "Of course," he said, the lie both completely honest and full of deceit.

"Trent and I are anxious to help in anyway we can," Winston said. "It's about time someone did a serious article on the history of this house—and its other-worldly residents."

"I appreciate you giving me access, sir. I think the article should be fascinating. We're planning to run it in the Sunday magazine."

Winston beamed, clearly delighted with the idea of sharing the mansion's oddities with the world. Strange noises at night. Furniture moving that no one would admit to rearranging. Doors swinging shut without even the hint of a breeze. And for the last year or so, the subtle scent of lilac that filled the halls every Friday night.

Those things were real enough—Trent had experienced each occurrence more than once. The mansion had a tragic history; he of all people should know that. It would almost be more odd if there *weren't* ghosts. The hauntings had simply become part of the fabric of life at Claymore Mansion.

What annoyed and puzzled Trent was that Winston wanted to share those family secrets with the world. Yes, he knew his father's fascination with the family mythology, but some things were best kept private.

Winston, of course, disagreed. "History is the past," he'd said. "There's no shame in tragedy, particularly when it is those very tragedies that have populated the house with spirits."

At that, Trent had rolled his eyes, but he'd been unable to dissuade his father. Ghosts were now the mansion's claim to fame, and Winston wanted to share the history and the phenomenon. Or so he said.

Now—seeing the way Winston beamed at Jenna—Trent realized his father had a second motive: Winston Claymore was matchmaking. In a weak moment, Trent had once mentioned Jenna's kiss to his father. Considering the woman was here, now, Trent had a feeling he was going to live to regret that moment of father-son bonding.

Trent shoved his fists deep into his slacks, irritated with both his father and, unreasonably, with Jenna. In the year since Alicia's death, he'd given up dating. Hell, he'd given up a lot of things, some things hard as hell to give up. But finally, *finally*, his life had returned to some semblance of normalcy. And he didn't intend to let his father interfere with the life he'd managed to rebuild. No matter how much his father wanted it—no matter how much Trent himself wanted it—he couldn't afford to let himself get close to Jenna.

But then his father dropped the bomb. "Anything you need," his father said, clasping Jenna's hands, "and you talk to Trenton. He'll make sure you don't lack for information...or company." His father looked up at him, blue eyes sparkling. "Isn't that right, son?"

Trent wanted to argue. Wanted to shout from the rooftops that she needed to leave and leave now before she opened up old wounds, casting the final, fatal blow to their family.

But he made no protest. His father wanted this; that much was evident from the wistful look in his eye. And so Trent would be a good son. "Of course," he said.

He'd show Jenna around. He'd answer her questions. And maybe, if he was lucky, it would all work out for the best. Maybe if he stayed close, he could keep her focused on the ghosts in the attic...and not the ghosts in his heart.

# 3

JENNA SETTLED herself in a chair across from Winston and pondered his offer—Trenton Claymore as her own personal guide through the mansion. Years ago, she would have fainted dead away by such a proposition. Now, she didn't know how to react.

For one thing, the offer certainly wasn't what she'd anticipated. For that matter, neither was the man himself. In years past, Winston Claymore had been formidable. He'd had money and enough attitude to stop a freight train. Never would he have made himself or his son subservient to a waitress's daughter. Not in a million years.

When Maryellen had intimated that Winston had murdered Alicia, Jenna had no trouble fleshing the story out in her head. Maybe Alicia had done something foolhardy, something that tarnished the family name. Winston took matters into his own hands and pushed her. Decisive and direct. That was the Claymore Code.

The scenario had seemed perfectly plausible, though definitely unsettling.

Now, though, Jenna didn't believe a word of it.

Winston Claymore was no longer the awe-inspiring man in the mansion she remembered from her childhood. Instead, he was a soft-spoken old man with a gentle manner. Surely he couldn't have...

*Could he?*

She hated the possibility, but she knew better than to completely rule him out. She needed to focus on the facts. And only the facts. And right now, in all truth, she had no facts at all. Just rumor, innuendo, and one dead woman.

Which meant she had to start from square one and face both stories—the hauntings and the murder—as a professional. Even more, as a professional without any preconceived notions about this place or its people.

It was that professionalism that sparked her current quandary. She needed independence in her investigation, but she also needed a guide. And Mr. Claymore had just offered up Trent on a silver platter. Which meant that she simply needed to graciously accept Mr. Claymore's offer of his son's assistance...and then rein in her own libido.

*Easier said than done.* She twisted in her chair, her eyes searching him out. She found him behind her, leaning against a shelf, his face expressionless. His eyes unreadable.

She took a deep breath and broke their gaze, turning quickly back to face Winston. She opened her mouth, not entirely sure what she was going to say. "Thank you for the offer." The words came out, and she listened to her own voice, processing the words at the same time the men did. "It's very kind of Trenton to offer to be my escort."

She thought she heard Trent snort, but she continued without looking behind her. "It's a wonderful proposition, but I have just one additional requirement."

"Yes, my dear?"

"I'd like to be able to interview the staff without Trent—or you—around," she said, her gaze not wavering as she held Mr. Claymore's eyes. "The, um, *ghosts* are supposed to be your ancestors, right?" She didn't wait for an answer. "I think the staff will talk more freely if no one from the family is around when I interview them."

She expected an argument—certainly, if she'd ever killed anyone, she'd argue about potential witnesses chitchatting with a reporter. But neither man protested, and Jenna felt her confidence rise another notch.

"Done," Winston said. And then he smiled. "And what else can we do for you, my dear?"

"Well, if I'm going to write about the ghosts," she said, flipping open her notebook, "I guess you should start by telling me their stories."

JENNA WALKED SIDE BY SIDE with Trent through the estate's topiary garden. Neither had said anything more than a cursory word since Winston had finished laying out what he knew of the spirits that haunted the stately mansion. As a child, Jenna had always been certain the place was haunted. How could it not be? With its dark, spooky alcoves, its gargoyles, and the turrets that seemed to reach into the heavens, summoning lost souls. She'd never been scared of the place, simply curious. And now her curiosity was piqued even more. As was her certainty that ghosts really did populate the mansion.

She'd already felt Alicia's presence; how many other ghosts were lurking within the walls?

At least a couple, she thought, if Winston Claymore was to be believed. His grandmother, the woman whose husband had built Claymore Mansion, was the property's original ghost. Her husband had died in a logging accident, and she'd lost her mind, wandering the widow's walk night after night until, finally, she leapt to the manicured grounds below. Her daughter, Winston's mother, died giving birth to her third child. On stormy nights, a woman's soft voice filled the halls; a faint lullaby carried on the breeze.

Jenna wondered how the other Claymore women had fared. What about Mr. Claymore's second wife, for example—Trent's mother? And why hadn't he mentioned Alicia?

Jenna didn't know.

She crossed her arms over her chest and rubbed herself as if warding off a chill, even though the temperature had risen into the low seventies. Maybe she'd find out tonight. She and Trent had made arrangements to spend the night together in the attic. For all Jenna knew, tonight she'd be having tea with the ghost of Alicia Farnsworth.

"You're quiet," Trent said as they paused in front of a dragon expertly carved from the shrubbery. "Pondering your story?"

She shook her head, trying to banish thoughts of ghosts and spirits. "Just thinking." She turned to him, once again struck by his dynamic presence. It wasn't just physical. There was an undeniable power about him, a vibrancy that had always fascinated her, although it had dimmed slightly. As if time and circumstances had dropped a thick veil of darkness on top of him and Trent's light had to fight to get through. What had done that to him? Growing up? The responsibility for the family business pressing against his shoulders? Or something else?

"I still don't understand why you're so against me writing this story," she said.

He laughed. Not exactly the reaction she'd been expecting, but she didn't alter her stance.

"Tell me, Trent. I really want to know. Why on earth do you have a problem with me writing a story about the ghosts?"

"Some things are best left buried," he said.

She squinted at him. "What things?"

He looked at her for just a moment, then started back up the path that wended its way through the green animals.

Jenna rushed to keep up. "Trent! *What* things?"

"It's not important," he said, still walking.

"Actually, yes it is. I'm writing a story about the ghosts. Your father wants their stories out in the open, after all."

Trent laughed. "So he says."

She stopped, watching his back as he continued up the path. "You think he has a different motive?" She couldn't imagine what. Guilt, maybe? Winston was her prime suspect. So maybe the old man wanted someone to find out about the murder? Maybe he wanted to be discovered so that he could redeem his soul? Maybe that's why he'd mellowed so much. It was a theory, but not one she really bought.

Trent stopped long enough to turn and look at her. "I don't know what's on my father's mind," he said, then started walking again.

Jenna exhaled in exasperation, and stepped in double-time until she caught up. This time, she closed her hand over his forearm and tugged him to a stop. "Then tell me what's on *your* mind. *What* things? What things are best left buried?"

For a moment, she was certain he wasn't going to answer. Then he reached out and took her hand. The world around her vanished, leaving nothing but the touch of his skin against hers. The sky above them was perfectly clear, but an electrical storm brewed inside her, the power surging and crackling through her veins. She shouldn't have come back. Even after so much time, she should have known any assignment that required her to come within twenty miles of Trent was a mistake.

Gently, he tugged her toward him, then sat down on a concrete bench in the lee of a topiary elephant. He urged her down beside him, and she complied, sitting with her feet on the ground, her knees together, and her hands folded in her lap. Watching him, she tried to remember that she was a grown woman now and not a teenager with a crush.

He let go of her hand, then crooked his finger under her chin, tilting her face up until her eyes met his. "I don't want you to write the story because it means that you'll be here, close to me, sharing my space and the air and filling my world." His voice was low, a sensual rumble that filled her up and threatened to carry her away.

She couldn't speak. She just stared at him.

"And you, Jenna darling, remind me of my mistakes."

She flinched. He might as well have slapped her. *The kiss.* He was talking about their kiss.

"I...I'm sorry," she said. It was a stupid thing to say, but he'd surprised her. "I should never have been so bold. But I wanted, well, you. And I—"

He pressed a finger to her mouth, effectively silencing her. "What are you talking about?" His brow was furrowed, his voice a low whisper.

Oh, Lord, he was going to actually make her talk

about it. "Well, that night. Our kiss," she said, talking to her shoes rather than his face. "It was a dumb thing to do. I saw how much champagne you'd had. And then I took advantage like that. And I was only a kid. You were just being kind—"

She clamped her mouth shut when she realized he was laughing.

"What?" she demanded. "And this time, you *are* going to tell me."

"You," he said. He reached over and cupped his hands over hers, giving them a little squeeze. Then he let go and brushed her cheek with his palm, managing at the same time to tilt her face until she had no choice but to look at him. What she saw in his eyes made her start to tremble all over again. Not from fear or embarrassment, but from hunger. Hunger for him. Hunger for Trent's touch.

"Believe me, Jenna," he said, his voice a sensual caress. "That kiss was no mistake. And I wasn't drunk. Not then. And you were a hell of a lot more than a kid."

He pressed his lips to hers then, and a heat ten times more powerful than the sun filled her veins, pulsating through her body and making her tingle. His lips were soft against hers, yet still demanding. And when he pulled away, his eyes fixed on hers, and she swallowed a little moan of protest.

"Was that okay?" he asked.

She didn't answer out loud. Just hooked her hand at the back of his neck and arched up to meet his lips once more. It wasn't words she needed. It was this man and everything he made her feel. The heat and life he brought to her body. The way his touch alone made her feel like she could set the whole world on fire.

His hand stroked her back, the other cupping the back of her head, his fingers raking through her short, thick hair. His mouth feasted on hers, claiming her, taking as much as she gave. And when she parted her lips, he didn't hesitate. He tasted of chocolate and mint. Rich and masculine. Pure ambrosia that she could live on for the rest of her life.

The kiss seemed to last forever, and when he pulled away, she heard herself whisper his name.

"I've been wanting to do that again for years," he said.

She blinked. "Really?"

Once again he cupped her chin, then bent to press a quick, hard kiss to her lips. "Don't ever say that our kiss was a mistake."

She leaned back against the bench, completely perplexed. "That doesn't make any sense. If the kiss wasn't your mistake, then what was? And if you've wanted to kiss me like that—and believe me, I hope you weren't faking that—then why on earth don't you want me here?"

He leaned back with a sigh. "There's never a right time, is there?"

"You tell me."

"When you kissed me after the party..." He trailed off. "Well, the truth is, I'd known forever that you'd had a crush on me. And if you'd just been a little older—"

"Really?" That schoolgirl thing was back. Jenna felt like the science nerd who'd just been asked out by the quarterback.

"But you weren't. And that night...well, even if you were almost seventeen, I was leaving the next morning. It was selfish of me, but I had to grab some of the moment. That's why I took you out. And I never once regretted it. That night with you at the truck stop...it was special. Something real sparked between us." He took her hand, kissed her fingertips. "Don't ever regret it or our kiss."

"I don't," she assured him.

He smiled, then continued. "I never imagined that when I came back for the holidays you'd be gone."

"We moved away. My mom moved in with her dad in Phillie and signed up for community college. She's an accountant now."

"Good for her. I always liked your mom."

"Thanks." Jenna pulled her knees up under her chin, her heels balancing on the metal bench. "She's a scrapper."

"Like her daughter."

"No. I'm like her." Jenna had been incredibly proud of her mom when she'd become a C.P.A. It had been odd having a mom in school, but nice, too. Each was the other's loudest cheerleader.

"At any rate, I never guessed I wouldn't see you in town again. But the fact is," he continued, "I don't think I would have done anything even had I known. My father would never have approved of you. Not then."

"I know," she said. "But what about now?" The question was out of her mouth before she could reconsider.

"Now, he's a different man. But then again, so am I."

She licked her lips and nodded, almost sorry she'd asked, then gestured for him to continue.

"So I just continued with my life. I met Alicia when I was at Stanford, and she was everything my father could have wanted in a wife for me. And I loved her. I really did. She loved me, too. But there was something not quite right even from the beginning. Some little thing that was missing between us."

Jenna's brow furrowed. "What?"

"I don't know. I still don't. But the day after we announced our engagement, I saw you. You were walking across campus. I doubt you would have noticed me, but I ducked back into a doorway just in case. And I just watched as you passed by."

"You could have said something."

He shook his head. "No, I couldn't. Because that was when I realized there was a gaping hole in what I had with Alicia. That was when I *knew* that even though I was marrying Alicia, and even though I really did love her, that somehow, I was settling."

She reached over and took his hand. "No relationship is going to be perfect, Trent."

"You're right. I know that. But now you're here, and you make me want things that I just can't have. That I couldn't ever have."

She frowned, once again confused. "But why not? Like you said, I *am* here. And we are still attracted to each other. We both feel it. We've both been fighting it. But *why* are we fighting, Trent? Why don't we give it a try? I want to. At least, I do if you do."

The smile that touched his lips was infinitely sad, and she knew the answer before he spoke even one word. "Now things have changed again. So this is just one more time when you've entered my life and I can't have you, no matter how much I want you."

"Trent, *no*. Whatever it is, we can work through it together." She clasped his hands. "Or maybe we can't. But don't you think we should at least try? There's something between us, Trent. Something that hasn't died in all these years. Don't you think we owe it to ourselves to at least see what develops?"

He drew in a deep breath, then stood up, shoving his hands deep into his pockets. "No," he said. "I don't think so."

"Why on earth not?"

"Because it's not something we can fight, Jenna. This house may be haunted, but its nothing compared to my own demons. And Jenna, that's a battle I have to fight on my own."

TRENT TURNED THE CRANK on the attic's casement window, chastising himself with every turn. He should never have told her how he felt. Trent knew that. It was a stupid, selfish thing to do. But it was done, and now he had to live with the decision.

Even worse, he had to live with it in the dark. In the attic. With Jenna right beside him.

He'd cut their conversation off abruptly in the garden. She'd wanted to know what he meant, and he could see the genuine concern on her face. He'd confessed to being tormented by personal demons, and she wanted to help him. She believed in him and wanted to make it better, and that outpouring of love and devotion warmed his soul.

And damned if he didn't want her help. But he had to hold fast. He had to stick to his resolve.

He just wished they weren't stuck in such intimate quarters together.

He glanced across the attic to where she was setting up their little campground near a collection of old trunks filled with his childhood playthings. A rocking horse looked back at him, and a few old bicycles—ancient by the standards of the day—leaned against the far wall. Furniture sat nearby, sheathed in white sheets, conjuring images of ghosts. And then there was Jenna.

She was smoothing out a clean blanket in front of the trunks and toys, the corners weighted down with pillows, a picnic basket, a bottle of wine for her, and a liter of cola for him. She sat down, one of the pillows propped behind her back, then aimed a questioning look in his direction. "You coming, or what?"

"You're sure you want to spend the night up here?" He'd lived most of his life in this house, and never once had he spent the night in the attic.

"Of course," she said. "I'm writing an article, remember?"

He remembered. How could he forget?

"Unless you'd rather not sit over here by me," she said. "I promise I won't attack you." She aimed a teasing grin in his direction. "I can't promise the same for the ghosts."

Shaking his head, he strode over to the blanket and sat down next to her. "Cozy," he said.

"We aim to please."

"No electronic equipment? No plasma detectors or flux enhancers?"

"I thought about calling the Ghostbusters, but I figured you could handle all the leg work."

"Thanks," he said dryly, pouring her a glass of wine and himself a glass of cola. She aimed a curious look in his direction, but didn't ask any more questions, and he said a silent thank-you that, for once, she'd suppressed her reporter's instincts. They were already in the attic with ghosts. They didn't need his demons for company, too.

"Of course, the ghosts are your relatives. No ghost-catching equipment should be necessary."

He grinned. "Let's hope they're in a good mood to-night. I don't want to be trapped in an attic with a couple of angry ghosts."

"You don't think they'll show up tonight, do you?"

"Never once in my life have I been able to find one of the house ghosts when I wanted one. So, no. I don't think they'll show up."

She licked her lips, her eyes darting down to the blanket. "What about your ghosts? Your demons, I mean. Will *they* show up?"

He felt his chest tighten and he took a long draw on the Coke. "They never left."

She scooted closer, then rested her palm against his thigh. The pressure shot straight to his groin, a persistent, demanding need.

"Tell me," she said.

Trent closed his eyes. He'd been dreading this moment. But now the dread was mixed with relief. At first, he'd wanted nothing more than to run away from her. But now...now he *did* want her help. Wanted her strength.

Resolve, be damned. He wanted her to know. Not necessarily everything. But some of it. *Most* of it. And if that was a mistake, then so be it.

"Do you know how my mother died?" he asked, then continued when she shook her head. "I was eleven. She went into the garage, started the limousine, and went to sleep in the back seat. She never woke up."

"Oh Trent. I'm so sorry. I didn't—"

"She left a note. Said she couldn't bear her life. Couldn't bear being a mother. Couldn't bear being my mother."

Again, Jenna squeezed his hand, and he saw tears pool in her eyes.

"I'd cleaned my act up a lot by high school, but I was a terror as a kid. A total pain in the butt wild child." He shrugged, feeling like that eleven-year-old kid once again. No matter how many times he told himself that his mother was ill, it never mattered to that little boy. "She left *me*," he said. "She wanted so badly to get away from me that she asphyxiated herself in the garage."

"Trent, no." She took his hand in hers and squeezed. "Your mom was messed up. It wasn't about you."

"Maybe," he said. "Maybe not. When you factor in Alicia, I have to wonder if maybe I'm not cursed. Certainly any right-thinking woman ought to stay far, far away from me." He watched her face as he said that, but he couldn't read a thing in her expression.

"What happened? Tell me about how Alicia died."

Trent looked away, his eyes closed. He wanted to tell her. God help him, he wanted to hold her in his arms and tell her everything. But he couldn't. Not all. Because as soon as he did, she'd leave. He'd see that expression of longing change to one of contempt. And then she'd walk away and never look back. He didn't want that. Not with Jenna. Not ever.

"Trent?"

"She didn't really love me," he said, telling as much of the truth as he could. "Or rather, we didn't love each other. We were friends, and we had a mutual respect, but it wasn't love. Like I told you, I thought it was in the beginning, and even after I realized it wasn't, I tried to give her a good life, but I guess some women just can't live like that. And one day, I guess it all caught up with

*Julie Kenner* 253

her..." He trailed off, not willing to tell her the rest of the story.

"Oh, Trent." She took his hand, pressed soft kisses to each of his fingertips. "I know what you're thinking, and that's so not true. Neither your mother nor Alicia was trying to leave you."

"And you know this how?"

A tiny smile touched her lips. "You know it, too, when you're not being obstinate. But it doesn't matter, anyway. Maybe I don't know about your mother, and maybe I don't know about Alicia. But I do know about me." The pressure on his thigh tightened. "And I want you."

"Jenna." His voice broke. "I promise you, I wasn't fishing. I wasn't—"

"Shh." She pressed a finger to his lips. "I know you weren't. But I don't care. Because I *do* want you. I always have."

He *hadn't* been fishing, but now he wanted to kiss her just for saying that. Hell, he *did* kiss her.

Her mouth yielded willingly to his, welcoming his tongue, opening up for him as he feasted on her. Gently, he tugged the wineglass from her fingers and set it aside. Then he eased her back onto the blanket, her head resting against the pillow.

There was no hesitation in her eyes as she drew him close, arching up to meet his lips again. His need for her was like a live thing, and he straddled her, his thighs pressed against her hips, his hand stroking her breasts through the thin material of her blouse. One by one, he freed the buttons, then slipped his hand inside. The warmth of her skin seeped into his body as he grazed her nipple, watching the way her body trembled from the contact.

"Please," she whispered.

"We shouldn't," he said, but he didn't really mean it. He'd craved this moment. Wanted to bury himself deep inside her. Foolhardy, perhaps. But...

"Oh yes," Jenna said. "I think we should." And as she pressed her lips to his, his futile protests died on his lips, and he lost himself in Jenna's arms.

# 4

NOTHING IN THE WORLD could feel as good as Trent's body pressed close to hers. That was one of those universal truths about which Jenna was absolutely certain. In his arms, she'd managed to reach nirvana, and she never, ever wanted to leave.

His hands roamed her body, peeling off her clothes with a subtle expertise until she found herself lying naked beneath him. Her senses were on overdrive, and every tiny touch, every simple caress, seemed to bring her closer to ultimate release. A delicious pressure was building in her body, and Trent was the only one who could relieve it.

All her life she'd wanted this man, but this moment defied all her fantasies. His hands, his mouth, his ministrations. This was perfection. *He* was perfection.

"Jenna?" His voice urged her out of her reverie.

"More," she whispered.

He chuckled. "More what?"

"Everything," she said, forcing the words out. Her eyes were closed, but now she opened them, wanting to see the heat in his eyes. He didn't disappoint. "More you," she said, spreading her legs for him.

He didn't need more of an invitation, and she gasped as he pressed against her, then eased inside, completely filling her. She arched up to meet him, desperate for him to fill her, and then rocked against him as a wonderful, sensual pressure filled her, spreading out to her fingers and toes and then springing back to that sweet point between her thighs.

With an urgency that matched her own, he thrust into her, again and again, until she came with an explosion of lights and colors.

Gasping, she clung to him as the wave built and then crested, finally breaking up into froth and foam.

They held each other, Trent stroking her hair, as they lay together. Somewhere in the back of her mind, Jenna knew she should try to stay awake. That she was supposed to be waiting up for the ghosts. But right then, ghosts were the last thing on her mind. Her thoughts were filled with Trent and only Trent. And as she fell asleep in his arms, she couldn't remember a time in her life when she'd ever been happier.

SHE DIDN'T KNOW HOW long they slept, but when she awoke, light was streaming in through the dusty panes of glass, and she was still pressed close to Trent. She drew in a deep breath, relishing his musky scent. With the tips of her fingers, she grazed his thin dusting of chest hair, feeling his heart beat beneath her fingers.

He shifted in his sleep, then reached up and found her hand. "Jenna." Her name was a whisper on his lips, and she wasn't certain if he was awake or dreaming.

"Trent?"

No response.

"Trent?"

This time he shifted a little more, his eyes flickering open.

"Good morning," she said, her smile showing him just how good she thought it was.

"It certainly is," he said.

"No ghosts last night."

"No," he agreed, rolling onto his side. "But then again, I don't know that I would have heard any moans but my own."

She grinned, then kissed his lips. "Touché."

"Shall we try again tonight?"

"I'd like that. But I'm afraid our good time may be scaring them away."

He shrugged. "I can have a lousy time if you can."

Playfully, she popped him on the shoulder with her fist. "Thanks a lot."

"Seriously," he said, holding up his hands in mock surrender. "Why don't I take you to dinner. And if we're inclined to have...*dessert*...we can have it downstairs. We'll come up here right at dusk. I promise you, we'll do nothing but talk."

"Talk," she repeated. "I think I'd like that."

He squeezed her hand. "Me too. So," he added, getting up and stretching. "What are your plans for the morning."

She cocked her head. "My plans?"

"You did say you wanted time alone with the staff, right? I figured I'd leave you alone until dinner. I need to make some calls and I'm sure I have hundreds of e-mails. I may be working from home these days, but I'm still working."

"Right. Of course." She felt silly. She'd practically insisted on time alone to investigate, and now she was all bummed out because she wasn't spending the day with Trent.

He kissed his finger, then pressed it against the tip of her nose. "I'll see you tonight. The foyer at six? We'll drive into town. Or even Portland if you'd rather."

"Town is fine," she said. "I'll see you then."

She dressed quickly and left the room, pausing at the top of the stairs to look behind her. He didn't look back, and so she headed on downstairs. And as she descended to the third story walkway, the air seemed to thicken, the sweet scent of lilacs buoying her along.

SHE FOUND MR. NEELY'S bungalow just where she remembered it, tucked away just off the path leading to the southeast edge of the property. The gardener had lived in the small two-bedroom house his whole life, his parents before him.

Jenna had gone to school with his son, Colin, and she'd come to the bungalow once or twice. Colin had hated the thought of working as a gardener—he wanted to be a mansion owner, not one of the servants. She'd lost track of Colin years ago, and she wondered if he'd managed to buy that mansion. He'd been smart enough, though a little lazy. But that had been high school, and people could surely change.

She stopped in front of the door and smoothed her outfit. She'd decided on a light pair of khaki's and a light blue blouse. Casual, and not too professional. She wanted information. She didn't want to intimidate.

As she raised her hand to knock, the door swung open, and Mr. Neely peered at her. "What?"

"Oh! You startled me."

"Saw you coming up the walk. What do you want?"

"Mr. Neely, I'm Jenna Daniels. I used to be friends with Colin."

He squinted at her, his leathery face crinkling. She must have passed muster, because he stepped back from the door, silently inviting her in.

The interior of the little house was tidy. Everything

in its place. All neat and organized. For some reason that surprised Jenna. The gardener's hands were rough and gnarled. For some foolish reason, she'd expected the inside of the house to be rough hewn as well, especially since she remembered that Colin's parents had divorced years ago. So the bright white slip covers and framed photos lining the walls were a surprise.

Mr. Neely nodded toward the fresh vase of daisies. "Got a lady friend comes by sometimes. Damn frilly foolishness if you ask me. Flowers belong outside. Growing."

Jenna smiled. This was the cantankerous old man she recalled.

"So how are you? Jenna, you said? You were one of them track and field girls, right?"

"I was," she admitted. "Slowest time on the team, but at least I was on it. I'm a reporter now," Jenna said. She paused in front of a framed collage, her eye automatically picking out Trent and Colin from the group of boys playing on the lawn. "Maryellen thought you might be able to help with one of my stories."

"Then I might be," he said. "I guess it depends on the story."

She licked her lips, trying to decide the best approach. "I'm doing a feature on the mansion's ghosts," she said. "And, well, it sounds silly. But I think Alicia may be among them. I think she may not be at peace."

Mr. Neely picked the battered stub of a cigar from an ashtray and shoved it between his teeth. He squinted at her as he gnawed on the end. "And Maryellen thinks I can help you out, does she?" he said, the cigar never leaving his mouth.

"Yes, sir."

"Don't see how."

"Well," Jenna said, trying to ease into it. "If there's anything you know about Alicia's death..."

He squinted at her. "Why would I know anything?"

Clearly he wasn't going to make this easy. She'd wanted him to bring it up himself, but if she had to, she'd yank the information out of him bit by bit. She looked him in the eye. "Maryellen recalls that you said something the night Alicia was found. Something that suggested maybe it wasn't suicide. That maybe Mr. Claymore pushed her."

He crossed his arms over his chest and stared at her.

"Mr. Neely," she persisted. "It might be important."

"Should never have said anything," he mumbled.

"But you did. Please. I already know what you said. Don't you think I should hear it from you directly rather than secondhand?"

At first, she didn't think he was going to say anything. Then he nodded. "I was out walking the grounds at night. And I saw him there with her. Clear as a picture. No doubt in my mind."

"You saw him push her?"

"Absolutely," he said, his voice emphatic. "It was dark, but I know what I saw."

She ran her fingers through her hair, pondering the information. "That just doesn't make any sense..."

"Are you calling me a liar?" His face turned red, his voice so harsh she backed up two steps.

"No. No, of course not. I'm just thinking out loud. Why would Winston Claymore want to kill Alicia?"

"Winston?" The brawny gardener barked out a laugh. "Who said anything about Winston?"

Jenna shook her head, confused. "What? I thought—"

"Alicia was with her husband that night," he said. "Trenton Claymore killed that girl. Just as sure as I'm standing here."

IT TOOK A FEW SECONDS for Mr. Neely's words to filter into her brain. She felt numb all over. She'd known from the beginning that Trent was a possible suspect, of course, but she couldn't bring herself to believe it.

Now, though...

Now there was a witness, and the ramifications were almost too much for her to bear. She'd fallen for Trent all over again. Was she now to learn she'd fallen for a murderer?

She wanted to leave. Wanted time to herself. Time to think. But she had to stay professional. Had to ask the right questions and pull together all the right facts.

"Are you sure?" Her words came out as a mumble, and she tried again. "Are you certain of what you saw?"

Anger flared in his eyes and then died. "Of course I'm sure. I'm not senile now, and I wasn't then. I saw Trent Claymore as plain as day. That's what I told Maryellen. And that's what I saw."

"But...but the police report. And the medical examiner. The consensus was suicide. Why didn't you speak up?"

He snorted. "What? And lose my job? Where else was I supposed to go? I go blabbing to the police about what I saw, and there's trouble for sure. I shouldn't even be saying nothing to you now." He shook his head vehemently. "No way. Once they said it was suicide, that was good enough for me."

She nodded, her mind whirling as she tried to find another argument. Something she could say that would make him realize he had to be wrong. That he couldn't trust his own eyes. But she couldn't think of anything, and in the end, she just thanked him for his time. "You've been a big help," she added.

"I'll tell Colin you stopped by. I bet he remembers you. Maybe he'll stop by the mansion. Say hi."

"Great," she said, unable to conjure any enthusiasm. "What's he doing these days?"

"Logging," Mr. Neely said. "I wanted him to keep up the family tradition, but he built a few flower beds for Alicia, and hated the work. A shame. A damn shame."

"Yes," she agreed. She didn't really care, but it seemed the proper thing to say. And she wanted to leave. "Tell Colin..." What? That she was sorry he ended up a logger instead of a bank president? That she wanted to see him again? She didn't. "Tell him I said 'hi,' too."

"You be careful, young lady," he said, as she stepped onto his front stoop. "Digging up old ghosts is one thing, but you're poking around in areas the family don't want no one snooping. That's dangerous stuff. You watch your back."

"Yes," she said, imagining Trent's hand pressed between her shoulder blades in a slow and sensual caress. "You're right, of course. I've got a lot of thinking to do."

SHE HEADED BACK TO THE house, passing the cook on her way. They nodded politely to each other, and Jenna realized she was starving. She checked her watch. Almost noon. Maybe she could grab a bite in the kitchen and talk to some of the staff while she ate.

She caught Melissa, the upstairs maid, on her break. "Now this is just between us, right?" the girl said.

"Absolutely."

Melissa took a small bite of her sandwich, chewed, then swallowed. "There were rumors back then that Alicia had been having an affair. No one remembers her being depressed, but..."

"What?"

A tiny shrug. "She just always seemed secretive, you know? And she and Mr. Claymore never seemed to spend a lot of time together."

Jenna pondered the information. "Who do you think she was she having the affair with?"

"Don't know. But I think she might have been...you know. Knocked up."

"Did Trent know?" Jenna asked, almost afraid of the answer.

"Dunno. But it explains why she offed herself, huh? How was she gonna explain some other man's baby?"

"True," Jenna said. What she *didn't* say was that if Trent knew, it also made one damn good motive for murder.

"YOU'VE BEEN AWFULLY QUIET all evening," Trent said. They were in a private room at La Trattoria, a family-owned Italian food restaurant that had been in Dryer Cove for forever. She'd hardly said a word since they met in the foyer, and he couldn't help but wonder what was going on.

Jenna shrugged and poked at one of the stuffed mushroom caps they'd ordered as an appetizer. "Just processing information, I guess."

"Learn anything interesting today?"

She looked up, meeting his eyes, and he saw pain reflected there. Pain and confusion and something else.

Longing? Desire? He wasn't sure. But his heart ached for her.

He'd spent the day thinking about Jenna. Not working as he'd planned to do. For that matter, as he needed to do. Things were heating up at the mill, and he really needed to be on hand to take care of it. But he couldn't focus on work. Couldn't focus on anything, really. Except Jenna. He *did* want to see what could develop between them. But he couldn't do that so long as he was living a lie. He'd decided to tell her everything. And tonight was the night.

The trouble was, she had worries of her own. And he couldn't help but fear that somehow she'd discovered his secret, too. He didn't think anyone else knew. But maybe he was wrong. Maybe someone had been waiting all this time, just waiting for the other shoe to drop.

He reached across the table and took her hand. "Jenna, please tell me. What's on your mind?"

"A lot of things," she said. "It was a hell of day in the land of investigative reporting."

His brow furrowed as he thought about her article. "Some scandal about the women haunting the house?"

"Something like that."

"What?"

A waiter breezed by to refill their water glasses. "And can I bring you a bottle of wine?"

Jenna raised a brow in question. "Want to split a bottle of merlot? I could use a glass."

"Help yourself, but I'm going to stick to cola."

As soon as the waiter disappeared with their orders, she tilted her head. "I don't think you need to stay sober to fight ghosts tonight."

"I gave up drinking about a year ago."

She licked her lips and a shadow fell across her face. "I see."

"Jenna," he urged. "Talk to me. Tell me what's on your mind."

Nodding, she drew in a deep breath. "This isn't easy," she said.

"I could tell."

"Did you know Alicia was having an affair?"

She blurted the question out, and the force of her words knocked him back.

"I see you focused your investigation on the most recent ghost," he said, sure now that she really had stumbled across his secret.

"Please. Just tell me."

"Yes," he said harshly. "I knew. I found out the night I...I found out the night she died."

The waiter delivered Jenna's wine, and she took a sip, closing her eyes as she swallowed. "You didn't know before?"

"No." A finger of rage curled in his belly. He was remembering that night. The way Alicia had come to him begging him not to divorce her. She was pregnant, but she didn't love the father. She knew Trent would hate her, but she wanted her child raised in privilege. She wanted him to raise her child as his own. "She told me she was pregnant. Since we hadn't slept together in months, I managed to figure out the affair part all on my own."

"I'm sorry," Jenna said.

"So was I," Trent replied, his voice tense, his hands clenched into fists at his sides. He and Alicia had suffered their share of problems, but he'd never once cheated on her. Her news had shocked him. But even more, it felt as though his wife had driven a knife straight into his heart. And Trent had lost himself, drowning the rage and the pain in alcohol.

Jenna twisted her napkin in her lap. "I talked to Mr. Neely today, too. He was around that night. He saw Alicia before—"

"Before I pushed her," he said numbly. Oh, Lord, it was true. He had killed Alicia. There was a witness. He couldn't deny it any longer.

"What?" Jenna's eyes were wide with disbelief. And, Trent noticed, with trust. "*No.* It can't be true."

"Yes," he said. "I think I killed her. I don't remember, but that night, I think I may have murdered my wife."

# 5

JENNA COULDN'T breathe. Trent's words had the effect of a punch in the stomach. A sucker punch. The kind that surprised you and kept you lying on the floor gasping for breath, trying to find your bearings.

"I don't believe it," she whispered. The words were a reaction. Automatic. But as she spoke them, she realized they were true. "You didn't kill her," she said with more force. "You couldn't have."

But Trent just shook his head. "I don't know what I did. But I must have."

Jenna exhaled, focusing on his words. He didn't remember, and that meant there was still hope. He couldn't have done this terrible thing.

In his own mind, however, she could tell that Trent had already condemned himself. "I *must* have pushed her, because I know Alicia. And no matter what, that woman wasn't suicidal. She wanted my help, my forgiveness. I told her to leave, but I hadn't answered her. Why would she kill herself until she knew what I'd say?"

"No," she said, leaning forward across the table, trying with the force of that single word to make him believe in himself. "You didn't kill her."

"But you just said Neely saw me." He sat up straighter and met her eyes. "I've been living a lie for a year now. I've been fearing this very thing. It's been eating at my gut. And now that I know the truth..." He trailed off. "I need to go to the police."

"*No.* There was no lie. I'll never believe you pushed her."

"There's no other explanation. And if Neely saw me with her..." He shook his head, and she could see both defeat and courage in his eyes. "Tonight. I'm going to the police tonight."

She shook her head. "There has to be another explanation." She squeezed his hands. "We'll figure this out together." She licked her lips. "Please, Trent. I want us to have a shot. I want to see if this thing between us can grow."

"God, Jenna." He pulled their intertwined hands to his lips and pressed a kiss to fingers. "There's a huge gap between wanting and reality."

"No." She shook her head, emphatic. "No. You don't remember what happened, which means it might not have happened at all. *This* is my new assignment, Trent. Proving you innocent. But you have to tell me *everything*. And you can start with why you don't remember."

SHE REALLY BELIEVED in him. Naive, maybe, but her passionate defense warmed his soul. Even more, it made him want to believe in himself.

"All right," he said. "I'll give you a shot. I won't go to the police until after you've poked around."

"You're giving *us* a shot," she said.

He smiled. "*Us.* I like the sound of that."

"Me too. I want you to keep hearing it for a long, long time."

So did he. More than anything in the world, he wanted to make a go of a relationship with Jenna Daniels. To do that, though, they had to get past this moment in time. He had to know that he hadn't hurt Alicia. It was horrible, terrifying, to think that he could have done that to her, to any woman. No matter what the circumstances.

He shivered.

No, unless Jenna was right—unless he truly was innocent—there was no way he could be with her. No way he'd want her to be with a man like him.

But with all the evidence that seemed to be piling up, innocence was a long shot. Still, it was a gamble he was willing to take. For her. For them.

"We'd been at dinner when she'd told me. We'd been drinking. She wanted me to raise the child as mine. I didn't answer. I just told her to leave, and when she did, I kept on drinking." He'd drunk a lot when he and Alicia were together, losing himself to the alcohol so that he could ignore the fact that their marriage was little more than a shell. That he'd compromised and that there were no second chances.

He'd given the alcohol up after her death. Hard as hell, but he hadn't had a drink in over a year.

"And then?"

"And then I broke things," he admitted. "I threw china, turned over furniture. Our dining room looked like a war zone. And throughout all of that, I managed to down an entire bottle of Scotch." He rubbed his hands over his face. "And that's all I remember. After that, there's just a big black hole where my memory should be."

"So you passed out," she said with a shrug. "You can hardly have done much damage lying passed out on the dining room floor."

"That was what my father told the police."

"But you don't believe it," she prompted.

"I woke up in my bed the next morning. Alone, of course. My head was splitting wide open. And as I stumbled to the bathroom, I saw grass on the carpet. I looked later, and sure enough, there were bits of damp grass clinging to my shoes."

Her lips pursed. "Anything else?" she asked.

"My father never told the police about the mess I made of the dining room."

"Okay. More?"

"No. I think that about covers it."

"So you had a fight. You drank. You threw things, and then you passed out—"

"Or blacked out."

*"You passed out,"* she continued. "And in the morning, you found out that your wife was dead."

He nodded, his body cold as he remembered the horror of that morning, and the terror at the realization that he may have sent Alicia to her grave.

"Maybe she really did kill herself," Jenna said.

He shook his head, vehement. "No. Not Alicia. Not if she was pregnant. I'll never believe that about her."

"And I'll never believe it about you," she added pointedly.

He frowned, silently conceding the point. He'd never willingly hurt a child, born or unborn. But he'd been angry, drunk. Had he...?

"No," she said, reading his thoughts. "You didn't kill her. I'll never believe it." She sat up straighter. "And if she didn't kill herself then she was murdered." She met his eyes, conviction burning bright. "We need to find out who her lover was. Perhaps someone you both socialized with?"

Trent ran his fingers through his hair, frustrated. He

appreciated what Jenna was trying to do. Hell, he wanted to snap his fingers and have the whole nightmare go away, too. But the pieces just didn't fit. "Not possible. I would have heard about it. The grapevine is fast and noisy. I would have known."

Jenna made a face. "Well, that's the best place to start, anyway. We'll find out who she was having the affair with."

"Jenna, you're wasting your time."

She shot him an irritated look.

"I'm sorry. But I know where this is going. We're not going to find the mysterious fellow, and in the end, you're going to have to admit that I did do it. I pushed her. And what kind of a man does that make me? Certainly not the kind of man you want to be with. Not the kind of man you can love."

In response, she stood up and bent over the table, pressing her palms to either side of his face as she placed a bold, slow kiss on his mouth. Deep and possessive, the kiss had one clear message—he belonged to her. This woman was claiming him. And damned if he didn't want to be claimed.

She broke the kiss, settling back into her seat with her eyes never straying from his. "I *do* love you, Trent," she said, the force of her words making his heart sing. "I think I love you now most of all. If what's between us is real—and I'm staking a lot on the certainty that it is—then it isn't going to go away just because of bad times. I want *you*. Not some cardboard cut out of a man that I've pulled out of my memories. *You*. Trent Claymore. Here and now. Good and bad." She licked her lips and smiled, soft and sweet. "You're everything to me, and I don't intend to lose you now. Not because you're too dense to realize that you don't have it in you to kill someone."

As he listened to her talk, Trent thought his heart would burst. Right then, he knew two things for certain. He loved Jenna. And he would do whatever he could to help her prove that he didn't kill Alicia.

He could only hope that her faith in him was justified.

Jenna tapped a finger to her mouth, clearly pondering something.

"What?" he asked.

"The pregnancy was news to me. How did they manage to keep that out of the papers?"

"It's a small town," Trent said. "And my father is a very big fish."

"He pulled strings, you mean."

Trent pressed his hand over hers, drawing strength from the warmth of her fingers. "Sweetheart, that's what I've been saying all along. My father pulled a lot of strings. Why do you think I'm sitting here and not negotiating plea bargains?"

"Because you're innocent," she said.

And for that, Trent had to kiss her one more time.

FOR THREE DAYS, JENNA talked to the staff, interviewed folks in town, and poured through boxes of Alicia's belongings. She learned a few things, but nothing that would exonerate Trent. Or, at least, nothing that jumped out at her as being important.

That was the problem. Every little thing might be important, but until she got all the pieces, she couldn't fit the puzzle together. And she had to make it fit. For Trent's sake—for their sake—it had to all come together seamlessly.

Jenna had been doing the poking and prying on her own; they'd both assumed people would be more inclined to open up to her than to Trent. But they'd compared notes every evening in her room. For three nights, they'd had dinner at the small table in her sitting area, and then spread out on the couch to go over what she'd learned that day. Nothing had seemed that important.

Alicia's interest in the arts, for example. She'd helped put together a charity art auction. But no one associated with the charity remembered anything that would suggest she had any sort of a relationship with any of the staff, volunteers or artists.

Exhausted, she laid back on the bed, then kicked her shoes off. She'd talked to Melissa again that afternoon. Nothing new there. And Colin had called. She'd missed him, but the message had said he'd be in town for a few days. She'd call him back. He might know something.

She closed her eyes, wondering how Colin had grown up. They'd talked once or twice in school. He'd hung with a different, wilder crowd, but he'd always been nice enough to her. She tried to picture what he'd look like now, and as she focused on his memory, the air became thick with the scent of lilac. She sat up with a scowl, wondering if she'd left the box of Alicia's stationery open. But as she opened her eyes, the scent seemed to dissipate. Jenna rolled her eyes. Clearly she had Alicia on the brain.

With a sigh, she crossed to the window, thinking about tomorrow. She'd try and catch up with Colin then, and hopefully she'd catch Donna in the kitchen after that. She'd been trying to talk to the cook for three days, and their paths never seemed to cross. Ironic, since just a few days ago she'd literally almost run the woman down on the path leading from Mr. Neely's back to the mansion.

Trent's sharp knock sounded through the room, and she smiled, spinning around to face the door.

*Tomorrow.* She'd worry about interviews and affairs and witnesses tomorrow. Tonight, she intended to relax with Trent.


JENNA LAUGHED, TUGGING the covers back over her bare hip. Trent tugged back, exposing her hip and pretty much all the rest of her as the morning sun drifted in through the window.

"Stop it." She laughed. "You're stealing the covers."

"Maybe I like the view."

She rolled her eyes. "Maybe I'm cold."

He rolled over on top of her, a position he'd been in for much of the previous night. "Maybe I can warm you up."

She wrapped her arms around him and held him close. "Maybe you can."

They stayed that way for another half hour or so, talking and laughing. Despite the circumstances, Jenna couldn't remember ever feeling this open, this comfortable, with any man. Or any person, for that matter.

He leaned over, then kissed her cheek. "What's on your mind?"

"You."

"Good," he said, a teasing note in his voice. "Hold that thought."

She grinned. "Okay. Can I hold anything else, too?"

"Mmm. I wish we had time."

"Tossed aside for work again. I tell you, a girl could get a complex."

She watched, appreciating the view as he slid out of bed and headed toward the window. He stood there, bathed in the morning light, as he slid into a starched white shirt.

"I always loved the view from this room," he said.

She got up to join him, slipping her arms around his waist as she murmured agreement. The view really was stunning. A sliver of the sea off to the right, and straight in front a wash of trees leading into a forested area of the property. Only two raised flower beds, now sitting dormant and unattended, marred the view.

"Shouldn't Mr. Neely do something about those?" she asked, nodding toward the beds.

"Not his fault," Trent said. "Those were Alicia's flower beds. She tended them herself, and after...well, I just haven't told him what to do with them."

She kissed him lightly on the cheek. "You fill them with flowers. She liked lilacs, right? That would be a sweet thing to do."

He turned in her arms, holding her close and pressing a kiss to her forehead. "You're a good woman, Jenna."

"And you're a good man. I know it. And we'll prove it."

A grin tugged at his mouth, and he gave her a mock salute. "Yes, ma'am."

"So what's on your agenda today? Can I find you in your study?"

He shook his head. "Sorry, no. I need to go up to the mill. There's a strike brewing, and I need to try and forestall it."

She frowned, disappointed. "Will you be gone long?"

"I'll probably be there at least two days. Unfortunately, it'll probably take forty-eight hours to straighten this mess out."

She shook her head. "What are you trying to do?"

"Negotiate a new contract." He tucked a strand of hair behind her ear. "It's exhausting, but oddly invigorating. Solid negotiations. Hours and hours."

Didn't sound invigorating at all to Jenna. "When will you sleep?"

"If I'm lucky I'll catch a few catnaps. Or maybe I won't. I won't really know until I get there."

"Sounds horrible."

He laughed, then leaned over and kissed her on the cheek. "I'll miss you."

"Hurry back," she said.

"You better believe it."

COLIN LEANED BACK IN HIS chair and downed a long swallow of iced tea. He shook his head, a smile lighting his face. "I still can't get over it. You turned into a hell of a looker, Jenna Daniels."

Jenna rolled her eyes. "Thanks, Colin." The man hadn't changed much. Subtlety was never his strong point. "So your dad said you're working as a logger?"

He nodded. "Yeah. I thought about doing the Ivy League thing and getting my MBA, but..." He trailed off with a shrug. "Why get fat and lazy behind a desk? I make good money. Real good. And I'm not spending my days looking at balance sheets, you know?"

"Oh, yeah," she said. "I completely understand. I never wanted desk job, either. That's what I like about reporting. It gets me out there."

"I never pictured you the busybody type."

She laughed, shocked. "I'm *not* a busybody."

"Sure you are," he said. "That's what reporters are.

In fact, my dad tells me you were poking around in his head the other day."

"*Poking around in his head?* Lord, I've never heard it put quite that way before."

"So what were you doing?"

She shrugged. "He thinks Alicia was murdered. I was trying to find out why."

Colin's eyes went wide. "My father thinks *what?*"

"I take it he's never run that theory by you before?"

"No. Of course not. Jesus, the old man gets balmier every day."

She stirred her iced tea, watching him. "What do you mean?"

He shook his head. "Sorry. I shouldn't trivialize it. He's had a couple of strokes. His doc wants him to quit, move away. But he won't do it. He insists he's fine. But I know he's turning nuttier than a fruitcake."

Jenna cocked her head, considering. Could Mr. Neely have hallucinated the whole thing? No one else had corroborated his statement, though Alicia's affair had been confirmed by numerous folks who'd heard the rumors. Maybe Mr. Neely had heard the rumors, too, and just imagined he saw a figure with her. Maybe he projected, thinking about how he'd feel if he were Trent. Maybe Trent really was innocent.

Maybe it really was suicide.

And maybe she'd just never know the truth.

AFTER LUNCH WITH COLIN, Jenna tried unsuccessfully to find the cook. No luck, and she was beginning to get paranoid. How much time could a cook spend away from the kitchen?

Next, she'd popped into the library and had tea with Winston. They'd talked about nothing in particular, and the whole time Jenna was itching to get up to her room where she could gather her thoughts and ponder where to look next. At the moment, she had nothing. Nothing except the niggling feeling that she was missing something huge. That if she could just find that one piece of the puzzle, everything would become clear to her.

But now she was back in her room, and she wasn't having any brilliant revelations.

She was stuck, and she missed Trent and she didn't know where to look next.

Not one of her finer moments.

Frustrated, she wandered to the window, then pressed her head to the glass and looked down. The trees were swaying in the breeze, the birds were hamming it up for the squirrels. And then she saw Donna. Damn it! She'd just tried to locate the woman.

She considered running downstairs to catch-up, but the woman was moving briskly down the path toward the gardener's house. And right then, Jenna didn't feel like running anywhere.

Her gaze shifted toward the flower beds, thinking that Trent really should fill them with lilacs. After all—

She froze, her hand on the pane. *Dear God, he already had.* But how could he have? He'd left right after they'd discussed it. Had he ordered one of the servants to do it? But even then, how could the flowers have grown so tall so fast?

She opened the window and leaned out, peering at the flower beds. Even though she was two stories up, she was suddenly consumed by their scent, and as she breathed deep, the flowers shimmered. Jenna blinked, leaning out further, her eyes fixed on the beds.

The flowers were gone.

*Alicia.*

With a little gasp, Jenna moved back, falling on her rump as the realization hit her. Alicia was *there*, with her, guiding the way. She'd been there all along, by Jenna's side, from the first moment Jenna had arrived. She wanted the record set straight—and she was pointing to the flower beds.

"Come on, Alicia," Jenna whispered, her voice urgent. "Help me out here. What are you trying to say?" But there was no brilliant flash of inspiration, no words miraculously appearing on the mirror.

Frustrated, she spread out on the bed, rubbing her temples. The answer was right there, she could almost see it, but she couldn't quite get it. She reached out, trying to grab hold. Something about the flower beds. Something important. Something—

*Of course!*

Colin had made those flower beds for Alicia. But he didn't do one other thing in the gardens. He didn't like it. Didn't want to. But still he built those flower beds. *Why?*

The answer was obvious—he made the flower beds for Alicia. For his lover.

It all made sense. Mr. Neely probably did see Alicia get shoved to her death. But the man he saw push her wasn't Trent; it was his own son.

*Colin.*

Alicia must have confronted him. Told him she was pregnant. Told him she'd wanted Trent to raise the baby. They'd fought. And it was Colin who pushed her to her death. Perhaps an accident, perhaps on purpose, but either way, it didn't matter. Trent didn't kill Alicia. Jenna was certain of it. And that was all that was important.

She paced the room, the scene running through her head in Technicolor.

As for Mr. Neely, he must have known about the affair and panicked. He was afraid the authorities would come after Colin. So he decided to pin it on Trent, started spreading rumors. As soon as the body was discovered and the gawkers appeared, he whispered his story to Maryellen.

But then the edict came down—suicide.

Colin was in the clear. And Mr. Neely wasn't about to push the murder story now, not when he knew the real truth. So he kept his mouth shut. And no one had been the wiser.

*Damn.* She slammed her fist into her pillow, absolutely certain that she'd got it right. After all, she'd been led to the answer by the one eyewitness in all the world. Alicia had helped solve her own murder.

In a flurry, Jenna yanked up the handset on the phone, dialing the number for Trent's office at the mill. No answer, but she got transferred straight into voice mail. "Trent, it's me. I've figured it out. I know what happened. Call me. Call me as soon as you get this message. I love you." Then she dialed his cell phone and left the exact same message.

Hugging herself, she paced the room some more, not entirely sure what to do with herself now that she'd made this startling connection. She knew she should wait for Trent so that they could do something together. What she wanted to do was run screaming through the hallways shouting at the top of her lungs that the man she loved was innocent.

Not exactly classy, but there you go.

With supreme effort, she managed to rein in the urge to make a total fool of herself. Instead, she took a long bath and then headed downstairs to try and find some dinner. After that, she was going to bed. The sooner she went to sleep, the sooner tomorrow would get here. And the closer she'd be to having Trent home again.

She found food in the kitchen, and was perched at the staff's butcher block table eating a bowl of Honeycomb cereal when Donna stepped in. "Oh, Miss Daniels, I've been looking for you."

Jenna's eyes widened. "Really?"

"You got a phone call a few minutes ago. I couldn't find you. Trent called."

Jenna's heart sped up. "Does he want me to call him back?"

"He said he's in meetings, and you'd never catch him. But he said that he had something very important to talk to you about...and something he wanted to give you." She beamed. "Does he know your ring size?"

"I..." Jenna's head was spinning. "He really said that?"

"He wants me to get you to the bench at the cliffs at nine tonight. He said he'd be home by then. I'm sorry if I'm spoiling the surprise, but I don't know how to get you there without just asking you to go."

*An engagement ring?* Surely not. But maybe...

Jenna realized she was hoping against hope that she'd have a ring on her finger by night's end. She needed to tamp it down, or she might be quite disappointed. "You're not ruining anything at all. Thanks for telling me." She sat up straighter, remembering her job. "By the way, I've been wanting to talk to you."

"I know." Donna laughed. "Our schedules just never seem to mesh. What about breakfast tomorrow?" The elderly lady winked. "And you can show me your new gift."

Jenna nodded, anticipating the weight of a diamond solitaire on her finger. "Perfect," she said. "I'll be here."

Donna smiled. "I'll be waiting."

*VOICES*. Screams. And a flood of anger so dense it seemed to fill his soul.

In bed, Trent tossed and turned, the dream tormenting him. He could see himself and Alicia. Fighting. So angry. And then she was gone, and the sound of glass shattering. He'd thrown his glass of Scotch against the mantle. Glass. Glass everywhere. Someone could get hurt.

*"Help her, Trent."* Alicia's voice from out of the darkness. *"Help her."*

And suddenly there wasn't any glass. It was grass. Wet, newly cut grass. Clinging to his feet and his hands. *His hands?* He was prone in the grass, half-asleep, drunk out of his mind. But he could see. He'd been following her, but he couldn't follow any more. She was there in the distance. And someone else was with her. Another man. Touching her. A man. Pushing her. *Colin Neely.*

Pushing Alicia.

Only it wasn't Alicia. It was Jenna.

"No!"

The sound of Trent's own scream yanked him from the dream, and he sat bolt upright in bed, his heart beating so hard he was surely going to crack a rib.

*"Danger."* Alicia's single word filled his head.

Oh, God, Jenna was in danger.

He scrambled for the phone and dialed, but no one

could find her. He left a message for her to call him on his cell phone the second she got the message, and then he glanced at his watch. Eight o'clock. If he lucked out on traffic, he could make it back home by nine.

He didn't even bother to pack. Just grabbed his keys and wallet and headed for the door. And as he pulled open the door to step into the hallway, his mind just barely registered the heavy scent of lilac that seemed to linger in the room.

JENNA TUCKED HER KNEES up under her chin as she sat on the bench watching the stars appear in the sky. Trent would be there any moment, and by the time he arrived, the sky would be sparkling with pinpoints of light.

At first, she'd wondered about Trent's choice of a meeting place. After all, the cliffs had brought him nothing but tragedy. But now she thought she realized his motivation. A new beginning. The conquering of old demons. A fresh start, and a beautiful setting.

And the setting *was* beautiful. Such beauty didn't deserve to be marred by ugly memories.

The roar of the sea below filled the air, and she closed her eyes, breathing in the heavy sea air, imagining Trent's approach. A gentle touch to the shoulder. A kiss to the cheek.

He loved her. She knew that without a doubt. And if he really was going to ask her to marry him, she was going to say yes. Whirlwind, perhaps, but she'd never been so sure of anything in her life.

A new beginning.

Tomorrow they'd go to the police and tell them her suspicions about Colin. And finally—hopefully—she and Trent could leave the past behind.

The subtle sound of footsteps drifted toward her on the wind. Slow and steady steps. Jenna smiled to herself, savoring the moment. And then she turned on the bench, facing down the path to watch as Trent approached.

His step quickened when she turned, and she aimed a little wave toward him. Darkness had fallen, so she couldn't actually see anything more than a shadow with a broad build and a steady gait. He got a little closer and she squinted, confused when she realized he was wearing some sort of hat. How odd.

She was about to call out to him, to ask if maybe they were going to fly up to San Francisco to see the Giants play at Pac Bell park, when she realized it wasn't Trent at all.

*Colin.* She was on her feet, ready to run, but his voice stopped her.

"I wouldn't go anywhere just yet, sweetheart."

Jenna swallowed, her blood turning to ice water as fear filled her.

"Trust me," he added. "Leaving could be very, very bad for your health."

Jenna wasn't sure that staying was going to prove all that healthy, but she remained still. "What are you doing here, Colin?"

"I've come to see you, of course."

"It's really not a good time," she said. "I've got other plans. Trent's coming. We've got a date."

"I don't think so."

"Yes," she said. "He's—"

"Coming to give you something. Something magical and romantic."

Jenna drew a shaky breath. "Yes..."

"I called," he said. "It wasn't hard pretending to be

Trent. Just kept my voice low and made sure the connection was filled with static. No trick there."

He was right by her now, and she could practically see the hum of dangerous energy that surrounded him. "Such a tragedy," he said.

She licked her lips, not wanting to ask, but compelled. "What's that?"

"You," he said. "Learning that the man you've fallen for murdered his wife." He shook his head, making little clucking noises. "Everyone thought you were stronger than that, but it's the Claymore curse. The women meet tragic ends, you know."

"I'm not a Claymore woman," she said. "Not yet."

"Close enough," he said. "Once you throw yourself over the cliff, I don't think anyone's going to haggle about semantics."

No, she supposed they wouldn't. "Probably true," she said. "Except I'm not going to throw myself over the cliff."

"Yes, you are," he said. "I think I can pretty much guarantee it."

TRENT RACED FROM THE house toward the cliffs, his heart pounding in his chest, his feet moving faster than they'd ever moved before.

During the entire drive from the mill, he'd felt slightly foolish. He had no reason to believe Jenna was in trouble. No reason other than a nightmare and an overwhelming feeling of foreboding.

But as soon as he reached the house, his fear proved well-founded. Melissa had looked at him like he was insane. "Jenna?" she'd repeated. "She's out at the cliff, waiting for you."

*Shit.* He hadn't even paused to explain. He'd just

raced out the door, hoping, *praying*, that he got there in time.

He slowed as he got close, counting on surprise as his best ally. The faint buzz of voices drifted toward him, and he said a silent thank you that he wasn't too late. He listened more closely, his stomach twisting in knots as he recognized the voice—Colin Neely. Just like he'd seen in the dream. Colin had been Alicia's lover. Colin had killed Alicia.

And now, unless he stopped it, Colin was going to kill Jenna.

*No!*

Crouching low, he approached, terror ripping through his gut as he saw Colin struggling with Jenna. He'd got her in a wrestler's grip and, bless her, she'd clung tight to him, her arms intertwined with his. *Good going, sweetheart.* So long as she was attached to the bastard like a leech, Colin wasn't able to toss her over the cliff.

She was no match for him, though. Colin had been logging for years. And soon, very soon, Jenna's strength would run out.

*Now.* A red hot fury filled his gut, and Trent knew he had to act now.

Colin's back was to him, and Trent stepped into the open, focusing on the man's legs. Jenna's eyes opened wide as she saw him, and the trust that shone in those eyes almost brought Trent to tears. He wouldn't fail her. *He couldn't.* He'd put that son-of-a-bitch out of commission and save Jenna. He couldn't even fathom any other result.

She looked away, her eyes focusing on Colin. And then she yanked her head back and forward, smashing her forehead against his nose in a move that surprised Trent almost as much as it must have surprised Colin.

Damn, but he loved that woman.

Colin didn't let her go, but he did howl. And his cry covered Trent's approach, a football tackle right around his knees. Colin tumbled to the ground, and Jenna rolled free, scrambling on her hands and knees away from the cliff's precipice.

Trent clung to Colin, refusing to let him get an advantage. They rolled over and over, until finally Colin growled and jerked free, leaping to his feet with a cry of rage.

He loomed over Trent, moving in for the kill. Trent drew a strangled breath, forcing himself to bide his time, wait for the perfect moment. He'd have only one chance. He had to make the most of it.

And then it happened. Colin reached for him, bending over to yank Trent up by his collar. But as he did, the wind kicked up, heavy with the familiar scent of lilac. *Alicia.* She was there with him. Fighting to help save him and Jenna.

The wind caught the dirt, spraying it straight into Colin's eyes. The man gasped, pitching backward. It was enough. And as Colin blinked, Trent brought his legs up and out, putting all of his strength into the blow. His heels caught Colin just above the groin, and the other man stumbled backward. A look of pure surprise flashed across his face, and he reached out, grasping at the air.

But it was too late.

He'd lost his footing. And before Trent could even climb to his feet, Colin had gone over the edge, landing with a dull thud on the rocks below.

"Trent!" Jenna ran to him, throwing herself tight

against him. He hugged her back, then gripped her shoulders and looked down into her eyes. *She was alive. She was fine.* Somehow, despite terrible odds, he'd managed to save her. With a little help, he'd managed to save the woman he loved.

"Trent, oh, Trent." She clung to him, and he stroked her hair, pulling her down to sit on the ground in the circle of his arms. "You came," she said.

"Of course," he murmured, never lifting his lips from her hair. "I love you."

"But how? How did you know?"

"Alicia," he said simply, expecting her confused expression. But there was no confusion in her eyes. Instead, he saw only understanding as she moved in closer to hug him tight.

The still-present scent increased, the air filling with the essence of flowers. A silent acknowledgement.

"Goodbye," Jenna whispered. "And thank you."

And then the scent dissipated, blown out to sea by the evening breeze.

*Closure,* Trent thought. And, now, a new beginning.

Taking Jenna's hand, he pulled her to her feet. "Come on, sweetheart. I think it's time to go home."

# Epilogue

JENNA had never been one for huge, ostentatious parties, but for her own wedding, she made an exception. The ceremony was performed on the cliffs, the sea blue and clear behind them. The entire town was invited, and two bands were set up—one inside and one outside the house. Flowers—including lilacs—were everywhere, both growing and in vases brought by the lucky merchants who'd gotten the job.

There were even doves, which Jenna thought was a nice, but extravagant touch.

"It's like a fairy tale," Maryellen said.

"It's happily ever after," Jenna agreed. "That's for sure." Even for Mrs. Farnsworth. The woman had declined the invitation to the wedding, but she'd sent Jenna a long letter, thanking her profusely for revealing Alicia's killer. For Colin, Jenna supposed, it wasn't a very happy ending. But he hardly deserved one. And as for Mr. Neely, well, Trent had asked him to leave. The old man had gone without question. Donna had spent three days crying in her room, mortified by her unintended role in the plot to kill Jenna. The woman had fallen in love with Mr. Neely, and he and Colin had used her as a pawn, delivering through her the message that almost got Jenna killed. When she'd collected herself enough to speak without crying, Donna had tendered her resignation, but Trent had refused to accept it.

"What about your article?" Maryellen asked. "The one about the hauntings?"

"Back-burnered," Jenna said. "The paper ran with the story about Colin, of course. But the ghosts..." She trailed off with a shrug.

"What?"

"They're gone."

Maryellen's eyes widened. "Gone?"

"Winston says the Claymore women have moved on and that the curse is broken." She glanced out toward the sea. "They're all at peace now," she added. Alicia had helped set them all free.

Trent came over then, Jenna's mother at his arm. "Now I know where you learned to dance," he said.

"Mom was just getting you warmed up for me," Jenna said. "She didn't wear you out, I hope."

"Too tired to dance with my wife? Never." He held out his hand. "May I have this dance?"

"This one," she confirmed, slipping into his arms and pressing a light kiss to his lips. "And every other dance in my life."

*If you enjoyed these two stories,
you've got to check out...*

*Don't miss:*

**963 LEGALLY MINE**
*by Kate Hoffmann
Available next month wherever
Harlequin books are sold.*

*Here's a preview...*

and her fantasies were back full force. "It's going to

# 1

"YOU CAN'T BE SERIOUS." Jane glanced down at the photocopy of the old contract, written in her own hand. When she'd signed it seven years ago, it had been nothing more than a whim fueled by a fair bit of champagne. He'd been drunk and feeling sorry for himself and she'd been swept away by a fantasy that the subject of her silly crush might actually show up in seven years, contract in hand.

And now he had. She looked up to see Will McCaffrey sweep a bouquet of roses out from behind his back. "These are for you," he said with a crooked smile. "English roses. Your favorite, right?"

A shiver skittered down her spine and her indignation wavered. All he'd ever had to do was smile at her and she'd agree to anything from doing his laundry to typing his term papers to helping him pick out flowers for the endless string of girls in his life. From the moment they'd met years ago, Will McCaffrey had always been too charming for his own good—and hers.

He'd been a man so completely unattainable he'd taken on mythic proportions in her mind—the classic profile, a body chiseled by the gods, hands so strong yet sensitive they promised to drive her wild in... Jane groaned inwardly. Just a few minutes in his presence and her fantasies were back full force. "It's going to take a lot more than roses and this ridiculous contract to make me marry you," Jane murmured.

He took a step toward her, his grin widening. "Then tell me what you want, Janie."

She risked another look at him. Features that had been almost boyish had taken on a more mature edge. He seemed powerful, determined. If he was really bent on marriage, then she was hip-deep in trouble—both legal and emotional. She cursed silently at her racing pulse and the flush that warmed her cheeks. "L-let's suppose for a moment that this contract is legal which I don't think it is. You were drunk and I was...under the influence..." She drew a shaky breath. "Why would you want to marry me? We haven't talked since that day you graduated from law school."

He slowly crossed the conference room and stood in front of her. The scent of the roses made her head swim and she held her breath, wondering just how much closer he'd come, praying that he wouldn't touch her.

There had been a time when she'd remembered every single occasion he'd grabbed her hand or brushed his shoulder against hers. She'd carried around a catalog of such events in her head for far too long and had taken pains to forget them all in recent years. Will McCaffrey was no longer the subject of a silly crush or her rampant fantasies. He was a flesh and blood man, a man who still had the capacity to trample her heart and shred her soul.

"Maybe not," he said with a shrug. "But that doesn't mean I haven't thought about you."

"That doesn't count," Jane said. In truth, she'd thought about him hundreds, maybe even thousands of times. Her attention flitted from his startling blue eyes ringed with thick dark lashes to the tiny dimple in his left cheek, once so familiar. There was still a bit of the boy left in him even though the neatly groomed hair and finely pressed suit made him the picture of respectability.

"Come on, Janie. You have to at least consider it. We were good together."

"Did you suffer a head injury recently?" she demanded. "Have you spent time in a psychiatric hospital? Or are you just seriously delusional? We were never *together*. You were together with half the girls on campus, but never with me."

"We were friends. You're the only girl—I mean, woman—that I've ever had a friendship with."

He reached out and smoothed his palm along the length of her arm. She'd watched him charm so many women, studied his techniques and imagined herself on the receiving end of his attentions. Well, she wasn't going to fall for his tricks! "Let's just be honest here."

"Great," Will said. "Now we're getting somewhere. Let's just lay it all out on the table. I'm all for honesty."

"For some reason, you suddenly feel the need to get married. Maybe you're in the midst of some early mid-life crisis. Or maybe you've run through all the single women in the Chicago metro area. Or maybe all your buddies have settled down and you don't have anyone to party with. But rather than dating a woman and going the traditional route, you dig up this contract and called a lawyer. I suppose you thought I'd jump at the offer. After all, a girl like me would be a fool to turn down a marriage to a guy like you."

He frowned, his brow furrowed with confusion. "What is that supposed to mean?"

"It means I'm not going to marry you! We don't even know each other." She paused. "Anymore. And I don't remember signing this contract." She crumpled the paper up and shoved it at his chest.

It was a lie. She remembered every moment of that night. She'd been the one to insist they had a witness sign as well, she was the one who actually wanted the document to be legal, dreamed that someday he might come back and try to enforce it.

Will drew a deep breath and let it out slowly. "You've changed, Janie. You used to be so..."

"Weak, pathetic, spineless? I'm not the same silly girl who used to hang on your every word, who used to bake you cookies and mend your shirts."

"That's not what I was going to say." He reached out and hesitantly touched her cheek, drawing his thumb over her lower lip. "You're not a girl at all, Janie. You're a woman. A very beautiful, passionate, stubborn woman."

Jane closed her eyes, losing herself for a moment in the warmth of his hand. Oh, God. This was it. This was one of her top five Will McCaffrey fantasies! In a few moments, he'd sweep her into his arms and kiss her, ravaging her mouth with his lips. She swallowed hard. And, if by some bizarre shift in the cosmos, her fantasy became reality, then she might as well start shopping for a white dress—and a bridal bouquet—and those little candy-coated almonds tied up in tulle that always sat on the dinner tables at weddings.

There was no way she was going to avoid falling in love with Will McCaffrey all over again...and right now, with her heart slamming her chest and her pulse racing, she wasn't even sure she'd ever fallen out of love with him in the first place.

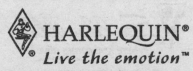

**Don't miss the exciting February 2004
Harlequin Temptation lineup!**

**CUT TO THE CHASE by Julie Kistler
BACK IN THE BEDROOM by Jill Shalvis
LEGALLY MINE by Kate Hoffmann
COVER ME by Stephanie Bond**

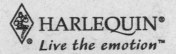

**HARLEQUIN®**
*Live the emotion*™

**Visit us at www.eHarlequin.com**

# Don't miss the exciting February 2004 Harlequin Temptation lineup!

**HARLEQUIN** *Temptation.*

**CUT TO THE CHASE** by Julie Kistler
**BACK IN THE BEDROOM** by Jill Shalvis
**LEGALLY MINE** by Kate Hoffmann
**COVER ME** by Stephanie Bond

**HARLEQUIN®**
*Live the emotion*™

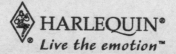

**Visit us at www.eHarlequin.com**

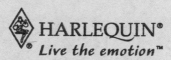

# HARLEQUIN®
## *Live the emotion*™

### *Give in to the indulgence*

...during The Decadent Escapes promotion.
Collect original proofs of purchase
from the back pages of:

**LIP SERVICE** 0-373-83630-9
**BEYOND SUSPICION** 0-373-83631-7
**STRANGERS IN PARADISE** 0-373-83632-5
**READING BETWEEN THE LINES** 0-373-83633-3

**and receive free books from our most passionate authors!**
**Each author-led bonus collection is valued at over $9.00 U.S.!**

Just complete the order form and send it, along with your proofs of
purchase from two (2) or four (4) of the featured books above, to
The Decadent Escapes National Consumer Promotion, P.O. Box 9071,
Buffalo, NY 14269-9047, or P.O. Box 609, Fort Erie, Ontario L2A 5X3.

098 KJV DXHY

Name (PLEASE PRINT)

Address                                                              Apt. #

City                      State/Prov.                      Zip/Postal Code

Please specify which bonus author collection(s) you would like to receive:

❑ I am enclosing two (2) proofs of purchase to receive 1 bonus collection
containing 2 FREE books by Lori Foster and Jill Shalvis
❑ I am enclosing four (4) proofs of purchase to receive 2 bonus collections
containing 4 FREE books by Lori Foster, Leslie Kelly, Julie Elizabeth Leto and Jill Shalvis
And don't miss out on exciting travel discounts that can be used all around the world!
Send us two proofs of purchase and check the box below to receive a Preferred
Member Hotel Accommodation Card for savings of up to 50% at hotels worldwide.

❑ I am enclosing two (2) proofs of purchase to receive 1 (one) Preferred Member
Hotel Accommodation card.

---

**THE
DECADENT ESCAPES
CAMPAIGN**
One Proof of Purchase
JANNCPPOP2R

Please allow 4-6 weeks for delivery. Shipping and handling included.
Offer good only while quantities last. Offer available in Canada and
the U.S. only. Request should be received no later than **April 30,
2004.** Each proof of purchase should be cut out of the back-page ad
featuring this offer.

© 2003 Harlequin Enterprises Limited

**Visit us at www.eHarlequin.com**